Growing Up

Growing Up

STORIES ABOUT

Adolescence

FROM THE
FLANNERY O'CONNOR AWARD
FOR SHORT FICTION

EDITED BY
ETHAN LAUGHMAN

THE UNIVERSITY OF GEORGIA PRESS
ATHENS

© 2021 by the University of Georgia Press
Athens, Georgia 30602
www.ugapress.org
All rights reserved
Designed by Kaelin Chappell Broaddus
Set in 9/13.5 Walbaum

Most University of Georgia Press titles are
available from popular e-book vendors.

Printed digitally

Library of Congress Control Number: 2020950812
ISBN: 9780820358710 (pbk.: alk. paper)
ISBN: 9780820358727 (ebook)

CONTENTS

ACKNOWLEDGMENTS

The stories in this volume are from the following award-winning collections published by the University of Georgia Press:

Tony Ardizzone, *The Evening News* (1986); "Idling" first appeared in the *Carolina Quarterly*

Debra Monroe, *The Source of Trouble* (1990); "The Source of Trouble" first appeared in *Great Stream Review*

Nancy Zafris, *The People I Know* (1990); "The People I Know" first appeared in the *Black Warrior Review* and also appeared in *Into the Silence* (Green Street Press)

Rita Ciresi, *Mother Rocket* (1993)

Alyce Miller, *The Nature of Longing* (1994); "What Jasmine Would Think" first appeared in *American Fiction: The Best Unpublished Stories by Emerging Writers*

Carol Lee Lorenzo, *Nervous Dancer* (1995); "Two Piano Players" first appeared in *Epoch*

Paul Rawlins, *No Lie Like Love* (1996); "No Lie Like Love" first appeared as "Washtucna" in *PRISM International*

Mary Clyde, *Survival Rates* (1999)

Kellie Wells, *Compression Scars* (2002)

Barbara Sutton, *The Send-Away Girl* (2004)

David Crouse, *Copy Cats* (2005)

Randy F. Nelson, *The Imaginary Lives of Mechanical Men* (2006); "The Guardian" first appeared in *Gettysburg Review*

Andrew Porter, *The Theory of Light and Matter* (2008); "Departure" first appeared in *Ontario Review* and also appeared in *The Pushcart Prize XXXII: Best of the Small Presses 2008* (W. W. Norton/Pushcart Press)

A thank you also goes to the University of Georgia Main Library staff for technical support in preparing the stories for publication.

The Flannery O'Connor Award for Short Fiction was established in 1981 by Paul Zimmer, then the director of the University of Georgia Press, and press acquisitions editor Charles East. East would serve as the first series editor, judging the competition and selecting two collections to publish each year. The inaugural volumes in the series, *Evening Out* by David Walton and *From the Bottom Up* by Leigh Allison Wilson, appeared in 1983 to critical acclaim. Nancy Zafris (herself a Flannery O'Connor Award winner for the 1990 collection *The People I Know*) was the second series editor, serving in the role from 2008 to 2015. Zafris was succeeded by Lee K. Abbott in 2016, and Roxane Gay then assumed the role, choosing award winners beginning in 2019. Competition for the award has become an important proving ground for writers, and the press has published seventy-four volumes to date, helping to showcase talent and sustain interest in the short story form. These volumes together feature approximately eight hundred stories by authors who are based in all regions of the country and even internationally. It has been my pleasure to have read each and every one.

The idea of undertaking a project that could honor the diversity of the series' stories but also present them in a unified way had been hanging around the press for a few years. What occurred to us first, and what remained the most appealing approach, was to pull the hundreds of stories out of their current packages—volumes of collected stories by individual authors—and regroup them by common themes or subjects. After finishing my editorial internship at the press, I was brought on to the project and began to sort the stories into specific thematic categories. What followed was a deep dive into the award and its history and a gratifying acquaintance with the many authors whose works constitute the award's legacy.

Anthologies are not new to the series. A tenth-anniversary collection, published in 1993, showcased one story from each of the volumes published in the award's first decade. A similar collection appeared in 1998, the fifteenth year of the series. In 2013, the year of the series' thirtieth anniversary, the press published two volumes modeled after the tenth- and fifteenth-anniversary volumes. These anthologies together included one story from each of the fifty-five collections published up to that point. One of the 2013 volumes represented the series' early years, under the editorship of Charles East. The other showcased the editorship of Nancy Zafris. In a nod to the times, both thirtieth-anniversary anthologies appeared in e-book form only.

The present project is completely different in concept and scale. The press has reached across nearly eight hundred stories and more than forty volumes to assemble stories that speak to specific themes, from love to death to holidays to transformation. Each volume has aimed to collect exemplary treatments of its theme, but with enough variety to give an overview what the Flannery O'Connor Award–winning stories as a collective are about. If the press has succeeded, the volumes illustrate the varied perspectives multiple authors can have on a single theme.

Each volume, no matter its focus, includes the work of authors whose stories celebrate the variety of short fiction styles and subjects to be found across the history of the award. Just as Flannery O'Connor is more than just a southern writer, the University of Georgia Press, by any number of measures, has been more than a regional publisher for some time. As the first series editor, Charles East, happily reported in his anthology of the O'Connor Award stories, the award "managed to escape [the] pitfall" of becoming a regional stereotype. When Paul Zimmer established the award, he named it after Flannery O'Connor as the writer who best embodied the possibilities of the short-story form. In addition, O'Connor, with her connections to the south and readership across the globe, spoke to the ambitions of the press at a time when it was poised to ramp up both the number and scope of its annual title output. The O'Connor name has always been a help in keeping the series a place where writers strive to be published and where readers and critics look for quality short fiction.

The award has indeed become an internationally recognized institution. The seventy-four (and counting) Flannery O'Connor Award authors come from all parts of the United States and abroad. They have lived in Arizona, Arkansas, California, Colorado, Georgia, Indiana, Maryland, Massachusetts, Texas, Utah, Washington, Canada, Iran, England, and elsewhere. Some have written novels. Most have published stories in a variety of literary quarterlies and popular magazines. They have been awarded numerous fellowships and prizes. They are world-travelers, lecturers, poets, columnists, editors, and screenwriters.

There are risks in the thematic approach we are taking with these anthologies, and we hope that readers will not take our editorial approach as an attempt to draw a circle around certain aspects of a story or in any way close off possibilities for interpretation. Great stories don't have to resolve anything, be set any particular time nor place, or be written in any one way. Great stories don't have to *be* anything. Still, when a story resonates with enough readers in a certain way, it is safe to say that it has spoken to us meaningfully about, for instance, love, death, and certain concerns, issues, pleasures, or life events.

We at the press had our own ideas about how the stories might be gathered, but we were careful to get author input on the process. The process of categorizing their work was not easy for any of them. Some truly agonized. Having their input was invaluable; having their trust was humbling. The goal of this project is to faithfully represent these stories despite the fact that they have been pulled from their original collections and are now bedmates with stories from a range of authors taken from diverse contexts. Also, just because a single story is included in a particular volume does not mean that that volume is the only place that story could have comfortably been placed. For example, "Sawtelle" from Dennis Hathaway's *The Consequences of Desire* tells the story of a subcontractor in duress when he finds out his partner is the victim of an extramarital affair. We have included it in the volume of stories about love, but it could have been included in those on work, friends, and immigration without seeming out of place.

In *Creating Flannery O'Connor*, Daniel Moran writes that O'Connor first mentioned her infatuation with peacocks in her essay "Living with a Peacock" (later republished as "King of the Birds"). Since the essay's appearance, O'Connor has been linked with imagery derived from the bird's distinctive feathers and silhouette by a proliferation of critics and admirers, and one can now hardly find an O'Connor publication that does not depict or refer to her "favorite fowl" and its association with immortality and layers of symbolic and personal meaning. As Moran notes, "Combining elements of her life on a farm, her religious themes, personal eccentricities, and outsider status, the peacock has proved the perfect icon for O'Connor's readers, critics, and biographers, a form of reputation-shorthand that has only grown more ubiquitous over time."

We are pleased to offer these anthologies as another way of continuing Flannery O'Connor's legacy. Since its conception, thirty-seven years' worth of enthralling, imaginative, and thought-provoking fiction has been published under the name of the Flannery O'Connor Award. The award is just one way that we hope to continue the conversation about O'Connor and her legacy while also circulating and sharing recent authors' work among readers throughout the world.

It is perhaps unprecedented for such a long-standing short fiction award series to republish its works in the manner we are going about it. The idea for the project may be unconventional, but it draws on an established institution—the horn-of-plenty that constitutes the Flannery O'Connor Award series backlist—that is still going strong at the threshold of its fortieth year. I am in equal parts intimidated and honored to present you with what I consider to be these exemplars of the Flannery O'Connor Award. Each story speaks to the theme uniquely. Some of these stories were chosen for their experimental nature, others for their unique take on the theme, and still others for exhibiting matchlessness in voice, character, place, time, plot, relevance, humor, timelessness, perspective, or any of the thousand other metrics by which one may measure a piece of literature.

But enough from me. Let the stories speak for themselves.

ETHAN LAUGHMAN

Growing Up

Farming Butterflies

MARY CLYDE

From *Survival Rates* (1999)

As Todd hangs car keys on his mother's PROUD PARENT OF
CAMEL-BACK HONOR STUDENT key holder, this is what he suddenly knows about his Aunt Deirdre: she can unflinchingly say
the name of the most private body part or reveal anything—that
her father wore Youth Dew perfume or that she once lost eleven
pounds on a grapefruit and horseradish diet—that she can announce her most raw secrets with abandon, according to myster-
ies of mood or logic or whim. Lately Todd has begun to suspect
women of having frequent bouts of whim. His mother's emphatic
fancies, Alisha's rehearsed impulsiveness.

Aunt Deirdre is also not really his aunt, but his mother's closest friend, just arrived for a visit with the family. Right now she's
telling him she's famished. She'd like something colorful to eat.
Orange circus peanuts or rainbow sherbet. "Joyful food," she calls
it. Her nose wrinkles in anticipation, a not unpleasant nose, but
the kind where you notice the nostrils first—a little rounder than
most people's. Her eye makeup is complicated. Todd has counted
three colors—easily—in shades of a healing bruise.

"I think we have some Creamsicles," he says. Then, "Help
yourself," which is a formality, because she's already doing just
that: unloading hot peppers, mashed potatoes, and deviled eggs

from the refrigerator. She kicks the door shut, and Todd watches the Pizza Barn magnet slide toward the floor. Next to it the library overdue notice and the dry-cleaning receipt shudder and then flap.

She says, "Imagine how much better spinach would taste if it were hot pink!" Then, pausing in mid-lick of the paprika on a deviled egg, she says worriedly, "Is your mom really skinny?"

One of the few things Todd learned about women in high school is how they can trick you with questions. Todd considers, not what the truth might be, but how he can say what Deirdre wants to hear without being disloyal to his mother—though he has only the vaguest idea of what his mother's relative skinniness might be.

"I don't know," he says. Shrugs. Her look—pleased, he can tell from the way her jaw relaxes, though she's still focused on her egg—tells him it's the right answer. He looks out the sliding glass door. In the backyard, starlings are fighting over wind-fallen figs. The deceptively cool-looking swimming pool water flashes hot glints of desert light. The blue sky is pale, as if exhausted from the heat.

Todd circles each of the brass rivets in his jeans pockets with his thumbs, a weird ritual he's found he does when he's nervous. He pulls the chain for the ceiling fan and hears a slight complaining sound underneath the hum. Deirdre's presence feels large and sticky. Not just because of the food all over the table, but there's something uncontained and risky about her, like sitting behind Lizzy Stocks in American Government and watching the straining outline of her bra hooks. Anxiety, but also shamefaced interest, even hope.

Deirdre spreads mayonnaise on seven-grain bread and then plops on a handful of hot peppers, saws the mess in two, takes a bite. The whole unappetizing sight makes the hair on the back of Todd's neck stand up.

Deirdre kicks off broken-down espadrilles and tosses them into the family's shoe pile by the door to the garage. "I've been on the road forever," she says. "When your mom and I were young we were always looking for a road trip. One day we got Mount Rushmore into our heads from watching Rocky and Bullwinkle. We left that afternoon. Rocky the Flying Squirrel, for crying out loud." She airplanes her arms, soaring like Rocky into some memory Todd hopes desperately not to hear, because his mom's behavior now is so relentlessly spontaneous and frequently inappropriate he can only imagine what it must have been like before she was someone's mom. *Now* his mom will shop for and buy a car in a single afternoon—last time, an extremely used yellow Mustang convertible. *Now* his mom walks half-naked from the bathroom to her bedroom, talks about her breasts, calls them "breasts" to show her "emerging awareness of her dignity as a woman." What happened back then when she was gallivanting around with Deirdre is certainly more than he wants to know. *Gallivanting.* Now he's *thinking* like them.

The ceiling fan is kicking up all the refrigerator's notices: a car wash coupon, the dentist's phone number, the phone bill. They flutter; they taunt.

"Should I call her at the hospital and see what time she'll be home?" he says. His mother works in the billing department at Good Sam. Her hours are the most regular part of her, but calling her would give him something to do besides standing here waiting for some embarrassing or frightening revelation of Deirdre's.

"The hospital! What drama." Deirdre peels fibers off a stick of celery. The strings curl like green hair. She dangles them in her mouth, wraps her tongue around them.

Deirdre looks like a vocabulary word, *precarious.* And she looks like sex too, not the sleek, sexy kind of Hannah Reed, but something harsh and natural and a bit reckless. Hannah Reed and her long, golden red hair are a closed mystery, while Deirdre

3

is a messy open secret, offering answers to questions Todd would rather not know.

He realizes Deirdre is saying something about cactus. "How can you not love the too-little yellow flower hats on a saguaro or a prickly pear shaped like green, thorny pancakes? Affectation and character—in *plants*! Did your parents tell you why I'm visiting? That I lost my job?"

Todd's parents are diligently, exhaustingly honest with their children. He and Alisha were given sex talks with diagrams. Todd's certain it is part of what's wrong with him, that his parents were too open. He suspects them of being calculating as well. For what better way to frustrate a boy's sexuality than by being explicit about sex? But his parents are also forgetful and spotty in what they remember to tell their children about routine matters such as motivations and schedules. He didn't know about Deirdre's job. Hell, he didn't even know she was coming until this morning when his mother asked him to rearrange his pool cleaning jobs to go pick her up.

"It was my fault they fired me," she says. "Sometimes I forgot to go in. I was helping my boyfriend farm butterflies. Painted Ladies. Orange and black. Pretty, but only in a bridesmaidish way. We had problems: poor quality feed, fluctuations in incubator temperatures. Then the eggs began hatching too soon, in the shipments. We were calling experts from all over. Until finally we found one in Minnesota who agreed to come out." Deirdre pauses and takes a dainty bite of her sandwich, chews it carefully. "What happened was she and Brian went off together. Flew away." She flaps her arms, this time like a butterfly. "Left me with six thousand butterflies in various stages of maturity. Can you imagine?"

Of course, he cannot imagine, not this or several other things, like why she's telling him about her love life or even why someone would farm butterflies. She doesn't make sense. Or the sense she makes is as unhelpful as his mother and father's. His father wants to tell him about condom use. Deirdre wants to tell him about betrayal. And all he really wants to know about any of that stuff is what to say to Hannah Reed on the phone now that school's out.

He looks imploringly at the oven's digital clock, trying to figure out when either of his parents might return. He thinks his unhappiness at being a high school graduate enrolled for the fall at the community college pales in comparison to Deirdre's misery or even the misery of playing her host.

Deirdre licks her finger and presses it down on some sandwich crumbs, then brings it to her mouth. "After Brian left, his absence started to grow like a weed in bad science fiction. Bothersome and indestructible, too. And then having those butterflies. Having to let them go. That didn't help me one bit."

Todd wonders why she doesn't ask him about his job or school. *Something.* It's as if she doesn't know what adults and teenagers are supposed to talk about. She turns her chair around and straddles it. The fiddle-back his mother refinished with a kitchen sponge and turquoise paint is between her legs. Her gauzy skirt hikes up worrisomely on either side.

"I called your mom right after I was fired. She invited me to come for a visit. I was helpless, just sucked up her sympathy like a hummingbird at a feeder."

This absolutely forces Todd to say, "Did you know I play the trombone? Trombone." He works an imaginary slide, the final phrase from the school fight song, then drops his hands defenselessly in his lap.

Deirdre rests her chin on the chair back. "Ump-pah-pah," she says. "Your mom told me. Were you a band nerd or just a cool guy who appreciated music early and had the maturity not to mind getting stuck with the school band stigma?"

"Actually, a band nerd," he says.

It's a small exchange, not much of a joke, but she gets it. Her

smile is happy and wide enough to show a mouthful of teeth—
teeth his mother says Deirdre used to open beer bottles with. He
feels the surprise of a connection, one of those understanding
links he assumed he'd always have with Alisha because they are
twins. Momentarily, he feels as if he fits again, all awkward six
feet of him. He's unexpectedly grateful.

"Deirdre," his father yells, coming in the door. He drops
his beat-up accordion briefcase, and he and Deirdre do a hip-
bumping, patty-cake thing that is so embarrassing Todd has to
look at his sneakers.

"Hasn't Todd grown?" his father says. His father is, as usual,
delighted with the most obvious observations.

Since graduation, Todd's been sifting and weighing and prob-
ing the experience, trying to make it feel more important than it
does. He thinks—hopes—you shouldn't slip through something as
big as graduation unchanged and unguided. He's scrutinized the
black-haired newscaster's commencement speech, but all he can
remember is some story about a guy naked under his graduation
gown, and he can't even remember the point of that.

One moment during graduation *has* stayed with him, but
it's so weird he's not entirely sure it happened or entirely sure
he wants it to have happened. It occurred as he was playing his
trombone and marching to his place on the apex of Camelback
band's sloppy triangle. There was a slide in the fight song, a slide
he'd played—at how many football and basketball games?—
but this time it was different. He remembers extending his arm
with a smooth, steady grip and feeling his soul somehow go with
it—a follow-through beyond the brass reach of trombone, beyond the aluminum bleachers, beyond where he was or where
he's been. Reality seemed to slip. He's suddenly on a San Francisco street corner, his trombone case open, a few dollars rustling

in the worn gray velveteen, the brim of a gentle fedora shading his concentration-closed eyes. He's playing "Mood Indigo," each phrase ending perfectly, opening to the rich surprise of the next. Freed from all clumsy technique, lifted into expansive expressiveness, he plays as he's only dreamed. His breath becomes music.

It's his imagination, he knows that. But it's clearer and feels more relevant than anything that really happened that evening. Now sometimes, while he's driving from pool to pool, he'll see the layered gray of a San Franciscan sky or a Chinese character in pink neon, flashing in a black reflection of plate glass, like a reminder or a sign. He feels foolish. He'd die if anyone knew, but it's so vivid. It scares and thrills him, a mysterious possible life, so exact in detail it must in some way be prophetic.

Alisha, who his mother has never tired of pointing out was his "womb-mate," has taken up with the drama club crowd. For some reason this seems to have cured her childhood stuttering, though now she is prone to repeat whole phrases, trying out different inflections and hand gestures. Todd thinks the stuttering was preferable. As babies, they sucked each other's thumbs and scratched each other's ant bites, but now Alisha has turned inward.

She is sunning by their swimming pool, though the only result Alisha gets from her tanning is an occasional swollen forehead. Todd used to call her Alisha the Beluga Whale when that happened, and she'd just throw her ice pack at him. Now he wouldn't dare say anything. She's unpredictable: hostile one day about the style of sunglasses he's wearing, tearful the next about lard in bean burritos. Todd brushes down the sides of the pool. Alisha sweats dramatically. Music comes from the headset of her Sony Walkman, insect voices whining about last chances of last dances. She takes off the headset, shades her eyes, squints at him. "Todd, you're beige." It's an accusation.

"Well, I find it goes with a lot of things."

"But you're outside all day. Why don't you get a tan? Are my eyes the same color as yours? Yours are blue-green." She says this with distaste, presumably because his eyes are neither one color nor the other. Alisha has begun to notice many dissatisfying things. There's a palm frond shadow across her leg, the silhouette of a giant comb.

"How're you liking Aunt Deirdre?" he says.

"I don't know how many of those dinners I can take."

Dinner *had* been wild. Their dad served his Bianca Florentine Lasagna, a towel over his arm in a corny waiter imitation. Their mom told Deirdre about the patient at the hospital who told a nurse she couldn't breast-feed yet because the doctor hadn't been in to poke the holes in her breasts. Then after mentioning that Todd had graduated in the top 5 percent of his class, their parents asked them to tell Deirdre about their college plans.

Todd had looked to Alisha to go first, but she wouldn't look up from the exclamation point she was making with salad croutons.

"I thought Mom was particularly ridiculous," Alisha says now.

For the first time in a long while, he sees they agree. It comforts him, in an old thumb-sucking way.

The beach towel Alisha lies on covers a multitude of rips in an old lounge chair. Her hair is fanned above her head. She speaks with her eyes shut, looking like a severe fortune-teller. He's tempted to ask her advice about Hannah. To ask if Hannah's lowered blond eyelashes are a good or bad sign. To ask if Hannah's laugh—like a car changing gears—is for him or about him.

Alisha says, "Did you see those pills she took? I think they're illegal."

"I doubt that."

"They're something *very* illegal," she says again, her chin up. Alisha likes to shock. When he doesn't respond, she opens one challenging eye. And he knows with a sad dip of regret that whatever he says will extinguish their fragile camaraderie.

"I think," he says, savoring the impossible simplicity of his hope, "she's just having a rough time right now."

"She's surfing for God on the Internet. She thinks she's descended from Anasazi Indians. 'Something has happened—what is it?' Blanche in *A Streetcar Named Desire*."

He suspects much of what Alisha says is to enable her to quote someone. He can feel the heat of the pool deck through his sneakers, like a warning. He remembers when they were kids cutting out pictures from *Better Homes and Gardens* of rooms they would build in their house when they grew up: ice cream parlor attics and billiard room basements.

"Anyway, it's too bad she lost her job," he says. He kicks a rotting orange. It is bloated and gray like a dead animal.

"I got my dorm assignment," Alisha says. She's headed north in the fall, into the mountains. She is so feverishly thrilled by it, he knows his unhappiness about the community college is genuine. "I want to get some Broadway posters framed," she says. "And a *real* coat."

On one knee, he scoops some water into the test kit tubes. Alisha's plans exhaust him, or not precisely the plans themselves, but the surety of them. Another mystery: how does anyone know so clearly what to do? He adds solution number four to the testing tube, shakes it to see the red swirl turn the water pink. He could do it without testing. Today the pool needs what it needed Monday and the Friday before, what it always needs: twelve ounces of muriatic acid.

It's arranged for Todd to take Deirdre on his swimming pool rounds. "Show her the ropes," his father had said. "Or I guess with swimming pool cleaning, it's show her the brushes." And his mother said, "It'll do you some good, Deirdre, to get out into that hot desert you like."

They were watching television news about a divorce lawyer's trial for beating up his client's ex-wife.

His dad turned his face toward Todd, but kept his eyes on the tearful attorney. "Tomorrow's okay, isn't it, Todd?"

"You deserve everything you're getting, buster," his mother said, hiking her chin to the lawyer, but it might as well have been to Todd.

Only Deirdre, he saw, was looking at him, smiling a shy smile, a blushing bride smile.

He looked desperately to Alisha. She glanced up from her hands, lined up finger to finger in steeples, and grinned with savage innocence.

"Dad," he says later, when he finds his father in the bathroom brushing his teeth, "I don't think it'll work for me to take Aunt Deirdre. You know, it's really hot. She's not used to it." He does not add that she's a time bomb.

His father's stomach hangs over the waistband of his pajamas, sags in a truly disheartening way. He brushes his teeth as if he's filming an instructional tape for the American Dental Association. "Son," he says—and how Todd hates to be called that—"Deirdre needs help getting her life back on course. Can't you just take her around? Stop and buy her a taco." He rinses his mouth. "My treat," he says, because life is so simple for his father, Todd thinks, that he really supposes someone can be bought these days for the price of lunch.

His parents have always treated their children like adults, which his friends have unwittingly called cool, because they had no idea of its obligations. You can't make another kid understand the burden of an unlocked liquor cabinet or the ordeal of twenty-four-hour-a-day access to adult cable channels. "We trust you," his parents said over and over, until Todd wanted to scream, "Please don't. I think I might be a maniac."

But the worst of it was he and Alisha weren't maniacs. They

acted like adults—parents, in fact—waiting up while their father and mother danced all night at the Rocking Horse Saloon.

His father now forms exaggerated vowel sounds with his mouth. He claims these are toning exercises for his neck. "*A-E-I-O-U*," he says. Lost, Todd walks out.

But later he passes the glassed-in patio and hears the hiccup of a sob. He sees Deirdre in the room, sitting at a small desk. Her back is to him, hunched as if protecting something. "Please," she says into the phone. "Brian, it'll be different." A pause. "I know, but I'll quit that. I promise." She strokes a geranium's jointed stem. Drops it. "But Brian—" Her words are cut off by her weeping. She nods, accepting, admitting whatever she's being accused of.

Todd has never heard such anguish, didn't realize it really existed. He thinks of his mother's grief at his grandmother's death, dignified and contained. And though Alisha evidences misery, it is as posed and vain as a party dress. Deirdre's sorrow is homely and unbounded. It seems to soar, a pain set free by hopelessness.

In his bedroom, he closes the door with both hands on the knob, carefully, tightly.

In the morning, Todd keeps glancing at Deirdre, worrying about how she's holding up, whether breakdowns are like David Andrew's epileptic seizures or like Jason Reily's diabetic lows. Would he even recognize a breakdown?

But Deirdre seems content, pleased with the day. His beat-up Nissan truck doesn't have much in the way of shocks and has no air-conditioning. She sticks her arm out the window, pats the side. "I wish we had some Jethro Tull on the eight-track and some beer in the back. Then we'd be like a couple of teenagers."

One of them actually *is* a teenager, he thinks, and he has no idea what an eight-track might be. But he's glad—and relieved—she feels better. He considers telling her about Mr. Petersen, his newly divorced biology teacher, maybe even setting her up with him.

When they pull up to a huge Spanish colonial, Deirdre hops out and carries the long-handled brush and net while he totes his bucket of chemicals and test kit.

"Will you look at this?" she says.

The pool, with its tiers of blue and white tile and twisted columns, resembles a Turkish harem. Todd fills containers like miniature buoys with jumbo chlorine tablets while Deirdre flicks away leaves slimy with pool water. She talks about her high school summers working at a hardware store, how she'd loved the names for toggle bolts and wing nuts. "Your mom had a more glamorous job," she says. "She worked at a Dairy Queen in a tight white uniform."

He sees his mother's past hovering over his own. Homecoming Queen Gives Birth to Band Nerd. He wonders what she does with her disappointment in him. He imagines it in the form of the impossible jewelry his father gives her—the brass fertility goddess earrings that she exclaimed over before they disappeared. Todd thinks she did something similar when he failed to even apply to a university. She shoved her discouragement into some drawer and pulled out something else to wear. Her proud mother badge. He wonders if it fools her.

Deirdre says, "Your mom says you have a girlfriend."

His scalp tingles. His wet hands sweat. Could his mom have guessed about Hannah?

"A flutist?" Deirdre says.

"Jenny? No, she's just a friend." In addition to a rather unsuccessful evening at the Sadie Hawkins dance with Jenny Allen, there was only a movie gang date. But besides being a flutist, Jenny is a poet. Though his mother doesn't read poetry, she's confident only worthwhile people write it.

"I'm certain I've got some bad love advice if you need it," Deirdre says.

"No," he says, quickly, stunned and shy at the invitation. "Anyway, I mostly like to figure out my own stupid stuff to do."

They nod together, almost in sync, a relaxed rhythm, as Todd brushes the sides of the pool.

"Probably better that way," Deirdre says. Then, "How come I haven't heard you play the trombone?"

"I don't usually play much in the summer," he says, though it isn't true. He's quit playing altogether—just at the point when he feels he's becoming more accomplished—because he fears the music will give him away. Atonal and unusually metered, it sounds confused and searching.

Deirdre pulls at the elastic of her gray jogging shorts. Todd thinks she will tan today, her skin color deepening with a cheap, alluring glow. He hands her the brush and nods toward the opposite side of the pool.

She says, "Are you going to play in the band when you get to college?"

He taps his jeans rivets. He thinks of sitting in the bleachers at football games, his music clipped to the stand with clothespins. "I don't know if I'm going to college in the fall," he says, for the first time speaking the truth of it and startled by his confession.

"When I graduated from high school I went to wax museums. Ten of them." She holds up all ten fingers. "There was one in Denver for women rodeo riders. Another one in Las Vegas had Marilyn Monroe's mole on the wrong side."

The Polaris vacuum cleaner makes a robotic patrol of the pool bottom. The sweep hose whips.

"I keep thinking about going to live in San Francisco for a while and just messing around with my music, seeing what happens." He's surprised how easy it was to say, how saying it makes it seem actually possible, but most of all he's surprised that Deirdre doesn't look surprised. She nods, or he wouldn't have been certain she'd heard at all. "I know it's a stupid idea. It probably won't work out." He has to say this, someone has to.

Deirdre slaps the back of her neck with pool water. "Well, you can't do something like that and still be a card-carrying band nerd, that's for sure," she says. She smacks her lips, a sound like approval. "But your mom and dad *are* going to kill you."

"Yeah, but first they'll talk me to death. They'll say how they know I'll make the right decision. They know I'll do what's best. They *trust* me."

She smiles. A breeze hot as a blow-dryer makes the palms sway obsequiously.

Todd says, "My parents won't accept failure. What chance do I have for any real success?"

Deirdre clears her throat. "I could go with you," she says. "It's not as if I have anything to go back to."

A construction wrecking ball, Todd sees in this, aimed at his parents' hearts. The only thing, he supposes, more worrisome to them than his going off to San Francisco alone would be his going off to San Francisco with Deirdre. It delights him.

"I'd get a job working for Ghirardelli chocolates," Deirdre says. "Don't you love those chocolate molds? Seashells, golfers, Scottie dogs. They have a trombone one too, don't they?"

"A road trip," Todd says.

"I know about road trips." Deirdre sits and puts her feet into the pool. Her sneakers must slurp up the water. "I've always done whatever came into my head and sometimes—often—it doesn't work out. But you can't be Alisha's womb-mate forever. Right?"

He sees himself stepping off a curb onto a gray wobble of cobblestone. He steadies a soft package of white butcher paper, smelling the sweet stink of fish. Deirdre walks along the curb, dipping a foot like a kid on a wall, balancing a basket on her head. Then she stops, turns to him, and laughs Hannah's laugh, the sounds of shifting from first all the way through fourth gears. It welcomes him; it embraces him; it convinces him: this bright laugh of adventure.

After cleaning eight pools, after watching his mother nearly swoon with horror and Alisha nearly swoon with jealousy at the sight of Deirdre's fierce sunburn, Todd is trying to sleep when he hears his mother and Deirdre talking. He looks through the tangerine tree outside his window and sees their legs, ghostly in the underwater pool light, weaving like bleached seaweed.

"I guess I thought butterflies were romantic, Debbie," Deirdre says, leaning into the water and fluttering her hands like a shadow-puppet butterfly. "I thought they were some kind of sign, an ancient Asian symbol of happiness."

His mother points her toe and brings it up out of the water. Silver droplets splash back into the lit pool. "Deirdre, you make too much of signs. Butterflies are, after all, insects." In her swimming suit, he sees his mother *is* skinnier than Deirdre. Fleetingly, Todd wishes he'd told Deirdre his mother wasn't skinny.

His mom says, "Deirdre, farming butterflies was the least of Brian's gambling. He drank too much. He was not a nice man."

"He was pigeon-toed," Deirdre says, helplessly. "How can a pigeon-toed man really be bad?"

Todd knows Deirdre won't mention San Francisco, though he finds he wishes she would. He can feel the tight tugging heat of her sunburn. She and his mother face each other in the water. He sees they are their own kind of womb-mates; a complex affinity balanced on something as opposite as a magnet's polarity. What are the allowances his mother makes for her friend? With him she's always looking for something to be proud of.

"Deirdre," his mother says. She pushes Deirdre's hair off her forehead. It is a mother gesture, but not a gesture of his mother's. "You're going to be okay, Deirdre." Then she swims toward the deep end.

"I don't want to go to college," Todd whispers to her swimming form. She floats on her back, brings her arms out of the water with surprising gracefulness, and he imagines her saying to him, "You're going to be okay, Todd."

In a room without shadows, black dark, or brilliant light, Todd plays with Duke Ellington's band. In the dream, Johnny Hodges is on alto saxophone, Jimmy Hamilton on clarinet. Weaving cigarette smoke filters the stage lights uncertainly, as Todd plays the blue note, filling his lungs until they ache. Sweat trickles down the small of his back.

Todd is unfamiliar with the score. It has a pleading quality, a question that makes his perspiration chill. Then suddenly he's playing solo for Hannah Reed, a bright phrase now, clear, but melting. He's amazed by his technique, effortless and magical, a glorious flight of sound. But imploring tones continue from somewhere else, with a human voice that must be the sax. Then the music becomes language, his mother's voice. "Todd, please wake up. There's an emergency. I have to go with Dad and Deirdre. The hospital. Do you understand?" He opens his eyes to his mother, confused by the hall light that silhouettes her.

"Yeah," he says, not sure what he's agreed to.

He's surprised to find his mother in the kitchen in the morning. She's in a tattered white robe he hasn't seen for a while, holding a mug of coffee in both hands. Her smile is overbright. "Deirdre's going to be all right. An overdose. She didn't mean to, an accident really" Her nodding is to make it true. "They have to keep her. You know?"

She picks up a spoon, stirs her coffee with a brisk clatter. "I've been thinking of the time Deirdre and I went to Mount Rushmore." She looks into the backyard, studying it as if it's the Great Plains of South Dakota. "We panned for Black Hills gold and ate buffalo jerky. I have a picture where I'm scalping her with a rubber tomahawk. We're a couple of skinny girls. But Mount Rushmore—" She taps the spoon on her palm, then holds it tightly still. "We got there after dark, sneaked in after the park was closed. And on top of the monument, by the presidents' foreheads, Deirdre walks over and looks down. Her sandal toes hang over and she says, 'Whew, this would be just too easy.' She leans over, and I see how dangerous it is—she is. I tell her to stop it right now. 'Come away from there, Deirdre!'" His mother's plea is sad, frightened, and filled with the anger only found in profound love. "Please," she says, quietly now to Todd. Her hair falls into her face. It's *his* hair, Alisha's and his, beige and bent in waves that don't curve regularly. The loose strand of hair scares him.

She puts the spoon down. "Deirdre's going to be fine."

But Todd knows she isn't. He feels a witness to her death, just as his mother has witnessed her past. Whether it's from pills or heights or cars or guns, it will come down to the same lost gamble: venturing too near to an edge. Some too-close attention to cactus or brightly colored food or butterflies.

His mother says, "If Deirdre would just—" But she doesn't continue. She reties the belt on the ratty robe and looks away.

Todd says, "I'm going to the hospital."

"No, not now." She says his name. Just his name. He hears the sharp *t*, the stop of the *d*, nothing more.

He drives to the hospital with an odd precision, carefully signaling lane changes, braking to gentle stops.

Departure

ANDREW PORTER

From *The Theory of Light and Matter* (2008)

That spring we were sixteen Tanner and I started dating the Amish girls out on the rural highway—sometimes two or three at the same time, because it wasn't really dating. There was no way of getting serious.

This was in 1992, over ten years ago, and things had not yet begun to change in our part of Pennsylvania. I think of that year as a significant one now, a turning point in our county, the first year the town of Leola started growing and becoming a city and also the first year the Amish started leaving, selling their property and heading west toward Indiana and Iowa.

There had been several cases of runaways among the Amish that year—mostly young men, barely in their twenties, tempted by the shopping malls and bars popping up along the highways near their farms. Leola was expanding quickly then, it was becoming more common, and it worried the elders in the Amish community. And I think it explains why that spring some of the Amish teenagers were given permission to leave their farms for a few hours on Friday nights.

Out on the other side of town there was an intersection on the rural highway where they would go to hang out. It was a remote area. A strip mall with a Kmart sat on one side of the intersection and across the road there was a twenty-four-hour diner. You would sometimes see them on Friday evenings traveling in a long line like a funeral procession, their buggies hugging the shoulder of the road as tractor-trailers rubbered by. They would park out of sight behind the Kmart, tie their horses to lampposts or the sides of dumpsters, and then the younger ones would go into the Kmart to play video games and the older and more adventurous would cross the street to the diner.

The diner was a family-style place, frequented only by local farming families and truckers, and it was usually empty. Inside, the Amish kids would immediately disappear into the bathrooms and change into blue jeans and T-shirts that they had bought at Kmart, clothes which never seemed to fit their bodies right. Then they would come out, their black wool clothes stuffed into paper bags, and order large platters of fried food and play country songs on the jukeboxes, and try to pretend they weren't Amish.

That spring Tanner and I had begun stopping by just to see them. We never bothered them, just watched. And it never occurred to us that there might be something unnatural about what we were doing, or even wrong. We were simply curious. We wanted to know if the rumors we had heard in school were true: that there were spectacular deformities to be found among the Amish, that few of the children possessed the correct number of fingers, the results of extensive inbreeding.

We would sit in a booth at the far end of the diner and glance at them from behind our menus. We were amazed to hear them curse and see them smoke cigarettes. Some of them even held hands and kissed. Sometimes other people, people from town like us, would stop by, just to watch—and you could tell that it worried them. People were still scared of the Amish then, they were still a mystery and a threat because of their wealth and the tremendous amount of land they owned—and so naturally they were disliked, treated as outsiders and freaks.

At eleven o'clock, they'd change back into their clothes and very politely pay their checks. Then they'd cross the street in a big group, climb back into their buggies and leave. And Tanner and I would stand out in the diner parking lot and watch them, still not believing what we had seen, but also somehow sad to see them go.

Once the other kids at school found out about the diner, they started coming regularly in their Jeeps and BMWs—not to watch like Tanner and I, but to mock and torment. It was cruel and it saddened us to see, though we never once tried to stop it. Instead we sat back in the corner and watched, angry, but also privately relieved that for once it was not us who were being teased or beat up. In the midst of targets so uncool and vulnerable as Amish teenagers, the popular kids seemed to have practically forgotten us.

There was one Amish kid who looked older than the rest. He could have been in his twenties. Tanner and I had noticed him the very first night because of his size and because of his face which always looked angry. He came every week with the rest of them, but always sat off by himself in a separate booth, smoking cigarettes and punching heavy metal songs into the jukebox at his table.

His anger scared us more than the others. That and his size. He had the body of a full-grown man, a laborer—his shoulders broad, forearms solid and bulging out near his elbows.

When the fights started he was always involved. They usually happened out by the dumpsters in back of the diner. The odds were never even: always five or six against one. Having been raised strict pacifists, almost none of the Amish would fight. But he would. And despite his size he would, of course, always lose—though he'd last longer than anyone would believe, moving with the grace of a young boxer, gliding, ducking. His style was to stay low and bring his punches up from way down under. He was quick, had a powerful jab, and knew how to protect himself. But the beauty of his moves never lasted long. Inevitably he'd lose his focus, turn his back or look away for a second, and there would be a pile-on.

A few minutes later, his face cut up and swollen, he'd retreat across the street to Kmart, followed by the rest of the Amish teenagers. And the next week, to everyone's surprise, he'd be back again—not even bitter about it, just sitting there at the edge of the booth, waiting.

It wasn't until late April that Tanner and I started dating the girls, but like I said, it wasn't really dating. They were all extremely shy and there wasn't a whole lot of common ground. Mostly we would ask them questions about their lives, and they would nod or shake their heads and giggle, and then we would sit and watch as they nervously stuffed their faces with cheeseburgers.

Later, we would walk them back across the street to Kmart, and then sometimes, if no one else was around, they would kiss us in the shadows. And then—almost like it never happened— they'd be gone again and we'd have to wait a whole week. Sometimes they'd never come back, and we wouldn't know why. We couldn't exactly call them up. Usually we didn't even know their names. So if they didn't show the next week, we'd try to meet two new ones.

Back at our school, pretty girls wouldn't look at us. We were unexceptional—failures at sports and our fathers didn't manage banks or practice orthopedic medicine. But out on the rural highway we dated the most beautiful of the Amish girls. They were attracted to our foreignness; and we, to theirs.

At school, there were jokes about us, naturally. Mainly inbreeding jokes. Someone had heard that our girlfriends had two heads, three nostrils, tails coming out of their backbones. It was almost summer and so we tried to ignore it, ride it out, though it made us think about what we were doing.

And it was not right, what we were doing. We were aware of that. And in a way we were still scared of the Amish. Even the girls. There was something unnatural about them. It's hard to explain, but they would only let you get so close—and it was always in private where no one else could see. Sometimes they would kiss you and then run away, or else you would be thinking about making a move, not even doing anything, and they would start to cry for no reason, like they knew.

I wonder now if it wasn't worse to let them leave the farms only once a week—if giving them only a small taste of freedom did not make the temptation stronger. Perhaps that's why so many never came back: it was simply too hard.

Tanner came from country people, though he had grown up in town like me. It didn't seem to make a difference. The wealthy kids still called him a hick and made fun of the way he talked and dressed. And you did not want to have the stigma of being from the country in our high school. Tanner and I both lived on the edge of the wealthy area, just across the street from it really. We were in the seventh grade when the school zone switched and the school district agreed to let us finish out our education at Cedar Crest High where all the beautiful and wealthy kids went, the only decent school in the county.

I had grown up with them, the wealthy kids, and even sometimes felt aligned with them when I'd see some of the dirty and disreputable country kids raising hell at our dances. But among them, sitting in class or walking in the hall, I was aware of our differences. Up until the ninth grade I had lied about my father's occupation, told people that he did a lot of work overseas, that his job was sort of secretive and I was not at liberty to discuss it. College wrestling coach didn't sound that great next to heart surgeon or judge. But I don't think anyone believed me anyway. They knew where I lived and knew that I was not a member of the country club, and that I was friends with Tanner. We were not one of them, Tanner and I, though we were not as low as country people either.

There was one girl I saw consistently that summer. Her name was Rachel. She wasn't shy or afraid of the outside world. And her hair smelled like tall field grass, a sweet smell. She was beautiful, too. She did not look like the other Amish girls; she lacked the full-bodied German figure, the solid thighs, the broad shoulders, the round doughy face. She was thin, small framed and with different clothes could have easily passed for one of the popular girls at Cedar Crest.

She was curious, too. Some nights she would want to leave the diner and ride around in Tanner's truck. She would beg Tanner and me to take her into town. Or else she would want to drive out to the Leisure Lanes bowling alley to shoot pool and smoke cigarettes. She was always excited, anxious, wanting to do and see as much as possible in the few hours she had.

When we were alone, Rachel wanted to know everything about me. She wanted to know what my school was like, what my house was like, what it was like to go to Ocean City. She wanted it all described to her in detail, almost like she was saving it up, collecting it.

Only once when we were parked outside the diner did she tell me about her family. It was an enormous family, she said. More than twenty of them lived in one house. Her father was seventy years old, the patriarch of the entire household, and he had set up rules and standards based on the very first order of Amish, now three hundred years old. These were standards that she was expected to uphold and pass down to her children. She had an obligation, she said, being one of the chosen very, very few. But she seemed upset as she told me these things. I could tell it made her feel guilty to think about her family, especially when we were together. And after that one night we never talked about them again.

———————

All summer the heat was getting worse. It had not rained for a record six weeks. Out in the deep country the crops were drying up and in town the grass on people's lawns, even in the wealthy areas, was turning into a yellow thatch. There was no escaping it. Even at night the air was thick with humidity and stuck to your skin like wet towels.

One thing Rachel liked to do was go down to the river valley where there was an old railroad track that had been out of service for more than fifty years. In all that time no one had ever thought to take down the tracks. They were rusted now, covered with weeds, and you could follow them for a mile or so to where they crossed over the river on an old wooden bridge, more than thirty feet high.

Rachel liked to have barefooted races across the planks of the bridge. The planks were evenly spaced, about two feet apart from each other. With a full moon it was easy, you could see where you were stepping, but other nights it would be pitch black and you would have to do it blind. It came down to faith. That and timing. If you slipped once, if your timing was just slightly off, your foot would slide into an empty space and you might snap a shin bone, or worse, if you were unfortunate and slipped through, you might fall thirty feet into the water. And of course we were young and confident and so we never once slipped, or fell, or even stumbled. The trick was always to get a rhythm in your head and to concentrate on it. But like I said, it mainly came down to faith, an almost blind trust that the wooden plank would be right there when you put your foot down. And it always was.

Tanner would sometimes come along with a girl he had met that night and we would all take a blanket and some iced tea down by the river and sit out underneath the stars. Some nights it was so hot Tanner and I would take all our clothes off and jump in the water, and the girls would watch us and giggle, never once thinking to join us; and we, of course, never asked. We knew the limits. We knew how far to push things and the truth was we never wanted to push, being inexperienced in those matters ourselves, and also not wanting to ruin what we had. We were young and somehow sex seemed intricately entwined with those other things—responsibility and growing up—and we were not interested in anything like that.

By then we had stopped hanging out at the diner altogether. It was no longer exciting to watch the fights and Rachel said it depressed her. More and more people had started coming out to watch the boy who always fought, and he was becoming a bit of a local celebrity. Rachel told me one night that she knew him: She said that his name was Isaac King and that she'd gone to school with him up until the third grade when his parents pulled him out to work. She said that during that past winter he had watched his brother die in an ice-skating accident and that everyone thought he had gone a little crazy from it. He had stopped going to church, she said, and it was only a matter of time before he left the community altogether.

Some Fridays we'd just drive, the three of us, with Rachel sitting between Tanner and me. Tanner liked to take his father's truck onto the backcountry roads that were all dirt and race it with the headlights off. It was terrifying and more fun than almost anything I've ever done—coming around those narrow curves at a high speed, not knowing what to expect, sometimes not even knowing if we were on the road or not, and then flying a little, catching some air when there was a bump or a small hill. Rachel loved it the most, I think. She'd close her eyes and laugh and sometimes even scream—she was not afraid to show her fear like Tanner and me—and finally, when she was on the verge of tears, she would beg Tanner to stop.

"No more!" she would scream. "Pull over!" And he would.

By July everything was changing quickly. Many of the Amish were already leaving, selling their farms to the contractors who had harassed them for years. Rachel never talked about it much, though I know that it was on her mind. People she had known her whole life were being driven off their land. Corporations even wealthier than the Amish themselves had moved in, offered sums of money that seemed impossible to refuse, and then, when that hadn't worked, had threatened them.

Rachel was beginning to change too. I knew she had strong feelings about leaving the Amish community by then, vanishing like the others had, though she never came out and said it to me, only hinted at it. For the first time, she had begun to complain about the tediousness of her life. Once she had even tried to leave, she said. She had packed up a bag with clothes and food but had stopped when she got to the highway near her farm, realizing she had no money and did not even know which direction led to town. With each Friday our time together seemed to go by quicker, and each time it got harder for her to go back home.

I think now that she wanted me to do something. It was not unusual for Amish women to marry at fifteen or sixteen, and I know that she was under a lot of pressure that summer to get married. Sometimes I tried to imagine what my parents would say if I brought her home with me, explained to them that she would be moving in. I imagined her coming to college with me and taking classes. I would get carried away sometimes, ignoring the absurdity of it, wanting to believe it could work.

It was a good summer for Tanner and me, our best, I think. Though we did very little until Friday nights. Days we stayed inside because of the heat and watched horror movies and drank iced tea by the gallon and nights we drove around by ourselves in Tanner's truck planning what we'd do the next Friday. We were wasting time, wasting our lives our parents said, and it felt good. That next year would be our last in high school and I think we were aware, even then, that we were nearing a pinnacle of sorts: the last summer we would still be young enough to collect allowance and get away without working jobs.

Our parents were never home that summer. There were cocktail parties and barbecues five or six times a week on our street and it seemed that almost every night the parents in the neighborhood got trashed, never stumbling home before one or two in the morning. Sometimes Tanner and I would show up at a party just to steal beer. We would stick ten or twelve cans into a duffle bag and then go back to my house and drink them on the back porch, and sometimes end up falling asleep in the backyard by accident.

In late July we started driving the truck out into the deep country during the days. The roads were all dirt out there and illegal to drive on. Occasionally we'd go out on a Saturday afternoon, hoping maybe to see Rachel or one of the girls Tanner had met the night before.

It was different out there. Aside from the humidity and the bugs, it was somehow depressing to watch all the young Amish kids working in the fields in such heat, fully dressed in their black wool suits, struggling with their ancient and inefficient tools, horse-drawn plows, steel-wheeled wagons. It seemed cruel.

One Friday night I borrowed Tanner's truck and took Rachel to the other side of town to see my house. We parked outside, just looking at it, not even talking. That night my parents were having a party and inside we could hear people laughing and the record player going. I could imagine my father slumped in his big leather recliner, surrounded by a circle of drunk guests, telling stories, and my mother carrying around trays of pierced olives and glasses of cold gin. Later on I knew my father would step outside and begin wrestling people, and everyone would yell "Go Coach! Pin 'em!" My father had been a wrestling star in college and whenever he drank, he'd start challenging his guests.

The thought of my father rolling around on the lawn with another grown man depressed me and I suddenly wanted to go back to the diner. But Rachel seemed happy listening to the music and laughter from inside.

After a few minutes she said, "Let's go inside."

I looked at her then and suddenly thought of what my father would do if I brought my Amish girlfriend into his house while he was throwing a party. My father, like most, did not like the Amish.

"Let's go," she said. "I want to try a beer."

I told her that it would be easier if I went inside and snuck the beer out to the truck myself.

A few minutes later I emerged with a couple of six packs and we drove down to the river and drank all twelve beers. Afterwards we lay down in a patch of grass near the water and acted silly. We felt loose and were affectionate with each other. It was Rachel's first time being drunk and she was being funny about it, kissing me in strange places: my elbow, my eyelid, my pinky.

Then at one point—I can't remember exactly—I started to understand that she was trying to tell me something: that it was okay. We could. That is, she would, if I wanted to. She was gripping my body tightly then, and it surprised me. And it scared me, too—because it did not feel tender anymore, but angry almost— and I know now that whatever she was trying to do, whatever she wanted that night, did not have anything to do with me.

And even though we never did, she still cried for a long time afterward, and I held her. And later, when I drove her back to the diner and we said good night, I was scared that I would never see her again.

In late August Tanner and I drove out into the deep country for the last time. Rachel had not showed up at the diner for two weeks and I had hopes of seeing her. I needed to talk to her. And Tanner, my best friend, drove me around all day.

We never did see her. Though we did see Isaac King as we were driving out toward the highway. It surprised us to see him and we stopped for a while and watched him working in the field.

He was the equivalent of a foreman, in charge of the younger boys, probably his brothers and cousins. It was strange to watch him at work. He was a different person out in the fields, not quiet like he was at the diner, but loud, animated. He moved around the fields swiftly, like an animal, and the young boys listened to him and even seemed a little scared of him.

We parked up on a hill, out of sight. We were still scared of him ourselves, even from a distance. I can tell you now that I did not really hate him. But those nights I had watched him take on four or five kids at once, I believed that I hated him. I hated him for never acknowledging the futility of the situation, for not bowing his head like the others and going home. For not accepting his place like the rest of us—like my parents did, like Tanner did, and like I did.

He must have spotted us before, because he came up slowly from behind the truck and surprised us. He might have thought we were two of the kids from the diner who beat him up every week, looking for some more action. But if he did, he didn't say anything. It was illegal for us to be on that land, even illegal to be driving around a car on those roads, but he never asked us to leave. He just stared at us until he realized we were not there to fight him and then he turned around and went back to the field.

Rachel finally showed up at the diner the last Friday in August. She was shy with me and distant. She told me that a lot of families in the community, including hers, were moving to Indiana at the end of November, after the harvest. The town was growing quickly, she said. It was just a matter of time before they would be forced to leave. She looked at me very solemnly as she said this.

"So what does that mean?" I said. "You're leaving for good?"

She nodded. "I think so."

I took her hand. "That's terrible," I said.

"I know," she said. "I know."

I've sometimes wondered what would have happened had I asked her that night to leave her community—to marry me and come live with me and my family. I thought of asking her even then, but it would have been a cruel thing even to suggest. My parents would have never agreed. It was an absurd thought, when you got right down to it. I was a pretty good student, after all, college bound.

Rachel had been begging me to take her to a movie all summer. She had never seen one before. So instead of spending our last night talking as we usually did, I took her to a rerun of an old Boris Karloff film playing at a place called the Skinny-Mini.

After the movie we drove around for a long time, just talking, though neither of us ever brought up that last night we had been together. I am certain now that she had been thinking about something else as we had watched the movie, and then later as we drove around. And somehow I could tell, even before she said the words, that she wasn't going to miss it.

We drove through town without talking. Rachel seemed disinterested, not even looking out the window. And the town seemed sad now, in the way every town looks sad right at the end of summer. It seemed cold already and empty, as if all the possibility Rachel had seen in it that summer had disappeared and now it contained only the same dismal potential it had every year.

It's strange, but I was not angry at her for leaving like this. I could tell she was not happy about it. And as we drove back to the diner I suddenly wanted to tell her how much I had enjoyed the time we had spent together, how much it had meant to me. I wanted to assure her that I would not forget her. But I never did.

When we got back to the diner, there was a crowd in the back lot, as usual. We walked over and saw Tanner watching. He was alone.

"Ten minutes," he said. "Fucking unbelievable."

Isaac King had been up for ten minutes. It was a record.

Kids were gathered around the circle, shouting, jockeying for position. I moved in closer to the group and found a spot near the edge. I could see that Isaac King was still up on his feet, his arms flailing.

What I never understood was why he never gave up. It shows that he was not right. Because even if he had been able to do the impossible—defeat five at once—there would be five more waiting on the sidelines. And then five more after that. And so on.

But that night it was clear that something was different. He wasn't going to let himself go down. In fact, he lasted a record twenty minutes. In the end, it took six or seven guys to finally get him off his feet and even after he'd been pinned down on his back he was still trying to move his arms and legs. Someone finally used a two-by-four to knock him out. It was an unnecessarily hard blow and even today I do not know which one of the kids delivered it. His head split open near the hair line. And when the blood started, everyone scattered.

I walked over to Tanner. "Hey," I said. "What the fuck just happened?"

"I don't know," he said. "I have no fucking idea."

It took a half hour to get him across the street and into a buggy. He was losing a lot of blood by then and had passed out. I suggested calling an ambulance, but Rachel said they never used the hospital. I tried to insist but she was stubborn about it.

"No," she said. "They wouldn't like it."

"Who's they?" I said.

But she turned away.

I never got a chance to say goodbye to her. When she left she was crying, though I knew it was not because she would never see me again.

Tanner and I went home after that and never went back to that part of town or talked about that night again. Instead we went into our senior year of high school and took the SATs, and then off to college like everyone else. I never saw Rachel again.

But a few months later I found out from Tanner that Isaac King had died of a brain clot six weeks after that night. It was a small article in the paper and no allegations were made.

These days almost all of the Amish have left. Most have sold their land off cheap to real estate agencies and contractors and gone west to Indiana and Iowa. We have new malls and outlet stores where their farms were, and out where Rachel used to live, actors dressed in Amish costumes and fake beards stand along the thruway, chewing on corncob pipes and beckoning carloads of tourists to have their picture taken with them.

I am twenty-nine years old now and not married. I am not yet old but some days I am aware of it closing in on me. Tanner lives in California now with a woman who will one day be his wife. But I can remember when he still lived in Leola, just a few blocks away. And when I think about Rachel now, I think mostly about those races we used to have out across the railroad bridge, thirty feet above the water, and I still shudder at our carelessness, our blind motions, not watching where we were stepping, not even considering what was below us.

What Jasmine Would Think

ALYCE MILLER

From *The Nature of Longing* (1994)

It was months before King was assassinated. It was the fall after the Detroit riots. Jasmine Bonner cornered me in the corridor at school. She came straight to the point. "You have study hall with Lamar Holiday, right?"

Lamar, Lamar, of course Lamar. Tree-tall, dark chocolate, with a three-inch natural and a wide, sloppy grin that could change your life. He wore black and green Ban-Lon shirts and a small gold medallion of Africa around his neck. He sat two chairs over from me and took copious notes from his civics book in small, curved handwriting.

"Everyone knows Lamar and I are 'talking,' but I think he's creepin' on me."

It felt like an accusation. "Lamar?" I was breathless, all legs and arms and curly unkempt hair.

Jasmine glanced behind herself briefly. "Yeah, with this little half-and-half Oreo, Jeanie somebody. She's been trying to beat my time. All I'm asking you to do is keep your eyes open. Let me know what they do in study hall. You know, anything *suspicious*."

I nodded vigorously. Talking to Jasmine in the hallway of our school was a promotion of sorts. Students passing by took notice, and I stood straighter.

"Cool," said Jasmine, closing the deal, and she smiled.

After that, I went on red alert. Lamar didn't know it, but we were now connected. Jeanie Lyons, the girl in question, sat by the window. She was high-yellow, with curly sandy hair and sea-blue eyes, but a flat, broad nose that gave her away. Not that she was trying to pass; everyone knew her father, our postman, black as the ace of spades.

I watched. Lamar didn't even pass her en route to the back table next to me where he and his friends congregated. And Jeanie, too sallow and freckled to be pretty, sat engrossed in *Valley of the Dolls*, and licking her long slender thumb carefully before each turn of the page.

Then, early one Saturday morning, on my way to a piano lesson, I spotted Lamar's white '63 Chevy convertible whistling down Route 10. No question that it was Jeanie crunched against him shamelessly, her sandy curls pasted by the wind against his dark chin.

I ran myself into a sweat getting home, where I dug in my schoolbag for Jasmine's phone number. My heart was in my throat when I dialed.

Jasmine's mother answered, sharply. "Who's calling, please?"

"Tish . . . Tish from French class."

"Tish?" Pause. "Just a moment."

The receiver clanked against something Formica-hard.

Time inched along. Nervously I chewed my thumbnail. Finally Jasmine picked up the receiver and spoke while crunching potato chips. "Uh-huh?" Her voice sprawled long and lanky on the other end. I pictured her spread out on a sofa inside her house on the other side of Main Street, large silver hoops dangling from under her halo of hair. Jasmine was one of the first girls at school to wear an afro and risk suspension.

"It's me, Tish." Conspiratorial. Hard as nails.

"Mmmmmmmmmm."

I threw out the bait. "I saw Lamar today."

"Ummmm-huh? Where?"

A woman's voice snapped in the background, and Jasmine said, "All right, all right." Into the phone she whispered, "I'm on punishment, talk fast."

This forced me to the point. Did she remember what she'd asked? Mmmmmmmm-hmmmmm. Well, I'd seen Lamar's car. Oh, yeah? Yeah, and Jeanie Lyons was in it. What did I mean in it? *In* it. You know, close to Lamar. How close? Close. Just close or very close? Very close. It got so quiet on the other end you could have heard a rat pee on cotton.

At last Jasmine said, "I knew his black ass was up to no good," and hung up.

That was it? I turned around and dialed my best friend Angela. Rarely did I have anything newsworthy to say; mostly it was Angela pasting together the meager details of her overlapping romances with the squarest boys in our freshman class. I acted casual, introducing Jasmine's name with the smoothest inflection. I repeated the whole conversation, word for word, without one interruption from Angela. A long silence followed on the other end.

"I didn't realize," she said cooly, "that you were currently friends with Jasmine Bonner. I know for a fact that she's two-faced and uses people."

"Maybe *some* people," I shot back.

"Sounds to me," said Angela sullenly, "like Jasmine isn't interested in you at all, she just wants information on Lamar. Besides, she doesn't like white girls, you better be careful."

"What do you mean, 'careful'?" I kept my cool.

"You'll find out," retorted Angela in that knowing way she had when she didn't know anything at all. "You don't understand you and Jasmine can never be *real* friends."

In our town, Angela and I both trod a thin line. Angela lived on the right side of town to be friends with Jasmine, but she still straightened her hair and worried about it napping up in the rain, and secretly thought the Revolution was just mumbo jumbo. Her mother wouldn't allow her to go dancing at the Boot Center where all the other black kids went. In all fairness to Angela, she'd been stuck with me as a best friend since grade school, old goody two-shoes Angela, who could least afford it.

Contrary to Angela's prediction (and much to her annoyance), Jasmine passed me a note, folded into a triangle, in French class the next day. "Just wanted to say HIGH," she wrote. Tuesday, another note followed. Jasmine Bonner had invited me to sleep over. As if it were the most natural thing in the world, Jasmine and me, matching the rhythms of our lives, as if she weren't two grades ahead, as if I were an equal. Jasmine of the rainbow fishnet hose and matching sweaters and pleated skirts, who sauntered the halls with queenly grace. She must have owned twenty pairs of pointed-toe shoes, purple, orange, lime, with fishing-line thin laces. Jasmine who with bold nonchalance popped a piece of Wrigley's Spearmint and calmly picked out her giant afro with a cheesecutter in the middle of French class while conjugating the present subjunctive of *être*.

I couldn't stuff my pajamas into a paper bag fast enough. It was a cool autumn night. My mother dubiously drove me south across the tracks, down through the park on Spring Street, past Angela's ranch house. She asked me what I really knew about Jasmine's family. Were her parents responsible people? Did Jasmine have a boyfriend?

"Jasmine makes good grades," I said, as if that proved anything. "She's always on the honor roll."

"And what about Angela?" asked my mother. She seemed to imply I could only have one friend at a time. "I haven't seen her around the house much lately."

I didn't dare condemn cautious, fraidy-cat Angela, carefully mincing her words at our supper table, easing my father's troubled conscience by her very presence. Angela, the Good Negro, agreeable and self-effacing.

When we got to Jasmine's I jumped out of the car, but my mother didn't drive off right away. I saw her hesitate, taking in the unfamiliarity of this end of the street, peering into windows darkened by early twilight, as if searching for a clue as to where exactly I was going.

Just before Christmas, Jasmine and I stretched ourselves across her unmade mattress inside the Bonners' gray shingle house at the bottom of Washington Street. As usual, the house was a pungent medley of frying fatback and greens and her younger sister Camille's hot-combed hair. Overhead, fine Huey Newton, framed inside his wicker fan chair, observed us skeptically. Jasmine rolled over on her stomach and came up on her elbows. I was envious of her perfectly round buttocks, slim hips, and long dark legs.

She studied me carefully, plucking wrinkles in her top sheet with long, slender fingers.

"I think Lamar's messing around with this white girl, Tish." Her tone was sepulchral. My flesh crawled. "She lives out on Gore Orphanage Road—in a farmhouse in a cornfield. Cindy something—Pavelka."

"You mean the one who hangs around Wanda and them and acts black?"

Jasmine nodded. "Little no-nothing triflin' tramp. She's got legs like bowling pins, girl. And she's been with just about every brother in town. They say she had an abortion last year."

"Why do you go on with Lamar?" I asked.

Jasmine studied me almost pityingly. Her eyebrows arched with older-girl wisdom, and then it dawned on me what she would never admit: that she and Lamar were connected sexually in some mysterious way only hinted at in the Motown 45s I knew by heart. I loved those melodies, the innocent lyrics shaded lightly with innuendo. Pure poetry and simple rhythms inciting the ache of fantasy. Without a word, Jasmine handed me Miles Davis for the turntable. We both lay back on her bed and listened somberly until twilight fell. That's how I passed my winter that year, vicariously learning the sting of passion without trust, a ragged wound torn open by Miles's horn.

There were evenings we'd drive around town with a stop at Dairy Queen for ice cream, with Jasmine peering through sleet-filled twilights in search of Lamar's Chevy. "He said he'd be at work," she'd say, "and he better be." A quick trip past Fisher-Fazio's parking lot proved he was: the pristine Chevy sparkled there like a diamond on the frozen blacktop. Jasmine's face would relax.

And sometimes, as Jasmine fussed at Lamar on the phone, twisting the cord with her fingers, I'd patiently feign interest in magazines, trying to pretend I couldn't hear the soft inflections of her voice, or understand their implications.

Evenings she wasn't off with Lamar, we listened to Miles or Coltrane ("traditional," Jasmine called it—she got the albums from her older sister Bekka, a student at NYU) and sneaked drags off the Kool Longs she stashed in her earring box ("Blow it out the window!" she'd hiss, fanning at the air around my face).

Sometimes she'd read me Sonia Sanchez or Baraka. As twilight moved to darkness, neither of us made a move for the light switch. Instead, we sank into silhouettes of ourselves, dark and indistinguishable shapes, consumed by words. We'd talk about who really killed Malcolm, and the importance of black economic power for self-determination and why the terms "Negro" and "colored" were passé, until Mrs. Bonner hollered through the curtain that hung instead of a door that it was two in the morning and we better shut that damn music off and let reasonable people get some sleep.

After Jasmine dozed off, I would lie awake, made nervous by the touch of her foot against my calf, wondering what on earth she could have ever seen in me, and promising myself to never disappoint her.

One afternoon after school a bunch of us drove to a frozen Lake Erie in Jasmine's father's black Ninety-eight to smoke and talk smack and look for someone named Peppy from Lorain who never materialized. Every time I spoke up, two of the girls exchanged glances and snickered. One of them pointedly stated she was sick of looking at peckerwoods every which way she turned.

Jasmine relished controversy. She seemed amused. "You talkin' about Tish? You don't know Tish," she snapped. "I got cousins in New Orleans lighter than her. Least she's got some wave in her hair. She *could* pass, you know that?" She reached over the back seat and ran her hand through my curls as proof. "See what I mean? Look at her mouth. Now try to tell me those are typical white lips."

I felt proud then, as proud as if I'd been black as ink. In grade school, stuck-up white girls like Kimberly Hubbard and Marjorie Grosvenor had called my mouth "bacon fat." Now Jasmine praised it. A full mouth was beautiful, couldn't be pursed like Kimberly's and Marjorie's into thin lines of superiority.

I began to sense I was someone other than the person I'd always been told I was. Over and over, the girl Jasmine saw inside me was being revealed.

But it all started long before when I came to understand that our town was really two. In one of Angela's more generous moments she had assured me, as if to assure herself, that I was really meant to be black, and she'd stuck her arm through mine and marched staunchly through the football stadium bleachers with me in front of everyone. Later, behind those same bleachers, she and three other girls jokingly christened me an "Honorary Negro." They each touched me and spoke words over my head, and I responded with "I do," to unite us forever. We were earnest, treating my whiteness like some cosmic prank that could be easily corrected. Then there were wisecracks about a fly in the buttermilk, which left us doubled over laughing. But deep inside I believed, and when you believe, the world shapes itself accordingly. Like the baptized, I saw through the eyes of the reborn.

On our way back from the lake Jasmine remarked, "You know, I take a lot of flack for hanging out with you."

"Then why do you do it?" I asked.

"Because," she grinned, smacking my arm, "you're different."

So I told her about my Honorary Negrohood and she fell out laughing so hard I thought she'd rear-end the car in front.

My family didn't grasp the incongruity of my presence in their lives. Instead they seemed to be blaming me for being other than what they expected. Sometimes I stared back at their puzzled faces, as we were seated around the dinner table, and saw only winter-pale strangers wearing masks of disapproval. The way my mother would turn to me sometimes and say, "Letitia, what on earth are you trying to prove?" pained me so much that I prayed they'd admit a terrible mistake had been made and confess to me who I really was. I was coming apart like a seam at the other end of a loose thread. I studied myself in the mirror, turning sideways, backwards, then facing myself again, trying to discern who it was that stared back at me. Not a person who belonged to these strangers. Just a person who knew the Revolution was inevitable. *By any means possible.*

"I don't know what you think you're doing," said my father, furious with me for announcing at the dinner table one evening that all whites would be dead by the end of summer. "I suppose this is what you call being 'cool'?"

The word slipped off his tongue like a mistake, and I cringed, secretly glad Jasmine couldn't hear the ignorance in his precise two-syllable inflection.

Keeping my eyes on my plate, I quoted Don H. Lee: ". . . after detroit, newark, chicago &c., we had to hip cool-cool/super-cool/ real cool that to be black is to be very-hot."

My father threw his hands up in disgust. "You see?" he said, appealing to my mother. "This is what happens when our liberal chickens come home to roost."

My mother shot me a baleful look. "I think it's Jasmine's influence," she said flatly. "I like Jasmine, but she's giving Tish wild ideas. We never heard this kind of talk when Angela was around."

My father muttered bitterly, "There hasn't been a white face in this house for over a year!"

Pain left me speechless. The countenances around me stared in silent accusation. What they couldn't know was that an unseen hand had reached inside and rearranged my whole genetic makeup, creating a freak of nature simply called Tish. Either side I chose I would lose myself. And living in the middle required becoming two people, split, like the baby Solomon threatened to cut in half. So I stared into my dinner plate until the Currier and Ives pattern of sleigh and horse melted into a swirl of icy blue and I was sucked into a storm of color so violent that I mistook it for redemption.

In June I, not Angela, was invited to Jasmine's seventeenth birthday party. My mother was dubious. Would adults be present? Would the lights be on? Would I leave a phone number?

It was a typical basement affair at Cintrilla Robinson's, with red and blue strobe lights blinking from the ceiling and a bowl of fruit juice punch spiked around eleven with Johnny Walker Red by some brothers from Lorain wearing three-quarter-length black leather coats and smelling of Old Spice. I slow-danced at least three times with Lamar's best friend Tyrone to seven scratchy minutes of the Dells' "Stay in My Corner." Tyrone sang into my ear in a precise, sweet falsetto and pressed me close against a hard place on his thigh.

He murmured approvingly, "Mmmm, you can keep a beat."

Jasmine and Lamar made out shamelessly in the corner by the

record player. From time to time their two silhouettes, topped by halos of thick hair, seemed to merge into one. Someone teased: "Y'all need to take that stuff to the bedroom!"

Awkward, I walked outside into a warm, starry night, holding my paper cup of spiked punch. Cintrilla and some senior girls I recognized from school stood talking on the patio. Cautiously, I joined them under the paper lanterns.

Tyrone followed right behind, but kept his distance. I watched him from the corner of my eye, pacing in the shadows, his hands shoved into the pockets of his St. Joe's letter jacket. He kept looking at the sky as if he'd lost something, but neither of us said anything.

Cintrilla smiled at me with surprise. "Aren't you in my French class?"

I tried to look as grown-up as I could in my flowered culottes and lime green shell. My eyes were so deeply outlined in Jasmine's mascara they felt brown and ancient as the Nile. "Mmmmm hmmmmmm," I said.

"You come with Jasmine and Lamar tonight?" Ruby Mason inquired in a friendly way. I nodded. It made an impression. The girls studied me with mild curiosity. When they asked questions, I found myself answering in a voice that could have been Jasmine's.

"Tyrone digs you," remarked Jasmine ever so coolly on the way back to her house. We rode in the back seat of her father's black Ninety-eight. She was trying to pull the collar of her blouse around her neck to hide the love bites.

I was so flattered I felt sick. "Yeah," I said, trying not to care.

"You know he's Lamar's ace boon coon. Lamar told Tyrone you're cool—for a white chick." She jabbed me with her elbow. I looked out the window at the small dark houses rolling by. "Lamar and I are back together for good this time," said Jasmine. "He gave me this opal ring." She thrust her left hand out to show me, and I saw a flash of milky white under the streetlight we'd just passed.

I understood then her sudden burst of generosity about Tyrone. Ring planted firmly on her finger, she gave me a conspiratorial wink. Tonight she could afford to share.

Call it guilt or mild yearning, the next day I made my way over to Angela's. She asked about the party in a deliberately offhand way. I described Tyrone. I made sure she understood this was a man with potential. For one thing, he was a senior, almost eighteen, and he attended *private* school. I described his hands moving over my back as we danced and the softness of his lips against my ear.

Angela dramatically threw her finger against her lips and hissed, "Shshshsh!" as if I had cursed in church. She rolled her eyes in the direction of her mother's bedroom.

"Your mother can't hear," I said, feeling myself rise tall above Angela. I was becoming less and less grateful for the friendship she bestowed on me in stingy little segments.

"You're getting in with a rough crowd" was all Angela said. "Mama says Jasmine's fast."

What she really meant was that she hadn't been included, but I didn't see that then. Disgusted, I got up and left. Angela didn't bother to walk me to the end of her driveway as she always did. Outside, the heat worked its way up from the pavement and burned through the soles of my sandals. They were sandals Angela and I had found in the College Shoe Shoppe two years before. We'd each bought a pair, agreeing we wouldn't wear them without telling the other. Now mine were showing the effects of two summers' wear, and Angela had shoved hers to the back of the closet, forgotten.

Angela's house on East Jefferson was an easy mile and a half from mine. By making a right on Lincoln, I passed Mt. Zion Baptist and a horse farm, and then a number of square brick low-income units where children rode bicycles in the street and front yard clotheslines were always full of bed sheets.

Just beyond was Jasmine's block; the houses were even smaller and poorer. The narrow streets, like many of their residents, were named for U.S. presidents. On the sagging steps of a turquoise house, some older black girls from school hung out playing 45's on an old phonograph. The humidity was cut by the scratchy rhythm of one of the summer's hottest hits, "Express Yourself" by Charles Watts and the 103rd Street Rhythm Band. Maxine Watson, the homecoming queen, danced in denim cut-offs in the dirt yard. When she saw me, she raised one light brown hand in greeting, and I thrilled at the acknowledgment.

But it was short-lived as a bright-skinned girl named Chick snapped, "What'd you speak to *her* for?" Chick had sat sullenly across from me one semester in ninth-grade algebra class giving everyone the evil eye. If she didn't feel like answering the teacher's questions on a particular day, she'd stage-whisper, "Kiss my black ass, bitch," so that the whole class would snicker. Now Chick was expecting a baby by her college tutor. Evil old Chick who lived ruthlessly on a higher plane than the rest of us, above fear of reproach.

I crossed Main Street, which divided our town exactly in half. The air sweltered. On Professor Street I passed the statue of Horace Percival Huckleman, honored posthumously for leading a troop of black soldiers during the Civil War. My parents lived up on tree-lined Elm Street, our house nestled among all the other professors' families. The yards here were midwestern-ample and the old three-story homes sat back from the streets in comfortable superiority. The gray summer air was still, silent, oppressive. Here, people kept to themselves. No noisy barbecues, no lawn parties, no children running and shrieking through sprinklers.

Up ahead two shimmering figures made their way slowly toward me: Kimberly Hubbard and Marjorie Grosvenor, in culottes and poor-boy tees. They were my two mortal enemies on the other side of the dividing wall. In reality, they lived on my street, but I might as well have been invisible, living a parallel life, unnoticed.

Kimberly and Marjorie could walk by you as if you were a leaf on the sidewalk, flipping their long straight hair with a casual flick of the wrist. They had a secret language of gestures and words that I had never been able to master. It was a language of privilege and confidence, designed to exclude.

At the beginning of ninth grade they took it upon themselves to corner me briefly by my locker. "So, Tish," Marjorie said, her teeth a flash of white in her summer-brown face. "We were just wondering, are you still going to hang around with Angela Winters now that you're in high school?"

I didn't understand, and my ignorance tested their patience. Marjorie gave Kimberly a significant look. "Angela's nice," she explained to me, "but you need to think about what's best for you now. We think you ought to know, and this as a friendly warning, that a lot of people think you're spreading yourself too thin."

Now, passing me, Marjorie and Kimberly fused together into one girl. "Hello, Letitia," their shared voice said, forced. I felt no compulsion to answer. Instead, I squared my shoulders, taking my courage from Jasmine. I never glanced their way, never even gave the impression of having noticed them, blowing them from my mind as easily as if they were chalk dust.

Jasmine tried to get me hired at the College Restaurant where she worked, telling Bud Owens, the black owner, that I was sixteen. But when I showed up he shook his head and shooed me out, telling me I was a chance he couldn't afford to take. I waited outside, humiliated, until Jasmine went on break and we wandered over to the college art museum, finding relief in the cool interior.

We sauntered by Del Washington, the black security guard standing awkwardly over to one side, sweating inside his uniform. Del was in his late sixties; for years he had done odd jobs for families in my neighborhood, and adults and kids alike called him by his first name. Now I felt ashamed to know him.

Jasmine couldn't stand him and went on to prove it. "Don't you think it's weird," she asked me in a voluble tone, "that white people hire black people to guard white people's art that they copied from black people?"

She pulled me over to a small Picasso. "Now there's one white man made a whole career off of imitating Africans."

Del pretended not to hear Jasmine's words echoing off the cool walls. We strolled back past him into the next gallery. "Some people are so damn worried what white people think of them. You know, don't you, you can't be a healthy black person and please white folks at the same time. It's a sickness, it's what makes black people go crazy, and then white folks can't figure out why niggas act like fools."

Jasmine's shoulder brushed roughly against mine, her eyes focused into empty space ahead. "We've been trying to please y'all for a long time, but now enough is enough. You watch and see what happens in Hough and every other ghetto this summer when they burn again. The Revolution is here."

To our left, Del was turning a deep purple.

"I'm going to have to ask you to lower your voices," he said, "or leave the museum."

"I was about to leave anyway," snapped Jasmine and grabbed my hand. "Come on, girl, I'm about to choke in here."

Outside, she threw back her head and laughed aloud.

"What's wrong with Del?" I asked, torn. Del used to give me chewing gum when he was cutting the neighbors' lawn.

"He's a Tom, that's what's wrong. That man has kissed so much white ass I'm surprised his face is still black."

I felt sad then, for all of us—me, Jasmine, and Del.

"That's the difference between us," remarked Jasmine. "You're over there feelin' sorry for Del Washington. Well, he hates himself for being black. He's the most dangerous of all."

The summer dragged for me. Jasmine was busy with work and her college applications. She was applying for early admissions to Fisk, Howard, Morehouse, and Spelman. She laughed when Harvard wrote to her and asked her to apply. "Why do I want to be some place where they either flunk you out or bleach you out? I'm not going to be part of someone's nigga quota."

We were on Jasmine's front porch watching the rain and I was greasing her scalp. A streak of lightning startled us both. Thunder followed right behind. "The Temptations in A Mellow Mood" revolved on the turntable just inside the door.

A phone call had put Jasmine in a bitterly rotten mood. Someone had seen Lamar at Rocky's Roller Rink Monday night, and Cindy Pavelka had left in his car. The old wound was reopened. "Why can't white girls leave our men alone?" Jasmine fumed.

I yanked her head a little to the left and carefully separated the next section of hair with the teeth of the comb. I kept the parts even, creating little irrigation canals into which I smoothed fingertips of Royal Crown. Jasmine's scalp gleamed like hematite. I pulled the hair on either side of the part straight up into rows, like stalks of corn. Cradling her head in my lap, I used the comb rhythmically like a lullaby. Her shoulders rocked gently against my knee.

"Tish, I'll be honest, I've never loved a man the way I love Lamar, and he's breaking my damn heart!"

With her right hand she guided my comb to a spot I'd missed. Little white flakes of dandruff lodged in the teeth of the comb. "Come out with Chick and Benita and me tomorrow night." It was more a command than an invitation.

"Where?"

"The Boot Center," said Jasmine.

I felt mildly panicked. "You know I can't go."

"Oh, come on. Say you're spending the night."

I must have hit a soft spot in her scalp because her head pulled a U-turn. The specks of amber in her eyes caught fire. "Watch it, I'm tender-headed."

"Well, don't mess up my lines." I tried to yank her head back into position, but she pulled away.

There was a long pause, marked only by the whirring of the fan from inside and the drumbeat of rain on the porch roof overhead. She reached her hand up to her scalp and felt where I'd left off. "You take too damn long." She stood up and paced. On one side of her head, where I'd been at work, her hair stood up in thick fist-shaped spikes. "I don't see why your parents think the Boot Center is so bad, except that it's full of *us*, a bunch of black boots. I bet if Kimberly and Marjorie were down there dancing to 'Turkey in the Straw' your parents wouldn't be scared to send you."

I ran my fingers down the greasy prongs of the comb.

"I'll try to come," I said, "but if my mother finds out. . ."

Jasmine bit her lower lip. "I'm telling you, if Cindy's there, I'm through with him!"

I felt the tension rise, along with the humidity and the smell of Jasmine's scalp oil on my fingers.

There was the unexpected sound of tires on gravel, and we both looked out to the road to see Lamar's Chevy pulling into the rain-soaked driveway. "Shoot!" said Jasmine. "Nigga knows he's in trouble." She grabbed the comb from me and began furiously to work her hair. "Tyrone's with him!"

My heart went heavy as lead as two figures splashed through the rain and up the steps. Jasmine kept her lips poked out sulkily when Lamar said, "How ya doin', baby?" I'd forgotten how tall Tyrone was, how good-looking. The combination terrified me.

"Mama and Daddy are down at their social club?" Lamar asked with a grin. "Thought we'd stop by."

Jasmine nodded. "I need to talk to you, Lamar. We can go listen to records in the basement. Tish, grab that stack of 45s, would you, girl?"

She picked up the record player. Tyrone and Lamar both smelled of cologne. I followed them down the steps like a sleepwalker. Immediately "Ooooh, Baby, Baby" was on the turntable and Jasmine and Lamar were linked together, murmuring to each other. Obviously Lamar was denying whatever it was Jasmine accused him of. Convincing. Smooth. Jasmine was loosening up.

Tyrone reached for me and I felt myself melting against him, as he guided me slowly toward the furnace. The record finished and Lamar started it over again. I heard Jasmine say, "You're gonna wear that record thin as a dime," and I felt the vibrations of Tyrone's chuckle in his chest as he pulled me closer while Smokey moaned.

My first kiss happened there in Jasmine's basement with Tyrone, but the experience was disagreeable. The smelly old sewer pipe ran straight out of the floor at our feet, and so that moment was permanently framed in my memory by a rising, heavy, sour odor too awful to consider. But I was in love with Tyrone, my heart about ready to explode.

Later, after they'd left, Jasmine, who seemed to be in better spirits, asked me, "Tyrone say he'd call?"

I shook my head, still overwhelmed that just moments before a boy's mouth had been pressing against mine.

Jasmine sighed. "What's wrong with the Negro? You're my ace honky."

I hated her holding the other mirror to me like that. "Shut up," I said.

A shadow crossed Jasmine's face. "Maybe Tyrone thinks your father will shoot him through the phone."

"I keep telling you," I protested, "my parents don't care."

"Don't be so naive about your so-called liberal parents." Jasmine frowned.

"My parents marched in Selma," I said, uneasy.

"So, then why don't you ask Tyrone to come by and have dinner? Get to know your folks?"

She was mocking me so I didn't answer. I didn't know why.

"See what I mean?" said Jasmine smugly.

Anxiety marked my veins like medical ink. "You're wrong," I insisted.

"I'm more right than you realize. Your parents would lose their minds if they thought you'd gone cuckoo for Cocoa Puffs." She lit a Kool Long and French-inhaled so that the smoke looped back through her nostrils.

We went upstairs where she heated up the iron to press her uniform for work. Overhead, on hangers, the dashikis we'd sewn hung like half-people from the light fixture. Jasmine's was black and yellow and red; mine was blue and white and green.

She mumbled to the wall, as if enjoying a private joke, "I must be outa my mind making a dashiki for a white girl." She winked at me as steam rose from the iron. "I'll have it ready for tomorrow night. You're comin'?"

Jasmine picked me up on her way home from work. She was still in her waitress uniform. My mother walked me out to the black Ninety-eight. She pointedly asked Jasmine if we were going out anywhere or if she could reach me at the Bonners'.

"We might go get Dairy Queen." Jasmine was sly!

"About what time would that be?" asked my mother.

Jasmine looked coyly at her watch. "Oh, maybe around ten."

My mother's eyes narrowed. "Jasmine," she said with maternal clairvoyance, "you know Letitia is barely fifteen years old."

"What are you trying to tell me?" asked Jasmine.

But my mother had turned abruptly and walked back toward the house.

At Jasmine's I changed into a short skirt and the dashiki. Now I was edgy as we drove past the Baptist church to pick up the others. I imagined coming face-to-face with my mother's car at every corner.

"Will you just relax?" said Jasmine. "I'm the one who should be nervous, what with Daddy being so fussy about his damn stupid car and all. One tiny scratch and I'm dead."

Mr. Bonner'd said if we weren't home by midnight he'd send the sheriff out after us.

"Your Ninety-eight ain't no Cinderella," Jasmine had muttered.

"Yeah, and you ain't meeting no Prince Charming neither," Mr. Bonner reminded her meaningfully. It was no secret he wasn't fond of Lamar, whom he called a "scalawag."

Jasmine was wearing blue jeans, her dashiki belted at the waist. On her long slender feet were slave sandals, the latest rage. I instantly regretted my short skirt, ashamed of my knobby knees. We split up a bunch of her metal bracelets, and crisscrossed our arms like gypsies.

Maxine and Jasmine made small talk up front. I envied their big afro silhouettes, blocking my view through the windshield. I was stuffed in back with Benita and sourpuss Chick. Benita commented sweetly on my hair. "You sure have some pretty curls. They natural?"

I thought how long I'd futilely envied the straight-arrow cuts of the white girls, every hair in place. Jasmine had picked out my hair, and now it bloomed around my head.

Chick scoffed from the corner by the window. "It just looks like some of that old flyaway shit to me."

As I leaned forward to check my eyeliner in the rearview mirror my leg accidentally brushed Chick's. She jumped back as if I had a disease. "Please keep your body parts to yourself," she said and crossed her eyes at me.

You could hear the Boot Center before you could see it. James Brown blared from speakers lodged in the open window frames upstairs. Shadows of dancers rose long against the walls.

"Ooooh, my song," said Chick and jumped out, full of baby, and headed up the stairs. "SAY IT LOUD!" she bellowed along with James Brown, "I'm black and I'm proud!"

Jasmine came up beside me and dug her fingernails into my arm. She hissed in my ear, "You better pray Lamar's at work tonight."

"Don't worry," I said, but I had serious doubts.

We tromped up the outside stairs, just as if we were a club. Girls accustomed to one another, who hung together. The music swelled from the packed dance floor. Across the room, through blinking lights, I recognized the black vice principal from our school, Mr. Foster, who'd been called down to chaperone after some fights between our town and Elyria. Everyone knew he Tommed. From what I'd seen, Mr. Foster faked it on both sides, playing "brother this" and "brother that" when it suited him.

The air was so close I immediately broke into a sweat. My head felt thick. Maxine yelled over at Jasmine, "See what happens when you get a bunch of niggas together?" She wiped drops of perspiration from her forehead with the back of her hand as proof.

Jasmine pulled me through the crowd like a needle dragging thread. We were headed toward Tyrone, standing alone in the corner. Jasmine thrust me at him in a way that made me suspect she had planned this all along. "Here's Tish," she said as if delivering a package.

James Brown over, Nancy Wilson began a lugubrious "You Better Face It, Girl, It's Over." The moody bass pulsed in my veins.

"I didn't come here to hug the wall all night. Would you like to dance?" asked Tyrone, the perfect gentleman. He took my hand in his. My fingers went cold.

I looked around for Jasmine, but she was nowhere in sight. Tyrone drew me close. "You feel good," he said. I went sleepy inside. Out of relief, I rested my head on his shoulder. His arms tightened around me and I closed my eyes. "Follow me," he whispered in my ear. "Keep the beat." An anonymous hand in the dark yanked my hair down to the roots, checking to see if I was or wasn't, but I played it off, a mistake, a miscalculation. I felt the sharp pain at the back of my head eased by the hypnotic movements of Tyrone against me.

But the trouble began before I'd fully regained my senses. The record was still playing when Tyrone gently nudged me and pulled away. I misunderstood at first. Then I looked in the direction in which he was staring. Just as Jasmine had predicted, just as she had known, Lamar strolled into the Boot Center with a bigger-than-life Cindy Pavelka. He was wearing a black fishnet shirt, a cap, and the gold medallion map of Africa.

Lamar's car keys dangled from his hand. He was trying his best to merge with the dancers, but Cindy hung close. When his eyes caught Jasmine's, his face registered first shock, then mild sheepishness. They stared at each other, moving toward that inevitable moment they'd created together. Tyrone murmured, "Uh-oh, my boy's in deep trouble," and gripped my hand tightly, as if to console us both.

Heads turned from all directions. Lamar kept moving. He gave the fist to several of his cronies, a forced smile across his face. Cindy wore a defiant look, like someone who'd won something. And the shameful thing was she hadn't even bothered to comb her hair, as if she'd just climbed out of his back seat.

Tyrone left me for Lamar. They clasped hands, grabbed wrists, then stacked their fists in the air, desperate to seem casual.

I found my way to Jasmine's side. Her features had all moved together in a mask of horrendous rage. She had known, hadn't she, all along, that this was why we had come tonight? Maxine and Benita and Chick stood over to one side, observing. Jasmine walked slowly toward Cindy. "You stupid white bitch." Her voice rose over the music. Dancing couples slowly parted, as more and more people caught on to what was happening.

Cindy's smile was forced and impudent. She heaved a bored sigh and put her hand on her hip, challenging. But the heavy pulse in her throat gave her away. "Get out of my face, Jasmine," she said.

Chick and Maxine and Benita closed around her like a fence. A murmur of "Fight, fight" rumbled through the Boot Center.

"Jasmine . . ." Lamar reached out. He tried to stop her, but Jasmine shot him a bitter look and struck his hand away.

"Don't you touch me!" she said and advanced toward Cindy. "Are you out of your mind?" A little push and Cindy looked startled. "Don't you know Lamar belongs to me?"

I squeezed in between Maxine and Chick. Cindy glanced nervously at me, then shifted all her weight to one side. "Look, don't you touch me again," she shot back helplessly. "It's none of your business what I do." She was losing her nerve.

Then Jasmine burst into tears, accepting defeat. I couldn't stand it. Before I knew what I was doing, I had drawn up my fist and pulled my elbow back as if stringing an arrow in a bow. At the moment my fist touched Cindy, the needle scratched like a scream across the 45. The music stopped cold.

Cindy stumbled back a couple of steps, her mouth drawing downwards. She looked back in hatred. Next to me, Jasmine grabbed a fistful of Cindy's hair and cried out like a wounded creature, "Leave Lamar alone, you honky bitch, leave him alone."

I started for Cindy again and would have shoved her against the wall, except that someone took hold of my shoulder, yanking me backwards.

"Have you lost your mind, girl?" It was Chick, her eyes dark and startled in her yellow face. "How can you?" she asked me. "How can you do that? This ain't none of your business."

Someone shoved me hard from behind. I heard murmurs of contempt. Mr. Foster broke through the crowd yelling, "Break it up, break it up. Disperse. Let's go." People began pointing, accusing. In the confusion, I turned to see Jasmine disappearing out the back and down the fire-escape steps, her body bent in the shape of heartache. Lamar threw down his car keys in disgust, as if inviting anyone to drive off in his Chevy. Mr. Foster's eyes smoldered as they came to rest on me. "Hey, you!" he said, starting toward me. There was nothing left to do except push past Cindy, the only person blocking my way, and get down those stairs as fast as I could to the street below where I wasn't sure what to do next.

The People I Know

NANCY ZAFRIS

From *The People I Know* (1990)

My mother is propped up in bed with the pillow shoved under her chest. She looks to be peering over the edge of a pool. This is how she always lies before she sleeps. Now she'll smoke cigarettes for at least an hour and talk to me until I drift off. Sometimes in fatigue she'll drop her head and smoke with one side of her face pressed against the mattress. With each puff she lifts her head slightly, like a swimmer catching air during his stroke, and blows the smoke away.

"Do you know what déjà vu is?" she asks me.

"Yes."

"I feel like I've got it all the time."

"You ought to. You do this every night," I say.

"Do what, baby?"

"Smoke, stare into space, tell me you've got déjà vu."

Without lifting her body, she wrestles the pillow from under her chest and smacks it on top of me. "I never told you I had it before."

I throw the pillow back to her.

"Maybe it's just déjà vu," she says, "for you." She bounces her hand in a piano-playing flourish to this rhyme and breaks into laughter. She's a heavy smoker and her laughter erupts in bursts of phlegm. She turns toward me and the hollows in her cheeks seem daubed with black paint. I feel hypnotized by those two holes of black; I realize, as if it's my last thought ever, that I'm a second away from sleep.

She leans over the aisle separating our beds and offers me her cigarette. I have barely enough strength to shake my head.

"What'd you say?" she asks.

"Nothing."

"What?"

I moan. "School," I try to whisper.

"What, baby?"

I can see I'm not getting out of this one easily. I gather my strength for one last sentence. "I never smoke after brushing my teeth." Then I'm gone.

If she could, she'd keep me up till dawn. She would like to sleep too, I think, but her body obeys the cranky rhythms of her mind. I am young, however, and my body still obeys its bodily needs. And so, right in the middle of her talk, I fall like a stone into shallow sleep. When I open my eyes, I don't know whether a few minutes or a few hours have passed: my mother has remained the same, staring, aiming her smoke over the top of the headboard. The coiling smoke has solidified into a thick gray cloud.

"You know what I'm thinking?" she says.

"Where are we now?"

"Him. We're back to him again." She means my father. "You know what I've been laying here thinking? That if I'd been smart like you I wouldn't have got duped."

"You're smart," I say. "Everyone says so."

"In medicine, baby. Along medical lines. That's not what I'm thinking about."

"Mmm."

"What?"

My eyes close.

"Okay, so don't answer me."

I jerk awake. "What was that?" The front door slams a second time.

"Sue's home. Lord help us."

"Mmm."

"Wait and see."

We hear a pot being thrown from the stove to the sink, then from the sink to the floor. Sue pounds up the stairs. "Here it starts," my mother whispers. Then Sue pounds down the stairs. The walls begin to shake with the sound of her stereo.

Sue is our roommate. It's hard to like Sue except in degrees. On the other hand, it's easy to dislike her wholeheartedly. She and my mother split the rent and try to share the apartment. It's not easy being in the middle of two thirty-six-year-old roommates. I watch them develop a hairline wrinkle one week, a gray hair the next, and in between regress just as fast as they're aging. Sue used to be a travel agent; now she's a waitress. My mother's a medical receptionist who has become increasingly sidetracked by schemes to get Sue's goat—calling from work to wake her up, signing her up for special offers she clips from *Parade*. This is a living arrangement I hope will end soon.

As music rattles the walls, Sue thumps up and down the steps. Against the noise of her stereo, this stomping emerges as trumpets in an orchestra, more felt than heard. Finally we hear a banging on our bedroom door. Sue sticks her head in. It's a small head; the shape of it in profile is all nose, no chin or forehead.

"Come in, Sue," my mother says.

"I can't stay," Sue says. "I just dropped in to remind you how many times I've asked you not to smoke while I'm home."

My mother takes a long drag before she answers. "When I can't sleep because someone's playing their stereo at 2 a.m., then I smoke."

"For God's sake! I work hard and I need to unwind!"

"The choice is yours."

"My God! You're so selfish!"

"Might I mention also," my mother continues in the excessively calm voice she affects with Sue, like a therapist with a neurotic patient, "that I have a daughter who attends high school early in the morning. Speaking of selfish, that is."

"Well, who could sleep with all this smoke? You can't even breathe."

"It's easier to sleep to the sound of smoke than to the sound of that music." By the way my mother takes a long indulgent suck on her cigarette, I can tell she thinks that was a damn good line. Sue slams the door and my mother rolls the cigarette around the rim of the ashtray. Sometimes she circles the whole rim. It's a habit of hers during contemplation. "What'd you think?" she asks.

"You were good," I say.

"I kind of threw the ball back to her court."

"You did."

She thinks for a while, rolling the tip of the cigarette into a pointed ash.

"That thing about the sound of the smoke, ooh that was good, that just came to me."

"Mmm."

"You know what it reminded me of?"

"What?" I ask.

"You know, *him*. That's like something he'd say. He could really use the English language. He could manipulate words."

These words themselves manipulate my sleep, the phrases drifting through dreams I can't recall, and the next morning in school when I'm still half-asleep and Mrs. Henmin says of a poet, "He knew how to use the English language," I feel that this is too coincidental not to be momentous. Something compels me to tell others of this coincidence, deprived though I am of the punch line that would explain its significance. The exact words, after all, have been used within hours to describe my father and a famous poet. But when I tell my best friend Natalie about it, she doesn't even pay attention. She's showing me some photographs she just had developed. "What do you think it means?" I ask.

"This is a really good one of me," she says.

She looks up for my approval and sees me staring at her.

"And you too," she says.

I continue to stare at her.

"I don't know what it means," she says.

In my heart I don't believe that he ever existed, biological necessity to the contrary. Nevertheless, references to my father always intrigue me. Because I have never seen him, not even in photographs, I dream of him in my own version of Braille—odors and shadows, and sounds (usually of a pan being thrown). There's never a face, though often the camera follows a pair of feet. Sometimes there are several pairs of feet. They follow behind me like visible footsteps of invisible men. And although Natalie claims to have prenatal memories (she remembers coming out and being slapped on the bottom), I can go even further: I can feel the temperature, the texture of darkness, and the aroma of my mother's seduction by the lone love of her life. Or so I imagine.

When I arrive home from school, my mother is sitting at the table with Jackie. Jackie always appears about ten minutes after my mother comes home, no matter when she comes. Jackie is like a Geiger counter that can, from a respectable distance, gauge any change in my mother's activities. I'd swear she watches us from her Venetian blinds if her Venetian blinds didn't hang three miles away.

Jackie is the type of person who says things like "Yahoo!" and "Hooray!" when she's happy, but I just think it's playacting because I don't think she's happy. But tell that to her—she thinks she's the happiest person on earth. When she sees a good-looking guy (or even a not-so-good-looking guy—let's put it this way: when she sees a *guy*), she says, "Yum-yum!" The worst is that my mother laps it right up and even says it herself. "Yum-yum behind you on your right," she said to Jackie and me at Burger King the other day. Isn't it obvious to her that people who say "Yum-yum" and buy unauthorized biographies and a half-gallon of malted milk balls to eat while they read them are people who, while they are usually old and sad themselves, make *you* feel old and sad? And when she and Jackie laugh together I feel so old and sad I might as well be stuck in a nursing home with a handicapped toilet as my only view. What is SO funny? I have to ask, but they can't answer me: they're laughing too hard.

I walk in just as Jackie is describing a heaviness in her legs. At first I'm struck with a tentative admiration: however slight, it is at least not my usual disgust. Jackie doesn't seem like one to admit her shortcomings, and heavy legs is one of them. She always wears stretch pants that have a strip of piping sewn down their center to mock a perfect crease. Under these pants she wears hose, which pulls her thighs into odd bulges like the lumps from removable football pads. Has anyone ever looked at her and said, "Yum-yum"?

Then I realize that Jackie is talking about a feeling of heaviness in her legs, not her actual heaviness. It's just the same old thing again. Jackie thinks my mother is a doctor simply because my mother works in a doctor's office. She is forever telling her about her ailments. Then she waits for a diagnosis. Jackie loves being diagnosed. She thrives on trying to have diseases.

My mother listens silently during Jackie's long description of this heaviness. I know that she wants to give me a hug, but she can't: it would break her concentration. Instead she holds out her cigarette like a peace pipe, and I take a puff. Then she studies the cigarette while she listens, tapping and rolling its ash to a point. Finally she poses several questions. This is the part Jackie loves best.

"Is this heaviness painful?" my mother asks.

"No, it's not real painful. It's more like a heaviness. But sometimes . . . I mean, sometimes it seems to hurt."

"But it's more a feeling of numbness?"

"Yeah, numbness."

"Is there a lack of sensation when you touch it?" My mother moves closer to her. "Look over there for a second. How many fingers am I touching you with?"

"Two," Jackie says.

"How about now?"

"Oh boy, I don't know. Feels like one. I couldn't really say."

My mother leans back and takes a quick tug at her cigarette and then crushes it in the tray. Jackie watches all of this with rapt and curious eyes. My mother trails her finger around the lip of the ashtray and lets it linger in the groove.

"What did it mean that I couldn't tell how many fingers?"

My mother shakes her head to curtail any talk. She's thinking.

"Ooh, sorry," Jackie whispers.

"Does the numbness radiate outward?" my mother finally asks.

"It seems to."

"How? Does it move in a progression—from here to here to here? Or does it sprout up in different parts of your body?"

"It sprouts up," Jackie says.

My mother lights another cigarette at the stove. She takes down a third cup from the cupboard and pours us coffee. "There are a couple of things that come to mind," she says to Jackie. "But what I would do is wait a few days and see if it's better or worse."

"What if it's the same?"

"Or the same."

"What if it is?"

My mother inhales and lets the smoke fork slowly out of her nose. It's another sign that she's thinking.

"What are the couple of things that come to mind?" Jackie asks.

My mother pours boiling water into a pan of lime Jell-O mix. "Varicose veins." She slices up a banana and drops the slices one by one off the edge of her knife. "Toxic shock syndrome," she says after the first slice plops heavily to the bottom and then fights its way to a floating position. In a few seconds there's a whole layer of baby yellow lifebuoys. When the Jell-O hardens, they'll sink like lead. "Multiple sclerosis," she says at last.

"Multiple sclerosis," Jackie whispers. "Wow." She is ecstatic.

Between Jackie and Sue, I'm about to go crazy. At least Jackie likes me all right, but Sue hates my guts. She despises my mother too. We're not so fond of her either, but it's not the main thing in our lives. Now we have another problem with her: she's left the night shift at the restaurant and become manager of the day shift. The only reason we've been able to live with her so far is that we never see her. Now we have her all evening long. She sits in the living room and sniffs the air for trouble with that nervous, upturned nose of hers.

At least I have an hour to myself after school. Thank God for small favors. But then Sue comes home. She immediately pours herself a Beefeater martini because she thinks it's sophisticated. After one or two drinks she puts a Weight Watchers TV dinner in the oven and drinks white wine while she waits. While she waits she usually accuses me of watering her gin. "Let me smell your breath," she says if she's had a drink too many.

When she finishes eating, she rinses out the foil dish with the water on full blast for as long as it would take someone else to wash a sinkful of dishes, and then fills it with cat food and gives it to her cat. She doesn't think cats should get addicted to human leavings, but neither does she think cats should be humiliated with animal bowls for their food. Frustrated as she is with no boyfriends, this becomes very important and gets mixed up with moral issues like sex, and suddenly she can become vehement and essentially hysterical about why cats should not lick

Weight Watchers lasagna. Afterwards she sinks back with a calm exhaustion and there is a slight smile on her face. We hate the cat almost as much as we hate her.

After the cat finishes eating, Sue rinses out the foil again, and after she's done this she just throws it away. Next she scrubs the sink with Soft Scrub, rinses it, and takes a paper towel and wipes away the beads of water. The sink is completely dry and shiny as a mirror. It says, "Please don't turn the water on me." When I turn on the water, Sue jumps visibly in the chair and her nostrils flare. "I'm sorry," I say.

"Don't be sorry," my mother warns.

Sue sips her wine and watches me. I go to the downstairs bathroom, but I know she can hear me. I run the faucet. When I come out, Sue smiles meanly. "Nice way to run up the water bill," she says.

"You should talk," my mother says. "That cat uses up more water than any human being." Sue's cat is named Shiva after the Hindu god of destruction. Behind her back we call Sue "The Goddess of Destruction" and we call her cat "Shitva" after the Hindu god of kitty litter. For days Sue has been worrying about whether she should get Shiva spayed. She says "spaded." She talks about it constantly when she isn't talking about Richard, her old boyfriend, or how youthful she looks for her age, at which point she gives my mother smug, accusatory glances. She talks in a high elated voice that is still oddly normal. It reminds me of someone on stage who has to exaggerate their voice and inflections and still sound ordinary.

It's the fifth day of Sue's new shift. She comes home bright and early. After drying the sink again with a paper towel and pouring a second glass of wine, she starts on her same three subjects. First, the cat. "I found out something *very* interesting today," she says in that theatrical voice. "Somebody told me that the male cat ejaculates within ten seconds of entering the female. The female *then* turns around *quite* often to claw the male. And I said, 'NO

WONDER! NO WONDER!'" At this point she throws out both arms in a wide expanse and I get the feeling that she never got over being the lead in the high school play. "*I'd* turn on a man who ejaculated in ten seconds too!"

Ejaculation leads easily into her second subject, Richard. "No one has ever felt the heartache I feel. I feel as if my heart is ripping in two right inside my chest—right inside, *ripping*. I need someone to hold me so I won't—*literally*—break apart. I *know* no one has ever felt this kind of heartache or everyone would be dead. I don't know how I'm still alive," she says.

"I don't know either," my mother responds in her quiet therapist's voice. She looks at Sue and aims slow jets of smoke her way.

This angers Sue and thus leads easily into the third topic: her youthfulness versus my mother's. "I don't know why men call you and they don't call me. I look so much younger. It must be that I don't look like an easy lay."

My mother calmly exhales a wad of smoke and says, "Or maybe you look too easy."

"I seriously doubt that," Sue says with a harsh laugh.

"I guess you're right," my mother says without a hint of sarcasm. It completely rattles Sue, who is gearing up. Her nose, darting the air for a fight, turns red at the tip and white at the bridge. We ignore her.

In bed that night my mother has a good laugh as she searches through her *Thirty Days to a Better Vocabulary*. "That Sue," she pronounces, "is a neurasthenic asshole. Sorry, baby. Had to say it." She stuffs her pillow under her stomach and returns to her vocabulary.

Whenever she takes a drag of her cigarette she turns her head to the side, as if she's being considerate of the book, and blows the smoke into nonoccupied space. The book, since it's a paperback, won't stay open. She turns it over and jerks it backward, but she only succeeds in breaking the binding. True, the book now lies obediently open, but groups of pages drop out and each page, as she turns it, goes its individual way. The edge of muci-lage grows wider as each page glides off. "Ah muchacho chiquita muchachos!" she shrieks in disgust. She thinks she is swearing in Spanish. "Chiquita!" she yells again. She thinks "chiquita" means "shit."

But now she sees the humor in it all. She strips off the mu-cilage like it's a Band-Aid and throws the loose pages in the air. Then she yanks the pillow from under her stomach and flings it on top of me. "Want to play '30 Day Pickup'?" Her laughter breaks into crackles of phlegm: the harder she laughs, the more she has to cough in the end. "Well," she says, "there goes my thirty days to a better vocabulary."

"Unh-hunh . . ."

"But I got a few good words out of it. Today, for instance, they made me wait so long at the bank I was going to be late for my next appointment, so I butted in at the front and said, 'This is a temporal matter!' Nobody said a word, they let me right in." She hits me with the pillow when I don't respond. "So what do you think?" she asks. She hits me again. "Why won't you answer me?"

"It's a temporal reason," I say.

"I love it," she says.

She gets distracted by the sleeveless nightgown which has slipped from her shoulder. Her chin compresses into itself as she tries to see the top of her shoulder. "Can you still see where my swimsuit strap was?"

"No."

"Chiquita. I'm all pale."

"You're still dark."

"Well . . ." she says, as if still thinking about her tan. "I think they're talking in the office like maybe I could start giving some shots."

"I thought you had to be a nurse," I say.

She shrugs. "They're talking about what a great job I do."

"Well, good."

"You think my legs look okay?"

"What are you talking about?"

"You know, OKAY. You know what I mean."

"You know they look okay so don't ask me."

"My stomach's starting to stick out though. Look."

My mother is the envy of all her friends because she's thin. But to me she doesn't look good. She looks too thin. Her collarbones protrude like a clothes hanger. On good days, when she has slept and eaten healthily, she has the angular features of a model, though still perhaps trimmed a little too sharply. On bad days her face is unrelenting in its thinness. On these days it makes me sad just to look at her. What wrinkles, I wonder, were plowed at my birth?

"I think I'll do twenty sit-ups every night," she says. "For a whole week."

Kindled by the doctor's praise and by Jackie's psychosomatic idolatry, my mother buys a white business suit that bears a definite resemblance to a doctor's uniform. That night, when I am startled from a deep sleep by Sue's shrieking ("For crying out loud! Can't I get a little peace in this world!"), I bolt upright in bed and call "Mom!" in a quick jerk of breath. But her bed is empty. It shocks me, and when I turn to see her skeleton hanging in the closet, I scream. My heart rushes in violent waves toward my throat: it is her white suit hanging on the bones of a clothes hanger.

The next day I tell Natalie about it. "So?" she says. "It probably looks nice on her."

"Thank you for just missing the point."

"Oh God, you're so argumentative."

"Okay, just forget it," I say.

"Fine with me." Natalie is a staunch supporter of my mother. If it weren't for the fact that she is black, people would probably mistake them for mother and daughter. Their relationship blossomed during our sophomore year when both of us went through a traumatic event: one day Natalie and I discovered our French teacher, Mrs. Lefebvre, dead on the floor. We had come in during lunch to do her bulletin board. There she was, flopped on the tile like a fish. Her eyes and mouth were open. She had choked to death on her turkey sandwich. It was the second day after Thanksgiving vacation.

Natalie went into shock and they had to take both her and Mrs. Lefebvre to the hospital. As far as I know, I've had no serious psychological repercussions from this event, but its consequence for Natalie was severe. She became so afraid of choking that she became afraid of eating. It wasn't that she didn't want to eat. She wanted to eat, but she was afraid to. I had to sit with her at lunch with my hands poised in the air. This was what I called the "Heimlich Ready Position." It was mortifying to Natalie to think that others might see her in this incapacitated condition (she was always very popular and bright), so she elected me as the only one privy to her humiliation. After all, I saw her go into shock, and if she had had someone else help her through that time, there would have been two people who had seen her helpless and two people, therefore, who had claim to a certain superiority over her. Besides, I don't think anyone else would have gone to all the trouble more than a couple of weeks, not even the Rondettes, who are her second-best friends.

The Rondettes are three black girls who, I must admit, make the drill team come alive. They are forever practicing their soul drills right in the hall. They look like very funky robots clapping once, saluting once, bending once, over and over again, all to a rhythmic chant. If they've got a crowd around them, they'll make the chant obscene. The white students love it more than the blacks. I don't really like the Rondettes, but I guess I'm the only one. Natalie's crazy about them. Whenever she's with them, her accent changes and she starts talking black. All of a sudden everything is "girl" this and "girl" that. Whenever she does this, I hate it.

The Rondettes were nice enough to Natalie during her trouble, but they weren't about to give up their lunch hours for her. The Rondettes are busy people. So it was left up to me to protect Natalie from choking. My mother helped too. Very calmly, she demonstrated the Heimlich maneuver to Natalie, explaining that no matter what went down, even turkey, it would come back up. She taught me the Heimlich maneuver too, and the three of us used to spend hours practicing it on each other. During these times Natalie would lose that skein of nervousness that always enclothed her, even when she was still (she was motionless like an animal sensing danger). My mother, bless her heart, would soothe Natalie and even make her laugh—she was the only one who could. Consequently, Natalie became dependent on my mother, and in some ways they're more like mother and daughter than we are.

On Saturday Natalie comes over and we get ready for the pool in our apartment complex. Sue becomes somewhat hysterical when she sees us. Someone has put water in Shiva's water bowl without rinsing it first. Two briquettes of cat food float about like pieces of poop, and Shiva refuses to drink it. So would I. "Whoever did this should clean it out," Sue says. When neither Natalie or I make a move, she screams, "*Dehydrated!* Do I make myself clear?"

I kind of nod.

"Do I?"

"Yes!" Natalie says quickly.

Now the two briquettes are starting to disperse in the water like brown tablets of Alka-Seltzer. Sue picks up the plastic bowl and slams it into the sink. "Cats are people too!" she screams. "They deserve a little respect! A little love! For God's sake, where's all the love in this world!" She pours herself some wine, pounds the cushions of her chair before sitting down, and glares at us.

Natalie and I dare not say a word or even look at each other.

"You're just like your mother," she hisses. It's supposed to be the ultimate insult.

"Let's leave my mother out of this," I say.

Sue takes another sip and stares into her drink. "You're a little piece of chiquita, as your mother would say."

Natalie and I glance at each other and then back at the floor.

"Yeah, I see you looking at each other. You're a little piece of shit, as I would say. Me, that's who. Me me me." She begins singing a little tune with "me me me" as the only lyrics.

"Let's go," Natalie whispers to me.

"Wait," I mouth back.

In another minute Sue sinks back into her chair in a refreshed stupor, a smile of exhaustion on her face. Her nostrils are dilated; I can see them from across the room.

"See what I mean?" I whisper to Natalie.

My mother comes home immediately after this. I see that she's wearing her new white suit and that she has the collar of her blouse turned stylishly up. Because she looks nice, the collar part makes me both sad and happy, the way I feel when a timid fat girl tries on a new skirt and smooths out her hips. I'm happy when I catch the girl's smile in the mirror because I can't bear to think of the alternative. My mother is starting to affect me this way though I don't know why.

"Girl, you look sharp in that suit!" Natalie exclaims as soon as she sees her.

My mother has a smile on her face. "Really?"

"She thinks she looks like a doctor," Sue says sarcastically from her chair in the corner. She's on her second or third glass of wine.

"Girl, you *do* look like a doctor."

My mother doesn't say anything, but she makes eye contact with me and grins.

Natalie presents her with a photograph of herself and me.

"What a picture of you two," my mother says. "I'm going to put this up in my office."

"What office?" Sue says.

"Natalie looks gorgeous."

"No, I don't."

"Tell the truth, Natalie."

"Well . . ."

My mother laughs and grabs Natalie in a hug. "How you feeling, girl?" she whispers.

Natalie looks at the floor, suddenly shy. "Fine."

My mother squeezes her shoulder again before letting her go. "Everybody ready for a swim?"

We lug ice, a six-pack of Diet Pepsi, chips, a couple of paperbacks, suntan oil, and towels to the pool.

"You're playing Russian roulette with skin cancer," Sue yells to us as we leave.

"God, I wish she'd dig a hole and crawl in," my mother says. She takes a seat in a chaise longue with her book. She oils up until she shines like a body builder. By the end of the summer her face will be wet leather stretched over a skull.

"Is that book good?" Natalie asks.

"No, but it's nasty. Ha ha, just kidding, girls." My mother steps off the chaise longue, which is divided in thirds, and arranges the parts so that they all click level like a bed. Then she turns over and lies on her stomach, head peering over the edge. The pose looks so familiar. It's how she lies in bed. I feel that same sadness as before. For some reason, when I see inconsequential things repeat themselves with her, moods or gestures circling the air above her, I get that feeling again, sad. Too sad, like when I cry at a song about breaking up when I've never in my life broken up. I watch my mother, stretched out, happy head up to view the sights, and I feel my eyes stinging.

"God, what is your problem?" Natalie says in disgust.

"Nothing."

"Don't start doing this now," she says.

"This is the life," my mother says. She deposits her ashtray, a foil disposable from Sue's restaurant, under the lounge chair. When she reaches for her cigarette, her arm wraps around the side of the chair and feels blindly along the cement. "Would you rub some stuff on my back, baby? Thanks." She lifts her head up like she's doing the breaststroke (it's as close as she'll get to swimming) and exhales some smoke. She checks her straps for a tan and then aligns her forearm with Natalie's. "Girl, you be dark as me," she says with her hoarse laugh.

"Girl, I wish I was that thin," Natalie says.

I can't believe it. Here I am putting oil on my mother and she's talking black and Natalie is talking black back to her. "Thanks a lot," I say.

"You're welcome for whatever it was," Natalie says.

My mother laughs and feels on the cement for her cigarette. I rub the lotion on her back until it shines. Then I move over to Natalie, whose complexion contrasts so sharply. My mother's tanned skin becomes thinly webbed with light creases as it thickens and puckers from the heat, but Natalie's skin grows into rich cherry wood with a gloss of burgundy shining on her shoulders.

"You're so lucky you don't get freckles," I say.

"I'm so lucky," Natalie says.

"So shut up," I say.

"Here, I'll put some on you."

"I'm going in. Aren't you going in?"

"I'm having a drink first."

"Natalie?"

"What?"

I flick at something on my thigh. When I look down, I discover it was a firefly. Why was it out during the day? On my leg is a fluorescent smudge.

"What?"

"Ooh," I say. "Look at that."

"Wha-aat?"

"Natalie?"

"What!"

"How come you don't ever talk black to me?"

"What are you talking about?"

"You talk black to the Rondettes, *and to my mother*. But not to me."

"Yes I do."

"You never call me 'girl.'"

"Yes I do."

"No you don't."

"Shut up," Natalie says.

"You like them more than me."

"God, who wouldn't the way you act."

"I'm serious," I say. "I mean it."

Natalie looks away and I see her jaw drop. I turn to see, oh please no, it's Jackie in a yellow bathing suit fringed with a little yellow skirt. Perfect for a dancing pink pig. Her legs shoot upward like giant sugar cones. They start out skinny but make up for it at the top.

"Hi, Jackie," my mother says dreamily. Her arms are spread out limply to catch the sun. On the cement her hands curl inward, palms up, as if she's doing the dog paddle.

When Jackie sits down, her butt appears below the chair, striped in green vinyl. "Yum-yum on your left."

"Definitely," my mother murmurs.

"Smack smack."

"Mmm."

"Not to change the subject," I interrupt, "but is ANYBODY going in the pool?"

"I would but my foot hurts," Jackie says.

"What's wrong?" my mother asks.

"A radiating pain."

"Another one?" I say.

"Where?"

"Right here in the center of my foot."

"Could be a plantar's wart," my mother says. "Is it a surface pain or does it have a core?" I jump in before I can hear anything else. I swim until I'm in the deep end where the ladder descends as deeply as the water. I follow it down and with the blue water surrounding me like umbilical fluid and my hair alive as Medusa's I look at the submerged bottommost rung and think, There she is—that's what she used to be like. The water is very cold. I'm shivering when I come up for air.

On Tuesday, with a week left of school, we have our final examinations. At the lockers before the English exam someone shows me the latest issue of the school newspaper. One of the senior profiles is of Natalie, but the photograph is horrible. At the time Natalie offered the school photographer one of her own pictures, but he shouldered her up against the window, turned the camera vertically, and snapped. Even I know that when you take pictures against the light, white people come out black and black people come out silhouettes. Poor Natalie's finely featured ebony is a featureless glob of newsprint ink; the light shafting through her hair has turned her processed strands into snakes.

I grab the newspaper and hide it. If she sees this before the exam, she'll fail for sure. As I take my seat behind her I can't help but marvel at what a good friend I am. It's those little things I do that should clue in more people than—oh well—they do.

Mrs. Henmin has warned us beforehand that if we write "Wadsworth" for "Wordsworth" we get an automatic *F*. I write: "I think this shows a negative attitude because you're assuming the worst. If I showed you a picture of half a glass of water, would you give me an automatic *F* if I said it was half full just because you assumed the worst and thought it was half empty? Sorry, but I just thought I should express my honest opinion."

Without thinking I tap Natalie on the shoulder and show her what I've written. She nods in approval and goes back to work. This little conference is treated as naturally as one treats a shoplifter who, with arms too full of a TV, asks the clerk to open the door for him. For once the room is full of quiet students who have done their studying; the usual goof-offs are the ones most frantic to have their say in court. They are nervous and earnest, like freshly shaved hoodlums before the judge.

I can hear the air currents from the vents, but the air remains thick with the hot dreaminess of a schoolday in summer. The slam of a door down the hall echoes a world we have left. I am losing my concentration.

When I come to a question about reincarnation and what poems illustrate it and how and why do I think that (please be specific), I can't remember. The answer gnaws at me like a forgotten previous life. I can't help but think how appropriate this is, more appropriate in fact than if I had simply known the answer—had simply led a single life—and so I write down this observation instead of the answer. When I finish, I drop my pen and exercise my fingers. I do in fact feel I've led several lives, I just don't know what they are or where they went. My father, I am sure, has not only led many lives, he's created many. A terrible thought occurs to me: my mother and I are just one of his many. Was he just one of her many? I decide to press her for the answer, to find out what really happened. She's always been vague about the subject. An even worse thought occurs: suppose she doesn't even remember?

I can hardly cope with this possibility. I light a cigarette and blow the smoke hard toward the ceiling. The newly demure rowdies don't dare draw attention to me. But it wouldn't matter. I don't really notice what I'm doing. Neither does Mrs. Henmin. She is staring out the window. That funny looking body of hers heaves in sighs or dreams. As she stares outside, her overlooked face deepens with sadness. Her stomach, which she so often grabs like a good luck charm, no longer seems set at that jaunty angle suitable for our laughs. It sags. She continues to look out the window, oblivious to the fact that I'm smoking. In fact, she herself has slipped a cigarette out of her purse. We are both, I seem to understand, thinking back to the same time. For Mrs. Henmin it didn't happen; for my mother it did. I make a mental note not to repeat either mistake.

Still at the window, Mrs. Henmin smokes the cigarette only so long as she needs it for her thoughts, stubs it out on the pane, and throws it outside. Furrowed student foreheads pop up like toast to witness this miracle. That bit of ash on the window squats more proudly than any of the bits of knowledge she has given us. It's probably the only thing we'll remember about her in a few years.

That afternoon I have a brief reign as a celebrity. Three or four boys tell me they would have asked me out if they'd known how I really was. It's too late now. I try not to look back with regrets, but why all these years did I confine my smoking to the toilet? Mrs. Henmin and I have come out of the closet, but the room is emptying in one week. Still, I am easily gratified.

"It's not too late, you can date them over the summer," my mother tells me.

"It's too late," I say. "So forget it."

"Here." She shakes up a cigarette from her pack.

"No, I've given up smoking."

"But I just bought that Topol toothpaste. It takes out nicotine stains if that's what you're worried about."

"No."

"Oh. Well, I'm not going to smoke if you're not."

"Go ahead."

"No. Not if you don't," she says sadly. She places the cigarette in the flat of her palm and looks down at it. Her pet fag that's died.

"All right, give it to me," I say.

We're sitting at a restaurant where she's taken me to celebrate my graduation. It's a restaurant above our means and I have the feeling that the waiters, the customers, the dishwashers—everybody—has immediately sensed this. We catch ourselves gawking as a waiter opens a bottle of wine at the table next to us and hands the cork to the oldest man, whose white hair, at each temple, has receded in finely speckled triangles. He breathes in the darkened cork with his eyes closed.

"Do you wish they were your parents?" my mother asks me.

"They're too old."

"You know what I mean."

"If they were younger, yes. Definitely yes," I say.

"I love it," she says. Then she calls the waiter and orders a bottle of house wine. She nods at me. "Two can play this game."

"You'll probably have to drink it alone, you know."

"Don't worry. You're grown up. Oh my God, I can't believe it: my little baby, all grown up."

The waiter opens the bottle in front of us and she smells the cork. "Mm-hmm, very nice," she says. He pours two glasses and she winks at me. "See? Here's to your graduation."

"Thanks. You drink both of them." Now I'll get her drunk and then I'll pop the question. Oh God, like father like daughter.

"You know what?" she says and puts her chin into her palm.

"What?"

She pivots her head both ways to make sure no one is listening. "I'm going to cry at your graduation."

"Why?"

"I don't know."

"I'm not."

"Well you're maybe not. But I am. Cause you're leaving me . . ." she says.

"I'm not leaving you."

"Yes you are."

"Just to go to school is all."

"That's enough."

"Don't say that. Now I'll feel guilty."

"Don't feel guilty," she says. And then, after exhaling, "Just don't go."

"Mom!"

"I can't help it. I'm going to cry if you go."

I look at her with my mouth open to speak, yet I don't know what to say. Because my mouth is open, she is confused for a second and thinks I'm the one who has cried out. But it's come from the table next to us. The delicate liver spots on the temples of the white-haired man have turned a flaming pink. His eyes and mouth are wide and round.

"Chiquita!" my mother whispers.

"Is there a doctor in the house?" the wife screams. My mother immediately stands up. She walks calmly over to the man, and in the midst of uselessly gesticulating people she grabs him from behind in the Heimlich maneuver and pops her fist against his diaphragm. She has saved a life. She really has. And she is wearing her white suit.

When she winks and gives me the thumbs-up sign, all action stops. Everyone turns to stare silently at me.

The Source of Trouble

DEBRA MONROE

From *The Source of Trouble* (1990)

I was in eighth grade, reading *Teen Beat*, an article called "Double Dare—What To Do When You Accept Two Dates for Saturday Night," and I threw the magazine down on my ribcord bedspread and looked at myself in the mirror, thinking Geez, counting on my fingers the months until high school, four. My mother says it's short, the time of pale formals covered with net and reinforced with push-up stays that make your cleavage deep, the time between when your date toasts you with his cocktail poured in your shoe and when your husband reads the paper while you pace the floor and the baby pukes. So I hung my red nylon windbreaker over the lamp to make the room dark and I stuck my gum over my teeth to cover my braces, and I thought about how the handyman at school once said to me, "Devita, I think about you every night."

I took my gum off my teeth, put my windbreaker on, picked up my pen and spiral-bound notebook, and went outside and sat on the porch and stared at the lake and made my Popularity Success List Plan: Be nice to boys, all boys, don't make fun of the hair on their chest or legs. Stop saying BALLS. Don't tell that joke about Tarzan's snake being in Jane's cave. Make friends with the smart and pretty girls at Butternut Consolidated High when you go there in the fall, but still be nice to Melissy Smith and Laura Plus (best friends from Glidden).

My mother walked onto the porch and said, "Devita, I got this letter from Butternut High which says you're going to take the tour next week so you'll know your way around in the fall." I threw my notebook down. "I forgot," I said. I'd envisioned myself in short colorful dresses, wearing makeup and heels, my hair long and flowing and boys standing next to their lockers and whistling through their teeth. I'd counted on having all summer to get ready. My mother sat down next to me and stroked my hair. I smelled her Dove soap smell and my love surged. I can't wait until I'm a woman. "I'll kill myself," I said. She said, "We'll order something from Montgomery Wards and it'll be here in time for the tour."

The next day at school, which in Glidden is a one-room building with kids from first to eighth grade, I passed Melissy a note which asked what she was going to wear. She put her hair in her mouth and said, "Depends on what's clean, I guess." So at noon I asked Laura and she said, "Jeans because if you overdress you'll look nervous." I'd considered a blue skirt and blouse with shiny pumps but Laura had a point; I told my mother to order the pale green shorts ensemble with matching sandals.

It turned cold and rainy that day and when I ran down the driveway to fetch the paper wearing my bathrobe and flip-flops, I came back shivering and drenched. My mother said, "Devita, you can't wear the new outfit." We had a fight and by the time Laura's dad was there to pick me up my face was puffy, my nose was running, and I was wearing the shorts outfit but with thick socks and oxford shoes and I had my windbreaker which I planned to ditch. Melissy Smith was wearing a wool dress. Laura wore jeans and sneakers and a sweatshirt that said ANDY'S FISHING LODGE. Genius, I thought: Butternut High is small potatoes, her clothes seemed to say.

We saw the gymnasium, the cafeteria, boys running lathe in shop class, and Mr. Darby dropped us off at the Home Ec room. "Wait here," he said. He came back a few minutes later with two girls. "Del Rae Thomas and Valerie Verholtz live right here in Butternut," he said, "and they're going to be freshmen next fall too." Mr. Darby left, and Del Rae got a box of vanilla wafers out of the cupboard and Valerie turned to us and said, "Have you met the girl from Fifield yet?" Del Rae rolled her eyes and, wiping cookie crumbs off her mouth, pointed at Valerie and said, "Valerie burns."

Valerie said, "I do not."

I said, "What do you mean, burns?"

Mr. Darby opened the door. "This is Bernice Isabell from Fifield," he said.

Bernice was wearing a Schlitz beer T-shirt and a pair of hip-huggers so low they had only three snaps. She smiled and her corner teeth stuck out. Mr. Darby counted us and said, "Okay, that's all the freshmen girls for next year." He shut the door and Del Rae said, "What about you, Bernice? Do you burn?"

Bernice didn't answer.

Del Rae sniffed the air. "Have you heard that theory that if your shampoo and soap and perfume and talcum don't match, and you use them all at the same time, you smell like dog shit?" Bernice put her hands on her hips and stared at Del Rae. Del Rae said, "And some people just roll in it."

Mr. Darby opened the door. "Have you girls made friends yet?" he said. "It's time for the pep rally."

A few weeks later, after school let out in Glidden, Melissy and Laura and I got the same letter, spidery, slant-forward handwriting on notebook paper: A Get Acquainted Before School Starts Next Year Surprise Party for Bernice Isabell, Bring PJs and Blankets. I took it to the living room to show my mother. She was wearing a wide dress with her crackly slip and pouring cocktails. "You drink too much," she said to my father, "and you fall asleep on the couch at eight o'clock."

He said, "I work hard all day, Arla, and I come home and I want to relax."

She said, "I'm sick of it."

I sat down next to my father and smelled him. I love his silky cheeks where he shaves. I showed him the letter. "Why is that familiar," he said, "that name? Oh. They own that tavern in Fifield."

A car pulled up in our driveway. "Arla," he said, "find out who that is and send them away."

My mother opened the door. "It's Jack Burns," she said. Jack Burns lifted her off the floor and twirled her. "Darla," he said. She smiled and straightened her hair. My father stood up and shook Jack's hand. "You're not going to keep us out until dawn drinking and carousing tonight," he said. "I'm tired."

Jack said, "Get me a highball." He smiled at me. "How are you, little girl?" I didn't answer. He said, "Aren't you glad to see me?" Again, I didn't answer. My mother said, "Have some manners, Devita." Jack Burns said, "And after I gave her my swizzle stick collection too."

Laura's dad gave us a ride to Fifield and on the way there I said, "Do you think Bernice is weird?" and Melissy pushed her glasses up her nose and said, "I never thought about it." Laura said, "She is, but Del Rae is mean." Mr. Plus pulled into the parking lot of Isabell's Castle Hill Retreat and pointed at the beer sign. "You girls stay away from the tavern," he said, "you're too young."

He drove away and we stood in the parking lot holding our stuff and no one came so we went inside and a fat lady with piled-up hair who turned out to be Bernice's mom said, "Where did you girls come from?" I said, "We're here for Bernice's Get Acquainted Surprise Party." She said, "Bernice's surprise party?" She wrinkled her nose. "Bernice!" Bernice walked into the bar-room and smiled. "Hi," she said. She said to her mother, "I asked some friends over."

We went outside and across this field, and Bernice opened the door to a small house, knotty pine with checked curtains inside. She said, "This used to be where we lived before we built the bar and put the house on top and now I use it for a clubhouse." She opened the top drawer of a dresser. "Look." There were packs of Marlboro cigarettes, a pint of blackberry brandy, all the makeup you'd ever need. I opened a tube of mascara and used the tip of the wire-coil wand to paint a beauty mark on my chin.

Someone knocked at the door. Bernice looked out the window. "Geez," she said, "I can't believe they came."

"Who?" I asked.

She said, "Those bitches from Butternut." Del Rae Thomas and Valerie Verholtz walked in. Del Rae said, "We're here for your surprise party, Bernice." Bernice said, "You know, I was so surprised. I had no idea. My mother planned it, you know."

We started putting on makeup and Bernice got these slips out and said, "These used to be my mom's when she was thin and they look cool with lipstick." She took her T-shirt off and stood there like she wanted us to see her knockers, and she took her jeans off too and put the slip on. She reached in the drawer for a cigarette and lit it and looked at herself in the mirror. "See what I mean?" she said.

A car pulled up. "Well," Valerie Verholtz said, "that's my cue. Good-bye."

"Where's she going?" Laura asked Del Rae.

Del Rae said, "With Rocky, her boyfriend, her parents try to keep them apart, it's so sad. But you know they do burn, I know for sure."

Bernice said, "How do you know?"

Del Rae said, "They did it once when she was on her period."

"How do you know that?" I said.

She said, "I just do. Bernice, do you have some snacks?"

83

Bernice said, "There's that blackberry brandy and me and De-vita will go get food." She tucked her slip into a pair of jeans and put a flannel shirt on, unbuttoned and hanging open. We were walking across the field and stars were twinkling and the grass was cool on my feet. Bernice put her arm around me. "We have a lot in common," she said, "like best friends." She opened the door to the bar and said, "Now get all the beef jerky you can and I'll go for potato chips."

We stood in the doorway and she looked around and her face lit up. "Peanut," she said. A tall guy in a plaid jacket walked over and set his beer down. "Bernice," he said, "you look dandy." Above the V her slip made her chest was delicate and pale. She gave me a quarter. "Play the jukebox," she said.

That's where I met Tim Koofall. He was drinking orange pop and playing pinball while his father drank beer, and it turned out we had the same favorite song: "Gentle on My Mind." Ber-nice and Peanut were standing in the corner between the bath-room and the pay phone and Bernice's mother yelled, "Peanut, I've talked to you about this before, now get the hell out and don't come back unless you can leave Bernice alone." He left and Bernice walked over and said, "I'm meeting him outside. Forget about the snacks."

In the parking lot Bernice and I stood next to Peanut's Clo-ver Leaf delivery truck and she shoved bags of pretzels under my sweatshirt. "I'll meet you at the house later," she said. I started walking away and the door to the bar opened and Tim Koofall said, "Would you like to go for a walk by the lake?"

We were standing on the pier and looking at the lights on the water, and he told me he was going to be a junior at Butter-nut High next fall, and he said, "If there was one thing you could change in your life, what would it be?" My hands were in my pockets and I kept my arms close to my sides to keep the snacks in. "I wish my pet rabbit hadn't died," I said. I looked at his profile, and he was wearing a hat with a bill and his nose was one of those fierce-looking ones like I never used to think was handsome. He said, "There's always one incident you can zero down to as the source of trouble and everything bad that happens after it happens because of it."

"An incident?" I said.

He reached for me and the bags of snacks crunched. "What's that noise?" he said. My heart thump-thumped. "Pssst," Bernice said from the bushes. "My mother's on the rampage."

We went back to the house and Del Rae and Laura stood with their hands on their hips. "How dare you leave me here," Laura said. Del Rae said, "I'm starving." Bernice said, "You'll have to wait." She opened the drawer. She reached in my shirt and got the snacks out and threw them in; she ran around picking up cigarettes and ashtrays and lipsticks, and she threw the dresser scarf in too because it had rouge on it. "The blackberry brandy," she said, "where is it?"

Laura handed her the empty bottle. "Melissy drank it," she said.

Bernice's mother walked in as we slid the drawer shut. "There better not be boys here," she said, opening a closet door. "Wasn't there another girl?" No one answered. "Yes," Del Rae said then, "she's sleeping." Bernice's mother walked across the room and pulled the covers back and looked at Melissy. She said, "Does she always wear silver eye shadow to bed?" She leaned closer. "Why are her teeth purple?"

Laura was at my house a few weeks later and we were sitting in the wicker chairs on the porch and she said, "We should keep in mind we're going to have boyfriends soon and we should practice kissing and the things we want to say back when they say they love us."

My parents were in the next room. My mother said, "There's

no decent restaurant for three counties." My father said, "So let's stay home." My mother said, "That's hardly the point." She walked away and a door slammed.

"Kiss each other?" I asked Laura. She looked at me. "No," she said, "let's work on our tans." We went down to the boathouse roof, which is flat and overlooks the lake from one direction and the county highway from another. We spread towels and put oil on and laid there, eyes closed, blue-flies buzzing around, and Laura said, "Do you think Melissy is slow?"

I said, "Retarded?"

She said, "About puberty."

Wheels screeched. We sat up. Peanut got out of his Clover Leaf truck. "I thought I recognized you," he said to me. He looked at Laura and all of a sudden it seemed sleazy that she was wearing a halter. She said, "Who's this?" I said, "Bernice's boyfriend." He said, "Nah, Bernice is like a kid sister to me." He tossed a pack of gum to Laura and said, "How about coming for a boat ride?" I said, "How are we going to tell my parents we're going for a boat ride?" He said, "Meet me at the public landing in fifteen minutes."

Laura walked that half-mile to the landing so fast my feet got scuffed, and Peanut was waiting in the boat. Laura sat down next to him and put her hand on his thigh. He gave her a life jacket. "Don't wear it," he said, "just hang onto it."

I said, "Do we have to jam into these high waves so fast?" Peanut said, "Have you seen the creek?"

I said, "She has to baby-sit at five."

Peanut slid the rudder to the right, then to the left. Water washed into the boat and suddenly we were in the creek, branches hanging low. He turned the engine off and threw a magazine to me, *The Bass Fisherman*. "I don't feel like reading," I said. He said, "If you wade to shore and walk through the woods for a hundred feet you'll find a road that'll take you home."

I got out and sank to my ankles in mud and when I reached the shore my cutoffs ripped on a brambleberry bush, and I turned around and saw Peanut untying Laura's halter. Sunlight was dribbling down through the trees and her knockers glowed, round and small, pale as snails. "Laura," I said. She said, "What is it?" I said, "If you don't come with me I'll tell." She grabbed her halter and jumped out of the boat. "Balls," she said.

She didn't talk as my father and I drove her home, and she slammed the door when we stopped in front of her house and she got out of the car. My father backed down the driveway and said, "You seem sad, Petunia." I didn't answer. He said, "It's a hard time." I bit my lip and nodded.

"We don't understand her," he said.

"Guess not," I said.

He rubbed his hand through his hair and sighed. "What's her trouble?"

"Who?" I said.

He shook his head and shifted. "It seems like it started as soon as we moved here."

My parents planned my birthday party so they'd take me and my friends across the lake on the pontoon boat to Andy's Fishing Lodge for dinner. Melissy and Laura arrived first and we were standing in the driveway when Del Rae's dad's car pulled up and she got out and handed me a box of donuts. "For breakfast," she said. "We own Thomas Grocery Emporium, you know. Valerie's not coming." She looked at the three of us. "I have the most dastardly secret."

Jack Burns drove up. "Darla," he yelled as he got out of his car.

My father came outside and said, "Jack, we're having a party for Devita but you're welcome to join us." My mother stood in the doorway. My father said, "Arla, it's Jack Burns." She came outside in a white dress with pink palm trees on it and she was wearing pearls. "Wonderful," she said. She smiled.

My father said, "Are we ready?" I said, "Bernice isn't here yet." He said, "The girl from Fifield?" I said, "I'm not going without her." My mother said, "It's supposed to storm so we better go now. We'll leave a note for Bernice on the door."

We were at the lodge eating chicken, and my father and mother and Jack Burns were at the next table, drinking old-fashioneds, and Bernice burst in the door. "Geez," she said, "I hardly made it. Peanut was going to give me a ride and then my mother wouldn't let him, and finally I got a ride with Tim Koofall and his dad." I looked up and saw Tim. He pushed his cap back and smiled. "Happy birthday," he said.

We finished eating and Tim and I took a walk outside and it was dark and he said, "I have this one dream over and over." We stood on the pier by the moored boats and listened to the far-away, tinkly music, and people in the lodge were laughing. Tim jumped onto our pontoon and gave its steering wheel a twist and the night wind blew his hair back, and he said, "I'm walking through these woods and branches scratch me and bugs bite me and it's humid, and I come to a clearing and you're in front of a house with a little rake. That's all," he said, "but I liked it."

"Devita," my mother called.

"I have to go back," I said.

I walked up the path and the music in the lodge stopped, and I opened the door and my father was standing in front of the pinball machine holding Bernice's arm with one hand and Laura's with the other, and they were swinging at each other. "Get the hell out," he yelled at Peanut who was skulking by the side door, "and if I get wind of you poking around fourteen-year-old girls again I'll have you sent up." Peanut got in his truck and drove away, and my father looked at me and shook his head. "And the goddamn Smith girl was trying to get Jack Burns to buy her lime vodka," he said.

My mother said, "It's time to go now."

We walked down to the pier and Bernice said, "I guess I'll ride back to Fifield with Tim Koofall and his dad because I couldn't stand to sleep near Laura." She took off running. "She has a ride home with someone else," I told my mother.

Melissy and Laura and Del Rae and I sat on boat cushions on the front of the pontoon and my father started the engine. Del Rae leaned close and said in a whisper, "Don't tell anyone but Valerie is pregnant and trying to get an abortion, and her parents are Catholic and someone will tell them and she and Rocky will have to get married and I'll be a bridesmaid. That's what I think."

Melissy chewed on her hair. Laura said, "That's interesting."

"You were outside with Tim Koofall," Del Rae said. "It's sad how his father used to be a drunk and then wasn't, and Tim's mother died and his father started drinking again and Tim hardly gets supper now or a place to sleep, and nothing but ugly clothes to wear."

Clouds were rolling across the sky at intervals and in the wake behind us water glimmered. Jack Burns was singing a song about a lady named Mrs. Bliss. "Hush, Jack," my mother said. "As I was saying, my husband and child, their happiness—it's my life."

On the first day of school I was wearing nylons and a new dress and Mr. Darby called us into his office, Laura and Melissy and Bernice and Del Rae and me. We sat in a row. He rubbed his hand over his crew cut and said, "I have something to say."

"It's about Valerie," Del Rae whispered.

He looked at us, his eyebrows wiggly, and he clicked his pencil on the desk. "Valerie Verholtz won't be attending school," he said. "I understand there's going to be a large wedding and many of you will be bridesmaids, punch-servers, whatever. It's an unusual situation for ninth grade and I hope you'll help us maintain a normal atmosphere here. And I urge all of you to make an appointment for the lecture with the school nurse."

A pep rally was going on outside, a bass drum booming, bonfires crackling. Del Rae said, "My father donated those hot dogs."

Someone knocked on Mr. Darby's door. "If you'll excuse me," he said. He left the room.

Del Rae turned around. "I talked to Valerie," she said, "and I'm maid of honor and I get to wear a pink dress. Laura and Devita, you're bridesmaids, with pink dresses too. You pass the guest-book, Melissy, and wear a blue dress. Bernice, you can wear anything you want."

Laura said, "A T-shirt. Or, for a formal look, a slip."

Del Rae said, "The dance is at your mother's tavern, Bernice, because no other place would let Valerie or any of us in."

Mr. Darby walked back into the office. "These are precisely the sorts of conversations I hope you'll avoid at school. Now go to the pep rally. Devita, I want to see you." I waited while the others left. He closed the door and folded his arms and sat on the desk. "If something's wrong at home," he said, "we'd like to help."

My father had his suitcase out. "It's a short trip," he said, "and I deserve it." My mother paced the floor and she was wringing her hands. "Our daughter is in the next room putting on her first formal, and for what? Prom? A party? No. A wedding for one of her pregnant school friends. I tell you I won't stay here. If you leave on this trip tonight you'll be surprised when you come home."

I knocked on the doorframe. "How do I look?" I said.

My father's tie was untied. He ran his hand through his hair and smiled. "Like a grown-up," he said.

My mother said, "You should borrow my new earrings, honey." She opened her dresser drawer and I turned to my father and said, "How long will you be gone?" He said, "Not long. You two will be fine." I said, "Will you be fine, Mother?" She waved her rat-tail comb in the air and smiled. "Of course," she said, "I'll curl up with a book."

It rained hard during the wedding, and afterwards we ran down the sidewalk in front of the St. Francis de Sales and got in a car and Rocky's friend, the best man, drove us to Fifield. The juke-box played a waltz, and we drank punch. I said, "Rocky was crying during the vows." Del Rae shrugged. Laura said, "How do we ditch these bouquets so we can dance?"

Tim Koofall tapped me on the shoulder. He was wearing a suit coat and a white shirt. "May I have the honor?" he said. I said, "I don't know how to dance." He said, "Then let me get you a fresh drink."

He walked away and I watched Rocky and Valerie kissing under a paper wedding bell and I thought how she was a woman now, her husband and new-coming baby the center of her life. "Melissy had her first date last night," Laura said, "with the handyman from Glidden School." Bernice's mother walked past, setting mint cups on tables. "Have you seen Bernice?" I asked Laura and Del Rae.

Laura said, "Let's go to the bathroom."

We went into the bathroom, which is a storage room with a toilet and a sink, and I held Laura's sash off the floor while she peed and I said, "The handyman from Glidden used to have a crush on me." Laura said, "You're not jealous, are you?"

Del Rae said, "You're interested in Tim Koofall now."

Laura said, "I hate his suit coat. What does he talk about?"

I said, "Nothing."

Laura said, "That night at Andy's Fishing Lodge?"

I said, "About a dream he had."

She stood up and looked at herself in the mirror. "His suit coat wouldn't be bad in the dark," she said, "if you were squinting."

"A wet dream," Del Rae said. "Do you know what that is?"

Laura said, "His nose is ugly."

I threw my punch in her face and it ran in pink streams down it, and she blinked and licked her lips. I went outside then and ran around and went down to the lake and stopped in front of the pier and took my sash off and tied it around my head and walked back and forth and thought about Tim's suit, how he just needed a tie. A branch above my head creaked and Bernice slid to the ground. "Geronimo," she said. "I thought you were Laura and I was going to kill you." I said, "I need a ride home."

So I was in the front seat of Peanut's Clover Leaf truck, barreling down the road, and he downshifted and said, "I don't know what it is about you but I've never had the urge." He pulled into my driveway and said, "God, I hope that's not your old man's car." Rain was falling hard and I couldn't see. I fumbled for my key and a single light burned, and I heard my mother singing. I opened the door. She was on the couch in her yellow dress with the ribbons and she was holding a glass.

"Is Dad home?" I said.

She shook her head.

I pointed to some shoes. "Whose are those?" In the next room, the toilet flushed. "Jack Burns," my mother said. He walked in.

My mother said, "Now get out of those wet clothes, Devita, and I'll bring you the hot-water bottle." I went into my bedroom and threw my dress on the floor and got under the blankets and waited for her. I listened to her laughter, its avalanches and slides, Jack Burns's bass echo, ice cubes clinking in glasses and the tall spoon scraping the pitcher. "So free, so free, so free," she said. I thought about my father rubbing his hand in his hair, Tim standing beside me on the pier, the one incident you zero down to, and the wind ripped through trees outside and the light through my window was spastic and my walls swelled and wriggled, and then it was dawn. And Jack Burns got in his car and drove away.

The Guardian

RANDY F. NELSON

The Imaginary Lives of Mechanical Men (2006)

FOR MILES

Okay, we're flying low now, delivering this bigmother Easter arrangement in the old panel truck looks like a hearse, decal across the back saying WEISS FLORIST—FTD 205 South Main Street in Morton WE DELIVER inside a black ivy wreath, which maybe should have been a red cross, on account of that's the way we work. Elrod's up front fighting to keep us between the lines. I'm in the back holding this purple and white bastard looks like an Indian headdress, ducking when we round corners so I don't get whanged by one of the swinging metal hooks we load casket sprays on. Thing must weigh thirty-five, forty pounds except for the short periods of zero gravity when we go airborne, and it's a little top heavy too on account of the Easter lilies, but do they ever think about that back at the shop? Hell no.

So it's inevitable. I mean we're headed south on Hwy. 115, right? Toward Baxter. Low cloud ceiling, visibility less than ten miles, and me without a parachute. Comes to the railroad crossing in front of the big denim plant, and what does the son of a bitch do? Takes the ramp like he was Fireball Roberts and this was his last chance at the leap of death. Then, voom, right out on the floor. The water, the Styrofoam, the peacock feathers, the ferns, and every kind of purple and white flower in the jungle, all over the inside of that green ratty-assed panel truck, and me screaming, "Holy shit! They fell out, El, they're floatin' out the back of the truck," but he keeps going like he's got plenty of fuel and just enough time for one more bomb run.

So what do you do? I mean, you're fourteen years old. The guy is retarded. You got an altar arrangement looks like it's been thrown up against a wall, and this is your first real life honest to God paycheck-paying job, which you deserve only because your mamma works there in the first place. And maybe his sister does own the flower joint and maybe you really are just a kid, but that won't change a thing because you're responsible for whatever happens next. Age doesn't have anything to do with it. So you've got to communicate in terms he can comprehend, right? "El! Hit the brakes, man! Oh God, we gotta go back. Jeezus Christ, El, it looks like somebody vomited flowers back here. I think I peed my pants."

"Pull over?"

"You not hear what I'm saying? The sum bitch exploded. We look like a free love bus turned wrong side out."

"Can't," he moans. At least that's what I think he says. The wind's catching everything and whirling it around me like a tornado.

"Oh God! El, you gotta listen to me, man. This ain't a cavalry charge; we in the florist bidness!"

"Church ladies gone meet us five o'clock. Then we got the hospital run."

It was the way he thought. Sort of like he'd got tuned in real good and clear on this one channel and didn't care to switch. Not retarded exactly, I take that back, but pretty damn focused on the here and now, if you know what I mean. Somebody told me he learned how to drive in the air force during the Korean War, though he didn't climb high in the ranks. They gave him a job trucking aviation fuel where the casualty rate was higher than actual combat.

And now here we are pulling up to the curb at Baxter Presbyterian, dripping and smoking right in the shadow of the steeple. El eases out from behind the wheel like he's the only Elrod Weiss in kingdom come and it didn't pay to hurry it any. And me, I'm trying to breathe. I'm pulling myself out of the water by one of the hooks, and I can see them through the side window, flouncing down the walk, the kind of foul-tempered biddies who show up Saturday afternoon dressed for church and wanting to inspect the big altar arrangement because they're on the Worship Committee or some damn thing and 100 percent ready to peck you to death, boy, if one leaf is out of place. That kind. Holding their pocketbooks out front like this. Lips that haven't touched nothing but lemon juice in the past twenty years. And me in the back believing in the power of prayer with all my heart.

So. He gets the door about half open and starts picking up flowers, no particular order, just picking them up and jamming them back into that liner two and three at a time. No hurry at all now, just two or three in his left hand, then half a dozen in his right, whap, back down in the Styrofoam. Church ladies getting closer and closer, El getting in a groove with the flowers, me saying, "Give it up, man. It looks like a bomb went off in here. Looks like I peed in my pants for a year. You not understand what I'm saying? El, we gotta get outta town before . . ."

When the tall pruney one in the navy polka dot lurches around that door like something out of Mardi Gras hell croaking, "May we take just one teeny look before you bring it in?" And whatever was left in my bladder? Bam.

"We must be sure the colors are right," piped another one.

El took his hat off, having been raised in the Depression, and opened the door all the way.

"Oh my wooorrrd!" said the third lady.

"Oh my," echoed the second lady.

"It's gorgeous. I believe it's the most beautiful piece we've ever had. I'm going to call Irene as soon as we get it inside."

And there you go.

We spent thirty minutes turning and centering and adjusting that avant garde train wreck on the high altar of Presbyterianism, me dripping blue preservative water, and them thinking it was beautiful, and El and me together finishing the hospital run before six-thirty. He had that kind of luck.

And for a time I did too.

During that same storm he said I got to go check she might've hurt herself, and I said she works in a bank for God's sake, what're you afraid happened, a paper cut? But he drove home anyhow, I mean the little house on Doster Street, and there she was, Patsy, alone in the bedroom her hand bleeding real bad and the mirror busted, with it wrapped in one of those ladies' handkerchiefs that won't soak up a thing. I said what are you doing home in the middle of the afternoon anyway while she stared into that hot dark stillness. I didn't feel well she said there's something wrong that feels twisted inside of me and just, Chad, please stay here while he fixes the fuses, just hold me until the lights come on. But your hand I said although she was warm and moist and her hair like roses but your hand. Will be all right she said if you just hold me. And so I did thinking that I was just holding her until the lights came on.

Elrod looked like a potato. Wore a gray fedora summer and winter, sweeping it off and crushing it against his heart on every occasion that demanded politeness, which, to his southern mind, was about every fifteen minutes. Black leather shoes that he never polished. Hawaiian shirts whenever he could. Pleated pants. White socks. Gray suit and bow tie for church. He had a nose that'd been broken enough times that you wondered what he did before you met him.

He spent his entire life looking for clues.

"Like my name," he said. "It ain't normal. Why would anybody call me that?"

It amazed him, his name did, and he printed it over and over in a blue notebook that he kept in the utility drawer of his worktable there at the flower shop. Along with a glass doorknob, a picture of his wife Patsy, broken watches, rubber bands, everything electrical that he could lay his hands on. And keys, hell yeah, maybe a hundred of them on a wire loop all worn smooth and forgotten. He just collected stuff. Sometimes he'd go looking for the one item he needed, just pick himself up and go, wham like that, maybe returning after lunch with a burned-out fuse, thinking.

Other days he might hit the brakes so hard it would stop time— you had to be ready for this—and he'd descend into the traffic to rescue a left-handed glove, a cracked mirror, a ribbon, a radio antenna. He cleaned and saved these things, arranged and rearranged his drawer, packed items away in those little boxes that cans of spray paint came in. Write in his notebook. Why should I care? He would let me drive as soon as we hit the city limits, on account of driving made him nervous. Or maybe distracted him from the search that eventually became his life.

Like the time we were five miles out on a dirt road that'd just been laid quiet by one of those summer storms. Searching for something—I don't remember really, one of those rural cemeteries maybe or a mailbox number—anyhow something that we weren't finding—so that we're just cruising, sort of lost in the warm, damp reordering of the world. And then there, on the other side of the windshield, at no particular distance from us, was a perfectly circular rainbow. For real. I didn't know the things existed.

I say, "Good God A'mighty, do you see that?" But of course he's been watching longer than I have; and who, besides El, could keep perfectly still and perfectly quiet inside of a miracle?

"You can't close it up like that," I insist. "You can't make no bull's-eye out of a rainbow."

"Sometimes you can," whispers Elrod Weiss.

Pretty soon I've got my head out of the driver's side window, squinting, one hand on the wheel, because for a moment it does seem like there's a figure in the center of the thing, the face of someone I might recognize. The air finally turning pure and cold in the after breeze, but I'm shivering from something else, and he's saying, "Patsy. That's my Patsy all up there in the yellow and blue. And pink. You see that? That's who it is." Not even surprised. "Better let me drive now; it's a rainbow here but a cloud over Morton, and she gets afraid." Though his hands didn't shake a bit.

Before Irene took him in, he drove a water truck for the county, one of those big tankers that sprinkles down the dust on gravel roads or washes dirt and trash off the regular highways. Big yellow boy with one of those black-and-white license tags saying "Bladen County—Permanent" like it was a monument or something. And thank God he didn't smoke and had a sister who could offer him a job when, you know, times got bad.

Because once he wheeled into Bub's Esso, said to the new guy fill her up, and headed off to visit Patsy during his lunch hour, before they were married I guess. And the new guy's yelling after him, "Filler up? Filler up? That mother holds five thousand gallon." Which would have turned a normal human being around, suggesting, as it did, frightening possibilities; but we're talking about Elrod Weiss here, who didn't veer one degree off course for anybody, yelling back, "Dus put it on the county ticket."

Well, that's what the kid does, because this is NASCAR country and, hell, anybody might need five thousand gallons of high-octane racing fuel. So it must have taken the whole hour to fill that tank until it was sloshing over the hatch and smelling like whiskey. Then here comes El back from lunch or whatever, hops in, and heads out to the bypass for his first run of the afternoon.

Okay, gets out to the new bridge, kicks on his sprayers just like always, and starts washing down the pavement with the highway equivalent of lighter fluid. He can't smell a thing, you know, on account of the busted nose, and he can't hear anything either on account of the radio. And he can't see anything either—like the road crew diving left and right—on account of he's in a groove now washing all that crap away like it was cheap sin. Pretty soon there're little rivers of gasoline. Then the port-a-john gets de-odorized. And maybe a few guys have their pants hosed down when they're too slow in vaulting for cover. But no more damage than that: God is watching over him just like always. So he drains the tank all the way down to empty over a three-and-a-half-mile straightaway without dropping a match, scratching a gravel spark, or backfiring. Then, same as always, he turns off the highway and heads back into town for another fill-up. Simple as that.

Which is when the far flagman starts sniffing and the site supervisor starts bellowing, "S'going on down there?" and the fellas wave their arms and yell back but don't come far out of the bushes. And the supervisor goes purple in the face howling at the flagman and the others, "You bastids wanna get fired? You think this is communis' Russia, you can take a corporate rest period?" Staggerwalking down the embankment at about the same time that the flagman clambers over the side of the half-built bridge that's sticking out into nowhere, figuring he needs to get his cigar going again in order to establish his full transportation department authority, and lights up.

It's like he lived a charmed life.

I told her I really did I said you think I don't know you're probably faking just to get attention. God knows you've got Daddy and Aunt Lib wrapped around your little finger and now you want to be my mamma too well you can forget it. I'm hanging around with whoever I want to hang around with okay because it's maybe all right to smile every once in a while and enjoy life instead of being you. We're not twins, not really, I mean is there a boy in the entire school who's ever touched you? I don't see how you can stand yourself I really don't you're such a faker. You think I don't know what you're doing in there, your own sister doesn't know, running to the bathroom every time so they won't think you're such a cow with that fake cough oh please. It's like you're being so pure you can't defile yourself with food or whatever, like you're the virgin bride or something, and then you think you can just preach to me like that? Let me tell you something pretty baby you ought to look in a mirror sometime. You are a cow. And if you want to starve yourself to death that's fine with me.

Every once in a while we'd pass a blur on the side of the road, and he might say tomato can or dead dog or chain gang, like they were all parts of the same puzzle, which if he twisted and turned just right would all at once fit together. A week might go by and then he'd say, "Remember that tomato can?" Like it didn't make any difference as to who was hearing him.

And one of the yahoos down at Bub's would say, "Damaters?"

"Yeah. Del Monte or Heinz?"

Guy would shrug, wink at the others, say, "Del Monte. Del Montier'n hell."

And this would be enough to send him into a trance, cleaning his ear with a toothpick, thinking, until maybe the one piece of information would fit with another piece that he'd saved for months. Squinting this time at me, "That a fig tree or a 'simmon tree we hit over to the War Memorial?"

I'd say, "Fig."

Then he'd narrow his eyes some more—"That's what I thought."

Of course the lady designers who worked in the back of the flower shop never understood. The atmosphere was too dense.

Back there a sort of chemical fog hung over everything. I hated the time we had to work inside. Inside the shop he was just another man, a drudge like those who worked the denim plant, breathing the same poisons, scurrying back and forth to do as he was told. Preservatives, dyes, glues, fungicides, spray paints, disinfectants floating everywhere. It was like a flower factory. I remember this clearly.

There were rules. Chrysanthemums got a shot of hair spray to keep them from shattering, or sometimes you dripped candle wax on the backs of the petals. Carnations got dipped in vinegar dye. Leaf-Cote made the greenery shine on Tuesdays and Saturdays; it smelled like varnish and alcohol. And long-stemmed roses—you already know this—are bred purely for color and tight buds. They take their scent from chloral benzoate and artificial perfumes. Even today. And snapdragons have got no scent at all. Gladiolus get sliced on the diagonal, the stems soaked in a solution of soda ash to keep the blossoms from wilting. While orchids get snipped and inserted into little syringes of water, taped down into their boxes like they're on life support. So that after a while nobody has to teach you the one thing that stays with you through the years—that all these flowers are dead.

So what is it that you smell? I mean that musky sweet summer greenhouse scent wafting out into the showroom that makes you wish you could take it home in a spray can, that smell? I'll tell you what it is. It's stripped leaves. Wilted baby's breath. Browned petals. Stem ends, brittle galax, dried lycopodium, dead ferns. Tons of Spanish moss that they use as packing material. Garbage. You can sweep and empty four times a day and there's still a residue, a green, mosslike stain in the linoleum. It's pollen and crushed stems. Dried rosebuds that have fallen beneath the tables. Old water. It smells sweet, the whole of it, like the perfume of some lost Eden. And it stays sweet in your memory, the way flowers ought to be, until you know.

That's what you smell.

———————

They moved to Morton oh I don't know 'bout ten, twelve years ago that's when Ed joined the Rotary and all but, no, it's not like I knew 'em real well. Had the one daughter a course and she lived at home and I mean boy she was a knockout you know what I mean? I mean a real knockout. Came there one time to pick up Ed when he was still attending and I'm in the living room waiting you know looking at all these pictures they got on the piano in the shelves and everywhere like they got stock in Kodak or something. And she comes through, Patsy does, and you couldn't help but make the connection. I mean hell I was just talking that's what I do for a living I sell things. Cars. And she said no that's my sister Clare she was killed in an accident. Just like that like she'd done give all the sorrow and tears she had to give and just didn't have any energy anymore. I mean Jesus like she was making conversation or something and you got to figure a car accident right so what could I say? Hell, mister, I wouldn't hurt anybody for love nor money I mean just standing there like that, what could I say? I never counted on twins.

Once in the autumn I saw leaves falling from a sugar maple close to our house. Some spiraling down, some blown by the first breath of winter; and every one, as soon as it released its hold, would burst into flames and hang in red-orange glory for a moment, like the sails of pirate ships set ablaze. Anyhow—what I thought. Every single leaf, a flame. A conflagration in every gust of wind. This really happened.

And there, standing in the street, waiting for El to pick me up, hoping for a whirlwind, I watched them fly. Flicker and flame. Catching one and feeling the momentary sting before it turned to ash in my hand. I still have the mark of it. And then he was there, the mirror on the right side of the truck almost bumping my shoulder, and him reaching across the seat and throwing open the door and saying, "You better crawl in, boy. You better crawl in before they set your hair on fire."

I'm not saying it was right and I'm not trying to make excuses or anything I don't want you to think I'm a hypocrite. It was wrong okay? I made peace with that a long time ago. It just wasn't as simple as you think. I mean good God she dated a damn criminal for a year and then turned around and married an ape what does that sound like to you? It was like she wanted life to punish her or something, which you can't even imagine with somebody that beautiful you know what I mean? There were days at the bank she came in with cuts, bruises on her arms or face when you just wanted to put your arm around her. She was so sad. Look I don't even know what I'm saying anymore I just know I would have done anything to make her smile for a second. I won't say I loved her but I did in a way and I would have done anything. . . . And I'll tell you something else I would have killed the son of a bitch if I'd thought he was doing it to her. But maybe she was hurting herself, you know what I'm saying? There's just no way to tell if you ask me.

He was terrified of dead people. He hated funeral homes even though they were the first places in the South to be air-conditioned, and we always made the cemetery run around noon just to be sure that we weren't overtaken by nightfall, but here's the funny thing. He knew the location of every grave in maybe two dozen cemeteries. Like he had a personal relationship with every corpse in Bladen County.

El never touched a casket. Never looked upon a body if it was in an open coffin. Never spoke in a room where there was a corpse, I don't know, maybe because he was holding his breath, I just don't know. And always he washed his hands after handling funeral flowers. Always. Used a big yellow bottle of Joy back there at the utility sink.

We had to go to Payne & Pinkerton one time, the colored funeral home there in Morton that took up three floors of a colossal white house on Houston Street, looked like a plantation. And the guest of honor was this fat lady, member of the Eastern Star or something, who just barely fit into her casket, which looked like a double-wide to me. They must have tucked her in with a crowbar and a shoehorn. Anyway, she's laying there sweet and serene as can be in a pink chiffon dress, white gloves, your pearl earrings, pearl necklace, and all your Eastern Star secret paraphernalia— except for one thing—the pink and white corsage that we've got to pin on her just before the service.

So what do you think, I'm going to do it? I'm fourteen years old and this involved touching a dead lady's breast in a colored funeral home that looked like Tara on an oiled-up dirt road where no sane white person would go after six o'clock on a Saturday night knowing that Roosevelt was no longer a favored name among Negro parents. What am I trying to say? I'm saying the times they were a changing, and you didn't want to handicap your future by maybe getting killed over some aspect of the new social order that you hadn't figured out yet. So I said, "Just leave the box on the front pew or give it to the oldest daughter, man, but let's hit the road before they bring in the forklift and she tips it over on one of us."

But no.

He had to do it. Take away everything else, and that's what was left. A gentleman. I can see his hands shaking to this day. See him swallowing hard. Taking that corsage up in one hand, the pin in the other, working his way up to the casket with slow shuffling steps. Till it gradually occurred to me what he was going to do as he took the pin. Eased it through the center of the bottom carnation until it stuck out the other side about an inch and a half. Then—whap—straight into her like a thumbtack.

Except I'm the one who squealed. "Oh God, no! What'd you do that for, man?! Jeezus Christ, El, you think they don't shoot to kill down here?"

"We got to go," is all he said. "It's after four."

"You got that right! Grab your hat, we gotta haul ass before the Fruit of Islam comes pouring through that door. Head for the border, you moron!" Just as she came in—all dressed in white— this younger version of the poor lady in the coffin, weeping.

She said El you think we could have stewed tomatoes tonight? I thought I saw a can of stewed tomatoes in the cabinet.

And now there is only one thing left, so I will tell it.

Patsy Burdette had long auburn hair and epilepsy. By the time she was thirty, I guess, she was working in the Morton Federal Savings and Loan, and I worshiped her. So did El. She painted her toenails, which you could see in the summer whenever she wore sandals, and never a piece of jewelry anywhere except the rings that El bought her when they were married, long before I started to work at Weiss Florist. And he was faithful as a dog. Never mind the rumors, he drove home for lunch every day so they could see each other for a few extra minutes. Sometimes there'd be guests, sometimes not.

He'd call Patsy every day to be sure she'd taken her medicine. We could be out delivering on the other side of the moon, and he'd pull in to some little country store and ask to use the phone, holding it out away from his ear like this because he had hearing like a bat, sort of talk into the mouthpiece like it was a microphone. You could hear her tiny voice on the other end saying, "What? Who is this? El, is that you? Who is this?"

And every Saturday I'd go with him, you know, to lunch at their house, an unpainted bungalow on Doster Street with a gravel driveway sounded like you were driving over crackers until you pulled up in the carport, and there she'd be, so happy to see us. And maybe one of her friends from the bank inside having lunch too, also happy to see us. El did almost all the housework; the place looked like a dollhouse, fussy clean, I guess on account of where she lived before they were married.

Then she died in December the year before I went away to

college. He just cruised in one evening, maybe later than usual, maybe after drinking a little, nobody knows for sure; I just remember people talking. Anyway he went home for supper to the house with the dark shutters and low-hanging pines and found her in the bathtub. She'd had a seizure, the long auburn hair floating in arabesques upon the surface of the water, perfectly serene and beautiful. He loved her so. Laid her out in the bed before the ambulance got there, in a satin nightgown, covers up to her neck, the thick silky hair brushed and dried, arranged in waves down to her shoulders. No one knows how he did it.

So now I'm one of them I guess I don't know what happened I just turned around took my eyes off him for a second changed my clothes and there you were my own son. But I can tell you this much no matter what they say this is a love story for your mother yes but also for you. Because when he finally slammed that battered door of the old panel truck and the looming echo faded and we had made the last hospital run of the day it was no longer the spring of 1965 and now I have to strain to get him back. He was Elrod Weiss. The funniest man I ever knew.

The Art of Getting Real

BARBARA SUTTON

From *The Send-Away Girl* (2004)

I don't think my dad was ever any age, any particular age. He never seemed old, didn't do stupid things that made him seem old. I can't see him licking a finger to separate the new twenties in his wallet after saying he'd spring for what everyone in the van has just ordered at the Burger King drive-through. Or getting into his Eddie Bauer pants and cruising the Home Depot all day Saturday. He never seemed young either—young like it was an act, like Andy's divorced father putting on his brand-new Gap cargo pants so he can dry hump the girls who come home with Andy's sister over Christmas break. My dad always seemed the age of some guy in the back of a car that you meet for five minutes at night—a guy crammed in with all these other people, a guy wearing some kind of special jacket, only you can't tell what kind of special jacket. My dad wasn't just no age: he was no canoe trips and no camcorders, no curfews and no catcher's mitts. The man was just gone—gone daddy gone, and fuck if I ever cared.

But then my dad is dead, and he is already sort of famous in the clan for being dead, for being only forty-three and dying of a heart attack. Because he died at forty-three in the way most guys die at seventy-three, he will always be thought of as "too young." I'm so sick of those words, and my mother's hiked the amp on the whole thing because "Forever Young" is a song on the Chris Isaak album she's been playing over and over these three days since he died. He hasn't lived with us in years, and in the three days of him being dead my mother hasn't pissed a tear—at least none that I've seen. But then I guess he was there, doing something or other at some present tense in her life, and I guess Chris Isaak's wailing is what cools her jets.

The only thing that made my dad interesting to me was why my mother married him. Everyone says this to their parents: "Why'd you guys get married? You hate each other." I know my mom wasn't pregnant when she got married, but I also know that her getting married is a subject I'm never supposed to talk about. "I'll tell you anything you want to know about the day you were born," she once told me, "anything about the greasy-spoon second you shot out of me, but don't ask me about the blackout during which I got married."

I don't hate the guy; you can't hate a guy like that. He was my dad; I look just like him, and I can't hate him for that either. What I hate is the idea that this has to be a big thing for me; what I hate is all these people hanging around, acting like they were authorized by the DMV to get under my hood. My grandparents are a wreck; they're the ones who need the cards that say "with deepest sympathy" and "in this time of sorrow." My dad was the loser of his family, but he was a miracle baby, born late to my grandmother after she'd had some miscarriages and was warned by the doctors that it was too dangerous to keep trying. His real dad also died too young, in his late forties, when my dad was still a baby, and then his stepdad was about the best father any kid ever had. But, there ya go, right? A wasted six-lane is a wasted six-lane.

Even though my dad was an only child, beyond him the clan is huge, with tons of his cousins and tons of their kids and everyone loving to hover. Me and my mom are holed up and don't know what to do. I don't want to do anything but go around like the seventh kid in a pack of eight or nine, just a walk-on, just like I was a few days ago. That forever-young dad of mine, he's done it again—fucked up the works by not being around.

People want to talk to me about this "congenital" thing, this "heredity" thing, this thing with my heart. Odds are I'll keel over at forty-three, just like my dad, or else have to suck up to rich teaching hospitals so that they'll let me buy one of the hearts they get from their organ pimps in Peru. People think I'm traumatized because I'll have to die or else suck up and then probably die anyway, but this is because all of them are way past forty-three, and the thought of dying freaks the shit out of them. To me, forty-three doesn't seem that young or that old, and dying doesn't freak the shit out of me. Even though there's a Pavement song that goes "simply put I want to grow old, dying does not meet my expectations," I'm not scared to die; I expect to die. All I want to know is who my relatives are forever comparing me to. They seem to think that the right way to act is a numerical constant—say, pi—which would mean that there are all these pi guys roaming around out there consistently doing the right thing. I'd like to know what the correct version of me looks like and sounds like and smells like. That's my big question, the one that pissed off my mother's brother, Phil the Drill, in regard to the "attitude situation" of yours truly: "Who's fucking pi, Phil?"

My mother was always sending my dad away, and he was always coming back from where he was sent—not right away, but he always came back. I picture it like having to cross a desert on a tank of gas: you could just drive straight through and pray you hit a Texaco oasis by the time you're on empty, or you could drive to some stupid half-tank spot and then turn around and come back, to get more gas. This is what my dad always chose. He never did anything bad to us, but that just went along with doing nothing at all to us. My grandparents paid his way, supported my mother and me, bought us this house. Now they say, "He loved you *in his own way*," and I wonder how they can say "love" when he never let me and my mother get in the way of anything he wanted to do, even though he didn't do one friggin' thing with his life. Most of my dad's older cousins have been playing *60 Minutes*, spilling their guts for the camera, saying that "down deep" the guy was "responsible" because when he was a teenager he taught their kids how to ride a bike. "Great," I said. "That's just great. He doesn't even know if I ever had a bike, but he teaches your brats to ride some merchandise, so he's suddenly Ward Fucking Cleaver. Did he teach them to chew gum and fart at the same time?"

The last time I saw my dad was at Christmas, and the cousins and their kids kept yapping about how I'd shot up, was already a head taller than him. Here I was getting pats on the back for being a successful sperm, and my dad just smiles, all mellow and faraway, like I had nothing to do with him, like I was just some Wonder Years graduate loading sacks of topsoil into his trunk. Maybe my being a head taller than him is what made him shake hands with me like I was someone he just met at a sports bar.

What my dad and I had in common the last time I saw him was Television, not the thing but the band. It used to be just the Band we had in common, but now it's these two things, even though with him dead, I don't suppose we have that much in common anymore. It was this past Christmas, and we were getting all scruffed up to shovel my grandparents' driveway. It's such a guy thing—hardly any talking—and it's always somehow fun in a way you'd never want anyone else to know about. We were in the garage picking out tools from my grandfather's stockpile, considering instruments like a dental hygienist thinks about which silver hook will best get the crud out from between the teeth you lie about ever flossing.

"What are kids listening to these days?" my dad asked as I decided on the shovel he should use. How do you answer that sort of ass-minded question? "I don't know what *kids* are listening to," I finally said. Then he said, "Okay, so what are *you* listening to?" I said, "I don't know. Stuff by Television." He banged the shovel on the concrete floor of the garage and said, "Man, I used to do that. That's what I listened to. I used to do that kind of . . . that way, I mean," and then his words trailed off, like he was all of a sudden remembering where he could go to get more gas for the desert.

My friend Andy listens to practically everything you can download—no discrimination whatsoever—just like any other watered-down shit who couldn't go twenty-four hours without taking four showers. My girlfriend, Alicia, likes good music, plus all that vagina stuff, but like she says, "Ya gotta take the shake with the fries." She's also always saying, "Call me your Pop Queen or bite my ass." The last time she said "Call me your Pop Queen" I said, "Okay, honey," grabbing an empty pretzel bag. "I'll call you my Pop Queen if you wear this here cellophane over your head, if you be my Bachman Lady." Alicia's my girlfriend because she laughs when I say things like this; she laughs and says, "Fuck yourself like you're really into it." I feel lucky about Alicia, because sometimes music feels like that's all there is, like it was the closest to you that anything could get. Sometimes when I'm in my room I smell the paper they print the liner notes on—I don't know if it's the ink or the paper or both—but this particular smell makes me feel safe, makes me feel good when I'm alone. Sometimes this is the only thing I like about any particular day.

I have no "role models"—that's what the guidance counselor tells me—but I wouldn't mind turning out like the guys at the used-record store near where my mother works, the used-record store that doesn't sell any used records, just CDs—promo CDs and all the crap people buy and leave for dead. Buy and leave for dead. I can't stand it, being around the store's idiot customers, but I like being around the record-store guys—Michael, Milt, and Heinley. Michael put me on to the Band, to MC5 and Television, that sort of stuff. Michael talks to me like he means it, like I'm not wasting his time.

They're all old, the record-store guys. I don't say this because their being old ever struck me from shooting the shit with them, but because they say it to each other and to people who come into the store, mainly Michael's on-and-off girlfriend, Gretchen, who retaliates by estimating the size of their dicks (Milt's and Heinley's, I mean) in millimeters. Once when Milt was complaining about how lately all his rubbers were busting on him, Gretchen said, "Go for the armor, Milt. Use a thimble." When it's just Michael, Milt, Heinley, and a couple dweebs roaming the bins, the conversation never goes in any specific direction, but it's always entertaining, like eight bucks for a movie without spending the eight bucks. Sometimes I think I'd like to write it all down, what they say, for no particular reason, just because I think I understand, even though I haven't been there and done that.

Michael is not one of those guys who hates practically everything that's happened to music in the past twenty years, but he really can't stand the trend to use tracks that are just some moaning white chick, what he calls "buttercream orgasm in a frosting can." "It's cheap," he told me, "it's such a fucking cheap thing." He said it reminds him of being in junior high, when one of his twit friends (all of his friends were twits, according to him) was excited because his dad had just bought this organ with all the synthesizer features a jerky family that loved throwing money away would want. Michael said that this twit friend pointed out the fact that the organ had come with color-coded, one-finger "sheet music" to the *Abbey Road* album, which back then had kicked its shelf life to death. This twit friend played for Michael "Maxwell's Silver Hammer" using one finger and a calypso beat, and Michael just about lost it, lost it with everything. "I thought, you know, 'I gotta get outta here!'" he told me. "And I meant, like, outta my skin." What I like about Michael is that when he's talking to me he'll use what he, Milt, and Heinley call Punk Latin. Michael speaks in Punk Latin to me even though when he's talking to Milt or Heinley he sounds like he's got shitloads of degrees, degrees in everything.

They all love to rag on me, rag on me for being my age, but it's never anything that makes me mad. Just last week Milt asked Heinley, "So, did ya get that K2 snowboard you wanted for Christmas?" And Heinley said, "No, man, but what I wanted was, like, that chick I saw riding one in a magazine—that chick with the Hello Kitty tattoo and the bra with the two orange smiley faces on her tits. That girl was mad awesome." Even though they'll rag on you, Michael, Milt, and Heinley are about the only older guys I respect. They know what they are, and they never try to make you believe they don't.

My mom keeps pissing off my grandparents by saying "the festivities"—this is what she calls all the funeral-home stuff we have to go through before they put my father in the ground. "What's next with the festivities?" she'll say, and everyone will look at her like they want her to go home, even though she's already in her home.

The worst part of my father's festivities doesn't have to do with funeral homes. It happened just this morning, when Alicia finally came over. Like, here she is my girlfriend, and it's been three days, and tomorrow's the wake, and the day after that the grand finale, the giant slalom into the hole, and today she finally finds the time in her busy schedule to drop by. She was at the back door with her brother's big plaid jacket and her hair looping down from the way her hair is usually brushed up. She wasn't wearing makeup, which meant things were bad, because usually she's got the mascara all smeared on purpose—that's how she looks when she says "Fuck yourself like you're really into it." "You sure look like money," I said to her, and she tucked her arms into her chest and sort of fell into me, crying. I mean, she was really crying, like it was someone that died on her. I asked her why she was crying—I said, "You saw my dad ten minutes, tops"—and she said she was crying because I wasn't crying, because I *wouldn't* cry. For me, that right there was bottoming out to China—my own girlfriend wanting me to be some way that wasn't real. At least she could've been crying at the thought that I'll probably be dead by forty-three.

Alicia's father is a real asshole; that's what she calls him all the time, to his face: "You are such a Papa Asshole, asshole!" And yet this morning she told me that she'd die if he ever died. She said "if he ever died" as if dying was something that only might happen to people, as if dying was as random as Ed McMahon stopping you in your driveway and sticking a giant sweepstakes check up one of your nostrils. Alicia's father is an orthodontist and has so far saved ninety-two thousand dollars for her college education. When she's eighteen he'll stop saving, and she can draw from the account to pay for her college or whatever she wants to do with her life. She says she can't wait till she's eighteen, to get the cash and get away. I know that this is a cool thing for a father to do, but still the man's an asshole.

What everyone says to their parents when their parents say some half-assed thing—like when they make some big fucking proclamation about what you're never allowed to drive again or what you've got exactly fifteen minutes to clean up—is "Get real." It doesn't really mean anything; it's just what you say. It's like filler for when there's nothing going on inside your head. If I think about what I myself would have to do to get real I get a wicked headache. It probably amounts to a religion if you can do it—a religion or some kind of art. Which is probably why everyone throws it at their parents, because if their parents could hack art then they'd be somewhere else, somewhere doing the big time, and would not have any kids to scream at. My dad never asked me to do anything, never gave me an order, but at Christmas when we were out shoveling my grandparents' driveway he said from the blackness a ways off, "Do this one thing for me, will you?" I remember I stood up straight and looked at him even though I couldn't really see his face, and he couldn't really see mine. I remember this was so weird, me waiting to hear the one thing he wanted me to do for him, because for a minute the world was so frozen and silent that it was almost not there. It was as if all the relatives crammed into my grandparents' house were in some Apollo or another and we were out dangling by strings, with no air, just us two out in the black galaxy, with nothing but a stupid job to do. "Don't ever give your mother a hard time" is what he told me. That was it, just not giving her a hard time. I remember feeling really bad and really alone then, and all I could think to do was bend back down to the shoveling and say "Get real," digging into my shitty filler as I dug into the shitty snow.

"What did you say to me?" he asked.

I sort of laughed. "I told you to get real," I said, and then the world seemed even more silent than before, because suddenly I felt like a milked-down bowl of oatmeal, being sad and mad and a prick-on-purpose all at once. "Chris," my dad said in a low voice, "that's the worst thing you could say to a person." I shrugged and said, "I didn't mean nothing by it"—said it all stupid, like some plank-brained linebacker caught pissing into a nice lady's shrubs. My dad was quiet again, and I could see him standing with both hands on the handle of the shovel, like those old pictures of farmers thinking deep thoughts about how to harvest a bowl of dust. "You're not even seventeen," he said. "You don't know shit. What's real to you is something I wish I could go back into, like a tree house. Like a tree house to hide out in. That's what's real to you. You can tell me to fuck off, you can tell me to stick the world up my ass, but don't tell me to get real. And don't tell your mother that either."

The last time I was in the record store a funny thing happened. I mean, it was a situation that started out funny but then went to someplace I wasn't sure of. I was talking to Michael—actually Michael was talking to me—when Heinley warned, "Prick up your ears, dudes. Fast approacheth Ye Olde Wretchin." "Wretchin" is what Milt and Heinley call Gretchen. It's a joke I half wish I could get a drag of, but I know by the sucking-lemon look on Michael's face that a low shit like me could not afford to laugh at "Ye Olde Wretchin." And besides that, Gretchen always looked to me relatively beautiful. They used to call her—all of them, before they got old—"Fetchin' Gretchen." This, according to Milt and Heinley, was before she'd even consider going out with Michael, when she thought that going out with Michael would be a joke, what you'd do if you were on Noah's Ark and needed a date for the Christmas party.

Like always, Michael and Gretchen moved a ways off down the counter, to talk that girlfriend whispery talk, with the girlfriend looking around suspiciously at the other guys making like they're busy. It's never that these other guys are trying to hear what she's saying—it's only other girls who want to hear what she's saying. The guys just like the sexy sound of this whispery girlfriend talk, and only if it's not their own girlfriend who's doing the talking.

"For Christ sake, Michael!" Gretchen shouted. "You're thirty-nine. Why can't you even think about doing something real for a living?" This sort of blew the whispery moment.

"This is a job that matches my life," Michael said looking down to the mess of empty jewel boxes in front of him.

"Well, yeah, that's exactly what I already knew," she said, soft for a change. "You know, Michael, you've finally completed the mission. You got me into this from the real world. You pulled me in from the outside. It's like I went out of my sane way to get a disease, and now I'm stuck with this disease. I spent too many years loving you for no reason, and now you've really done it—you went and broke a diseased heart."

Once Gretchen was out the door, Milt said, in a lame version of his usually perfect vice-principal voice, "Now that was completely uncalled for." All three of them stared after her through the store's mud-streaked window, stared after her as she walked off under the snow-blinding sunlight, stared after her like she was the last female on the desert island and was leaving them for another desert island. I felt my throat tighten, what I remember feeling as a kid, what I remember feeling those times that the whole fucking world seemed to be leaving me for dead. On our side of the store's mud-streaked window it felt like a sad old movie, mainly sad because I wasn't around in the old days of Michael, Milt, and Heinley, wasn't around then to see and understand how this could be happening. I guess I felt like crying because my sadness was for them, not for me. I felt like crying for Michael, because he was so decent, and for absolutely no reason I can tell he just fell through some big crack in the world, and for Gretchen, because she was relatively beautiful and had a life going on someplace else, and yet she still came into this shitty used-record store that didn't even sell used records anymore.

If I cried over my dad I'd be crying for someone who didn't even exist, because I'd have to cry for the dad I didn't have, the dad of that kid loading the sacks of topsoil into people's trunks. They say it's my age that makes me "heartless"—that's what all of my father's cousins have been mumbling, "heartless," all these dicks who didn't shoot out of their mothers with one diseased heart preinstalled. They say it's my shit-for-morals generation, that's what they say. But I know that Michael would act the same way I'm acting, even though he's almost as old as my dad was just three days ago. I think of that day that Michael didn't cry, standing there over the empty jewel boxes, a bunch of plastic with no music inside. If I was Michael right now I'd have about four years left, and if I was Michael with four years left, I wouldn't know how to find a real thing to do with my life either.

This is what I plan to think about during the wake tomorrow and the funeral the day after. This is what I'll think about when I'm supposed to be sobbing like a simp or else looking like I'm holding it all in for the sake of my mother, who's supposed to be throwing herself and her coat and her shoulder bag over the top of her husband's coffin, like they do in Mafia movies.

It doesn't bother my mom that I am the way I am, and no
one has to tell me never to give her a hard time. When I tell my
mom to get real she throws a dish towel at me—a dish towel or a
sneaker or one of the two Little League trophies I got for merely
showing up—and I like this. Sometimes she rolls her eyes and
yells "Jesus-fucking-Christ-Almighty!" before she throws a tro-
phy at me.

I think people cry because they're afraid of getting real, because that might mean thinking about how much they don't love
their loved ones. And I think maybe that's the reason Michael
didn't cry that day at the record store. He would never put on an
act. But then I also wonder about crying, because if people can
cry when they're happy, then they can also not cry when they're
sad. And the more I think about all of this, the more I just don't
know—don't know if I'd just stand there being real when a relatively beautiful girl was walking away from me, or if, with just
four years left, I'd close up my jewel boxes and do something else,
anything else, to get her not to leave, to get her to stay with me
till it was over, till the end.

Compression Scars

KELLIE WELLS

From *Compression Scars* (2002)

The summer the bats came, Duncan began wearing only blue and my breasts grew a whole cup size as if I were feeding them better. The day I first noticed the bats, I had gone outside to watch the Roto-Rooter men dig up the Dorsetts' backyard. Mr. Dorsett paced back and forth as the muddy men lifted parts of the lame septic tank out of the hole. I admit I was sort of glad about it. I could tell the whole thing embarrassed Mr. Dorsett because he was stinking up the entire neighborhood. It was the end of May and even though it wasn't too hot yet, neighbors were shutting their doors and windows and turning on the AC.

Mr. Dorsett looked over at our yard periodically to see if my dad had come out to watch the cavern that Mr. D's backyard was becoming, and I'd wave and smile like we were old pals. Across Mr. Dorsett's yard, I saw Mrs. McCorkle. She was kneeling in her garden, tugging at something. When she looked up, Mr. Dorsett waved nervously at her, and she smiled and yelled, "Hello, Ivy." I smiled back.

No love is lost between Mr. Dorsett and me. When I was eight years old, he wouldn't allow his twelve-year-old daughter, Judy, to play with me anymore. He claimed he was afraid she would pick up infantile habits or her brain wouldn't be properly stimulated if she didn't hang out with kids her own age. Personally, I think he didn't like me because of my unorthodox religious views. I think he was just steamed because I told Judy that when I prayed, I said it to my stomach, because that's where I thought God was—on the inside somewhere, maybe swimming in my small intestine or spinning around in my pancreas.

Judy told me the next day she was poking herself in the stomach, on the lookout for signs of a higher power hiding inside her, when her father asked her what in Henry's name she was doing. Judy, a hopelessly brick-headed literalist, told Mr. Dorsett what I'd said and asked him if God in the pancreas portended problems for the body later on (having just covered insulin and bile production in science class). She saw divine diabetes in my future and probably pictured my organs sagging with the weight of being occupied so intimately. I think she was hoping to find the tumor of God inside her stomach so she could push him up into her arm or cheek or some other harmless spot where he'd be less likely to interfere with her bodily processes.

Mr. Dorsett was a deacon at a church where going to movies, even *The Million Dollar Duck*, was a sin, although it was A-OK to watch television. You weren't supposed to dance either. It was probably a sin if you were even caught swaying a little. And music was definitely out unless the lyrics mentioned rising from the grave or the blood of the lamb or something. I went to this church. Once. I sat between Judy and Mr. Dorsett. The minister didn't talk, he yelled, like we all had a hearing loss of some sort (after several Sundays of that, I think we would have—probably an evangelical strategy for quick, resistance-free supplication: deaf lambs don't bleat back, a way to shut the mutton up). He leaned out over the pulpit and practically screamed the Word. His face was puffy, and the thick folds of his cheeks filled with red. I don't I think he got enough oxygen. He exhaled quite a bit, but I didn't see him inhale much. He had gray cowlicked hair that kept flying forward in an arc over his eyes. It's funny how some people think they have to look like they're having a stroke to convince you of the incontrovertible god's-honest truth of what they're saying. I remember shaking and kicking my feet during the sermon, and Mr. Dorsett slapped my knees.

So I was secretly pleased about this septic tank thing because I thought it definitely pointed to Mr. Dorsett's ailing karma. Actually, I am only a selective believer in karma. I believe in it when I think people are getting what they deserve, which, let's face it, is pretty rare. But I still have a hard time accepting the idea that hungry babies with bubbled, empty stomachs are in that predicament because they were maybe serial killers or jewel thieves in a previous life. Babies are blank, nearly smooth-brained, with a wrinkle for complacency, a wrinkle for fear, and a crevasse for hunger and thirst. So it's not like they'd learn a lesson or anything.

Anyhow, as I watched Mr. Dorsett pop Tums like they were Sweet Tarts, I saw them, I saw the bats. I didn't know what they were at first. I was picking a scabby fungus off our sycamore tree, half expecting it to bleed, and thinking it was odd the tree already had a few dead leaves. Then, a little higher up, I noticed these yellowish-brown bulbs, and it appeared our sycamore tree had suddenly grown peaches, like it was tired of simply being a sycamore and thought it might get more respect as a fruit-bearer.

I reached up to examine one of these dead leaves, and as I touched it, an electric feeling zipped up my arm and across my cheek. This leaf was soft and angry. It started shaking and screeching. I instinctively fell to the ground, in case it got the idea to dive bomb my head or something. It unfolded wings that were like little flannel rags, then it and a few friends dropped from the tree and flew off. As they screamed by, I actually glimpsed their faces, these furry little crumpled-up cartoon faces. They looked like one of those pictures you'd see in the backs of magazines or on the insides of matchbooks, and if you drew it and sent it in, somebody, somewhere, for a small fee, would tell you whether you should go to art school.

I examined the tree more closely and counted about fifteen bats total. Some were hanging freely on the branches convincingly miming dead leaves and others were curled up tight like tiny fists beneath real leaves. They ranged in color from yellowish to orangish brown, but none was black like bats are supposed to be. After I fully realized what I was looking at, I got a little spooked, thinking maybe they got their coloring from blood feasts. Then I noticed how beautiful they were. They looked like yellow flowers gone to seed. I reached up to touch one tucked beneath a leaf.

"You all right?"

My heart dropped into my Chuck Taylors. Mr. Dorsett. He scared the befreakinjesus out of me. You know how you're getting ready to touch something, maybe a smashed snake or an unidentifiable dark object lying in a corner, and some wiseacre comes out of nowhere and says something, or maybe your own stomach growls, and for a nanosecond you think the thing spoke to you, you think you just had a genuine brush with the godhead? Jeezoman, that's what I felt, until I heard the gate close.

"Ivy?"

"Hi, Mr. Dorsett." I brushed myself off and bent forward so my hair fell over my quadruply pierced ears, potential lecture fodder. "Too bad about your yard," I said. "Quite the terra carnage." I felt a thin smile spread across my face despite my best efforts to straighten my lips.

"What were you doing?"

"I wasn't dancing." I thought of that old joke about Baptists, who won't have sex standing up for fear it will be mistaken for dancing. Even though it had been eight years and Judy was now the sort of young Republican Type A personality urban professional overachiever I would never hang with anyway, I was still a little peeved at Mr. Dorsett. I didn't feel like being overly civil.

"What were you looking at?" Mr. Dorsett moved in closer and looked up at the tree.

"I was just looking to see, um . . . if that new tree food was working."

"New tree food?" Mr. Dorsett looked intently at my face, as if he couldn't believe his eyes, as if my nose had just fallen off and a big tulip had bloomed in its place.

"A couple of months ago, we got this revolutionary new botanical grow food they were selling on television. You know, it comes with Ginsu knives, or Popeil's Pocket Fisherman, I forget, if you order early. You sprinkle it around your tree and within a couple of months, you get fruit, apples or peaches, or sometimes even mangoes. Look." I pointed at the furry orange balls dangling from a high branch. Mr. Dorsett gave me this dour no-nonsense look like he'd had just about enough and if I didn't come clean soon, he was going to march me over to my parents and demand I be locked in the laundry room or shipped off to a reformatory for inveterate smart alecks or something, in the interest of the community.

"Bats," I relented. The way he dropped his jaw and began to back up, you'd think I'd said jackals or two-headed goats. "They're really neat."

Mr. Dorsett grabbed my shoulder and pulled me back from the tree. "Bats are dangerous," he said. "Disease-ridden."

"No, they're not." I didn't like how Mr. Dorsett was all nosy and pushing me around in my own yard. "They're little, harmless bats. They get bad press, but they're not actually going to morph into Barnabas Collins or Bela Lugosi for Christsakes." My heart raced as I said this last part—it came out of my mouth before I could put on the brakes—because I knew it was going to make the blood zoom in alarm to Mr. Dorsett's face.

"You listen here, missy . . ." Just then there was a minor explosion next door and black, foul-smelling goop started erupting from the hole in Mr. Dorsett's backyard.

"Looks like you got a gusher. Maybe you've struck black gold," I said as Mr. Dorsett raced out the gate.

I decided to go over to Duncan's to tell him about the bats. I knew he'd think it was totally gravy that we had bats hanging out in our sycamore tree. Duncan is my best friend. He moved to What Cheer from Medicine Lodge when we were both ten years old. The day after he moved in, he came over with two turtles, and he let me paint a red I for Ivy on the back of one. We tried to race them, but they kept going in opposite directions. Duncan said that was their secret strategy, that they whispered to one another, "Odds are better if we split up." Duncan and I have been inseparable ever since. Now, nearly every day, Duncan's father will ask, "You two attached at the hip?" And Duncan's mother will wrinkle her nose and say, "No, dear. They're attached at the heart," and then she'll wink. It's a little nauseating. Duncan's mom is super nice, but she can get on your nerves. She's the type that asks you every ten seconds if you're warm enough, cool enough, hungry, thirsty, etcetera, always on the lookout for ways to serve and placate. I think she took the gleefully self-denying good gal lessons of the *Donna Reed Show* a little too much to heart when she was growing up. Once Duncan and I made signs that said, YES, WE'RE WARM ENOUGH, OUR BODY TEMPERATURES ARE HOLDING STEADY AT EXACTLY 98.6 and NO, WE'RE NOT HUNGRY WE'RE FULL AS TICKS AND COULDN'T POSSIBLY EAT ANOTHER MORSEL. Mrs. Nicholson smiled and said, "Oh, you two," but she still asks.

Mr. Nicholson is a world-class cornball without equal. He's the kind of guy who steals little kids' noses, tells them that eating beets will put hair on their chests, as if that were a perk, and assigns them dippy nicknames that make them feel as though they're wearing their underwear outside their pants. Of course Ivy is an easy target. "That girl's poison, Duncan," he'll say. "You better hope you never get the itch for her." Yuk, yuk. When I was younger, he used to call me Intravenous de Milo, a nickname filched from *Spinal Tap*, which he'd been forced to watch countless times with Duncan, and he'd say, "I need a love transfusion, I.V." Then he'd make me kiss a vein. Once I said to him, "Boy, we'll never starve around here so long as you keep dishing that corn," and he quit razzing me, cold turkey, for days. I didn't say it with even a drop of malice, but I guess it took the fun out of it to have his behavior suddenly named like that, so now I just swallow it wholesale and roll my eyes like he likes. Mr. Nicholson calls their five-year-old neighbor Jill Shipley, Henrietta, for no good reason except that it makes her madder than hell.

If the caption WHAT'S WRONG WITH THIS PICTURE? were beneath a Nicholson family photo, you'd pick Duncan out in a second. Duncan has nappy, brown hair that curls off the top of his head like it's trying to escape. It's cut real short on the sides and there's a yin/yang symbol shaved against his scalp in the back. His favorite thing to wear is a Zippy the Pinhead T-shirt that says, ALL LIFE'S A BLUR OF REPUBLICANS AND MEAT.

Some of the beef-necked deltoids at school pick on Duncan. They wear buttons that announce they are the FAG-BUSTER PATROL. The insignia on the buttons is a limp wrist with a circle and slash. They call Duncan fag-bait and say, "Bend over, Joy Boy, I'll drive." And I say, "You realize the implications here are much more damning for you." I whisper confidentially, "You're obviously suffering from Small Penis Syndrome." Then I put my finger on one of their big, clunky belt buckles, run it down the fly, and say, "You really ought to have that looked at." Of course, they shoot back, agile and witty as the redwoods they resemble, with, "Stupid lesbo" or "Shut up, cunt." These guys listen to Guns and

Roses instructionally and dream of the day they'll bury their girl-friends in the backyard. Real princes.

Duncan, on the other, less simian, hand, is beautiful, completely beautiful inside and out. His skin is white as Elmer's glue, and if you look into his gray-green eyes too long, you'll slam your foot down because you'll feel like you're falling. It's like having a semi-lucid dream where you've just voluntarily stepped off a cliff, and one of the things you're thinking about on the way down is how they say you can have a heart attack if you let yourself splat because you're *so* into it. But me, I always bounce. I'm into it too, it's just that I believe in options. With Duncan, I know anything is possible.

So about Duncan. After I watched Mr. Dorsett race around the heaving hellmouth in his backyard for a while, I went to see Duncan. Mrs. Nicholson answered the door, and she busted out crying when she saw me. "I'm sorry, Ivy," she said. "Come in." She hugged me hard and for a long time, like she'd just recovered me from a kidnapper, ten years and forty thousand milk cartons later. She pushed my hair behind my ears and cupped my face in her hands. "You kids are so young," she said, and I could tell her voice was only a few syllables away from giving out. "Duncan's in his room."

As I walked up the stairs, my mind raced, trying to compute the meaning of such a greeting. I became paranoid, which is my stock response to inexplicable distress in adults, followed closely by either blind self-blame or -defense, depending. I was worried that maybe Mr. Dorsett had told them he feared I'd joined a strange new cult, a druidic splinter group, that worshipped at the altar of tree-roosting bats. Mr. Dorsett tended to see rank-smelling theological peril everywhere he stepped.

But as I entered Duncan's room, I instantly forgot what it was I had just been stressing about, like some corrective, cosmic hand had reached into my head with one of those pink erasers and I rubbed out those brain cells. Duncan was sitting on his bed reading *Death on the Installment Plan*, listening to Fad Gadget, a recent bargain-bin coup. *I choke on the gag, but I don't get the joke.* Somehow Duncan's skin seemed even paler, as if the glue had been watered down; his lips looked almost blue. "Hey, Dunc, what's up? Your mom's tripping."

Duncan stood up. "Look," he said, and started unbuttoning his jeans.

"Wow, is there some sort of planetary misalignment that's making people wig or what?" I made a feeble attempt to avert my eyes. I was in fact very curious about what kind of underwear Duncan wore—one of the few subjects we'd never covered. Striped boxers. Cool. He hiked his shorts up a little and pointed at his thigh, the scars from his moped accident. "I've seen your scars before. I like them. Except for this fading one on my cheek, I don't have any good scars." He turned around. The scars wound around his thigh and ran down his legs in widening, white lines past his knees. There were three lines that stopped at different places, as if they were racing. The lines were eerie, almost fluorescent against his milky legs. They looked like symbols or rebus, like they were trying to tell us something, like maybe they'd spell out a message when they reached the appropriate point. Duncan put his jeans back on. "Jesus, Duncan. Your scars are growing. What's the skinny?"

"So much for swimsuit season," he said. He tried to smile. I hugged him. I hugged him like Mrs. N. had hugged me. Even though Duncan had put his jeans back on, I kept seeing those lines, as if a flashbulb had gone off and branded the image on my retinas. I saw the lines lift off his legs and circle around my head, curling in through one ear and out the other. I saw them slip under the surface of the skin in my face, making fleshy speed bumps across the pavement of my cheeks. I thought about the movie *Squirm* and the electrified worms that terrorized people, getting under their skin, literally. I wanted to make the droopy, gray crescents under Duncan's eyes go away.

"Hey, Dunc, remember that scene in *Squirm* when that woman turned on the shower and the worms started oozing out the holes in the shower head, and then she turned the faucets back off and the worms retreated?" I laughed.

"They think it's some bizarre thing called morphea, or sclero-derma, they're not sure. They looked at pictures in dusty books they hadn't cracked since medical school and scratched their chins, told me they were just nose and throat guys, not weird disease experts. But they think it's one of those one-in-a-million deals. Unbeatable." Duncan pulled me toward him and kissed me. It was a desperate kiss, as if he thought it might have some therapeutic or medicinal benefit. His tongue went everywhere, touched everything, took complete inventory. I believe if he'd had more tongue, he would have kept going straight down to my esophagus, blazing a trail inside me.

I pushed him back. I wondered if this was one of his games. Sometimes Duncan is so childlike, almost obsessive-compulsive, a magical thinker. He makes up these games or rituals and convinces himself that his wish will come true if he completes his task. Like if he can successfully throw and catch his boomerang twenty times in a row while juggling cantaloupes, it's a sign he'll get accepted to UC Berkeley or receive manna, or something like that. The spooky thing is that it almost always works. I guess the psychologists would say it's just a self-fulfilling prophecy, but it's still kind of unsettling. I mean Duncan's no Nostradamus or Uri Geller or Tiresias or anything, he just knows what he wants.

"Morphea?" I said. "That sounds like science fiction. You're making this up?" I said hopefully. We sat down on his bed. I was starting to get seriously creeped out.

"No. I'm not."

"Is it some kind of sleeping sickness?"

"No. Misnomer."

"Spill it, Dunc-man. You're making me nervous."

Duncan fingered the shaved path of the yin/yang symbol shorn into his scalp. "I don't know if you remember the niggling details of my injury or not—who knew it was going to matter—but these scars I got aren't from being cut or anything like that, they're from the impact. You know, from being pressed up against the curb. They're called compression scars." Duncan stopped and looked at me like what he had just said was dangerously illuminating, the key to sudden understanding, and he was waiting for me to say a slow and knowing "Ohhh" and nod my head.

"Yeah, keep going."

"I guess we should have held out for more insurance money. Evidently these compression scars can come back to haunt you, big time. They can lie dormant like some goddamned ghost wound hibernating in your leg. And you don't know, you think you're fine. You just think you got some awesome scars to show the grandkids later on. Then these scars, they, like, come to life and spread across your whole body, and after they're done striping the outside, they can tear through your insides too, clipping the sharp edges off your internal organs like goddamned scissors. Fuck." Duncan bent over his wastepaper basket. "Maybe you ought to go, Ive. I think I'm going to be sick. I don't have a stomach for tragedy," he said.

"Wait. I don't believe this," I said. "I've never heard of anything like this before. This sounds like some made-up disease from another planet, something you'd get inoculated for before traveling to, I don't know, Neptune or something. Surely there've been like a bazillion people who've had these compression scars, right? I mean how come I've never heard of this?"

"I don't know, Ive, I guess it's not very high up on the research priority list." Duncan wrapped his arms around himself. "They just don't know shit about it. Fucking doctors. They're not even willing to commit themselves to this diagnosis. You could hear their malpractice-fearing knees knocking together every time they uttered the word *morphea*." Duncan began rocking slowly back and forth on the bed.

I twisted the spirals of hair that hung over his forehead. "Why didn't you tell me about this, about these scars?"

"Because. I didn't really know anything until today."

I felt my stomach start to knot in a way only a Boy Scout could appreciate, hundreds of tiny hands pressing against the walls. "So is it for sure . . ."

"Time to feed the worms? Should I prepare for the big dirt nap?

I nodded.

"They don't know. You could fill a thimble with what those bastards know about it. They said it might stop spreading and maybe it will never go inside. They said it could take a few months, a few years, few decades, maybe never happen, maybe happen tomorrow. Real conclusive stuff." Duncan looked straight into my eyes and softened his voice to a whisper. "I'm afraid to move," he said. "It's like I have this big rip in my pants or something, and if I move, I could die." He kept looking and looking at me, and I felt like he could see my thoughts, could see me thinking, *If you die, Duncan Nicholson, I'll, I'll cut off my hands and feet and sit in one place until I can come too.* His bottomless eyes. I steadied myself against the bed.

Duncan reached out and pressed his hand against my left breast, the larger one. "I don't want to die a virgin," he said.

I always thought this would be a great moment, that I'd feel velvety needles prickle against my skin. But it wasn't like that at all. It wasn't like anything. I couldn't feel it. If I hadn't seen his hand on my breast, I would never have known it was there. My breast felt novocained, heavy, but it definitely did not tingle, not a single goosebump, and I bump easy. I wanted to say, "Yes, Duncan. I love you, Duncan. Take me, take me," or whatever it is you say between hot gasps in moments such as these, moments that until this one I had only experienced vicariously through the lives of Chelsea Starling, secretly passionate nurse, and Vanessa Vandehorn, bored but sexy rich girl. But I couldn't. Had I wanted to,

I couldn't even say something stupid like, "Could I please have a pretzel first?" My brain and mouth were momentarily disconnected. All I could do was stand up with my numb breast and dysfunctional lips and walk out.

Things can get so strange so fast.

The sun was going down and the cicadas were throbbing. I wondered if the sound bothered the bats, if it disturbed their sleep. I sat very still on the picnic table. I decided to keep an eye on these fraudulent leaves. My brain was still buzzing from the strange bomb Duncan had dropped. *Morphea*. It sounded like a name for a host of late night horror flicks—Morphea Bloodletter or something. I know I should have stayed with Duncan and tried to comfort him somehow, but I just had to bolt.

The bats were still snoozing. Mr. Dorsett still had a septic gorge in his backyard. I considered mentioning something about sky-tram rides across the smelly chasm next time I saw him, but decided against it. I guess I felt even Mr. Dorsett deserved a break. He was probably at church praying his head off, begging God to have mercy on his crummy plumbing.

I watched for signs of life from the wrinkled, brown leaves. You couldn't even see them breathe. I thought about their metabolism, how it must slow during sleep so they can preserve energy for flying and foraging. I imagined their lungs as delicate bubbles, filling only once or twice a minute, their button-sized hearts beating slow and steady as a bathroom sink drip.

I thought about Duncan, about Duncan before all this. I thought about the night we rode our bikes toward a storm. The lightning in the distance was constant and bright. We counted the seconds between lightning and thunder and stopped riding when the flash and bang were almost on top of each other. We parked our bikes and walked along a dirt road that sliced a huge field of corn in two. The air smelled hot, burnt, and my mouth tasted like metal. We stared silently at the lightning, appreciatively, like we were at a laser show. You didn't have to be looking in the right place to catch the silver zags either, because they were everywhere. And then I noticed the fireflies that hovered over the field, a blanket of yellow blinking above the corn in an uneven rhythm, a floating net of intermittent light, bright and fleeting stains against the black sky. I don't know how long I'd been holding my breath, but all of a sudden I started gasping. Duncan pulled me toward him. He widened my mouth with his hands, turned his head, and put his mouth on mine. I was surprised at how well we fit together, no overlap, better than clasped hands. Then he breathed. He just breathed. I wondered where his tongue was and what it was doing, but it was only air that passed between us.

My stomach burbled with the memory, and a strange feeling like lit fuses sparked and trailed from my nipples down to my thighs. I wished Duncan were here touching me. I was sure I would feel it.

The dead leaves began wagging. The bats were dropping off one by one and flying in an erratic, noisy mass above the tree. The sycamore suddenly appeared a lot healthier. Up in the air like that, the bats looked like jittery little birds. The streetlights snapped on. The bats flew over and circled the lights, swooping into the buzzing glow periodically, feeding on mesmerized moths and June bugs.

Then I heard screaming, and my first thought was, *Oh, no, they've gone and attached themselves to someone's carotid artery*; this was clearly the residue of Mr. Dorsett's repulsion. But it was Mrs. McCorkle. "What?" she yelled, as she moved slowly across her backyard toward the pit of tamed sewage in Mr. Dorsett's yard. She kneeled at the edge and looked in. "Harlan? Are you in there?" She wrestled a spidery vine out of the mud wall. "We'll have to clean this up. Mercy. Come on now," she said. She walked back to her house and disappeared through the back door.

Then I heard screaming again and things shattering. I walked around front and across Mr. Dorsett's meticulously groomed front lawn toward Mrs. McCorkle's. She was yelling at some invisible person, something about bluebells and pork roast, and smashing glass on her driveway. She lobbed an armful of plates and cups and jars onto the concrete and shook her fists in the air. She ran into her house and pulled her gauzy curtains off the rods. She ran back outside and started ripping them into thin strips. She spotted me at the end of her driveway and looked at me with narrowed eyes and tense lips, like she wanted to club me. My heart was pounding hard inside my chest, as though it wanted to get out before it was too late. I was 100 percent clueless as to a reasonable plan of action. I knew Mrs. McCorkle had these spells if she forgot to take some kind of medicine. I think she intentionally neglected to take it sometimes just because she was bored or lonely and needed her other self for company. Once last summer Mr. Dorsett was about to get into his car to leave for work when she ran over and started clobbering him over the head with a newspaper. She'd thought he was trying to steal her gladiolas. I admit I thought it was sort of amusing at the time, but now it felt like the whole world had completely kooked out, schizoid squared, like the planet had wobbled clean off its axis, and it was beginning to spook me but good. I wondered if some unstable isotope had been released into the atmosphere of What Cheer, or some volatile chemical that could take a once uneventful existence and turn it into something Lon Chaney would surely star in if she were alive (something Morphea Bloodletter would introduce on the Late-night Creature Feature). Or maybe the magnetic field reversal was finally here. Life, as I had known it, was out of whack.

"You," Mrs. McCorkle said, still sneering at me. "You. Where's Harlan? What have you done with him?"

"He's at Medicalodge South, Mrs. McCorkle, the nursing home. Remember? He's been there for a couple of months." I stretched my arm out toward her for reasons I can't begin to understand. I think the only reason she would have taken it would have been to rip it out of its socket and beat me about the head with it. Mrs. McCorkle snorted a few chuckles and ran inside. When she came back out, she had a large ceramic vase and a wall mirror. I backed up into the street. Mrs. McCorkle threw the vase and mirror onto the pile of shards. The crash was loud and sounded final; glinting splinters of mirror shot across the pavement like sharp bullets of light. She smiled and kicked off her shoes. She raised her dress above her knees, and I could feel my panicked stomach trying to push free of my body. "Don't!"

She hopped onto the sharp rubble and pranced around like she was stomping grapes, smiling and stomping, dress in hand, as though she were just entertaining a tour group with this quaint, old world custom. Then she went down on her hands and knees.

I think I may have screamed, but I couldn't hear it. I walked unsteadily toward Mrs. McCorkle, my legs springy like pogo sticks. I made myself think, willed thoughts outside this scene to come into my head. I thought of the bats, wondered if they were watching and if they were glad to be bats with their breezy lives, hanging in trees, eating easy meals, ignorant of the unseen perils of power plants, compressed skin, and old age. I would have traded places with them at that moment. I wanted to rise, lift up and out of this life, and would have given it all up—Duncan; my bootleg albums, the Soft Boys, Captain Beefheart, the good old noisy collectible stuff strategically swapped for at used records stores; the archive of articles I'd been compiling since I was a kid on UFO sightings and the Viking Voyager expedition; my memory of Grandpa Engel and his magical teeth; my face, my breasts—the whole shmear. Would have given it up in the beat of a tiny wing.

Maintain, I told myself. I made my way slowly to Mrs. Mc-

Corkle. I grabbed her off the razory debris and wrestled her to the ground, which was no easy feat. Those age-worn arms and legs held surprising strength. Crimany. At first I was afraid if I handled her too rough, I might crack her bones or something, and then I was afraid she might crack mine.

I finally wore her down and began picking the spurs of glass from her hands and feet. She held her hands up and smiled like a child who's made a mess of herself with spaghetti or ice cream. She looked pleased that we were both now covered in blood. Mr. Myers, next door on the other side, finally came out to investigate the commotion, and when he saw the blood and shattered glass, he started running around the yard screaming, "Oh, my god! Oh, god! Oh my god, Effie!" He picked Mrs. McCorkle up. She was playing itsy-bitsy spider on her shredded fingers. I could tell she was miffed when he made her lose her place. He carried her inside his house. My stomach finally made its way up into my throat, and I spit bile into the bloody grass.

I wished the bats would swoop down and pick me up by the collar and carry me off to some cold, quiet cave and feed me flies.

Duncan came over the next night and apologized like mad for being so pushy and forward and unromantic and all. He said the uncertainty of his body's future gave all things nascent and physical a kind of guerrilla urgency. It made me feel crummy because I thought I should be the sorry one. I mean, I was the one who had abandoned him in his moment of need. It wasn't like my sense of propriety had been wounded or anything. I think I just went concrete at that moment; maybe I was scared his skin might start falling off if we did it, like that grisly film of the aftermath in Hiroshima they made us watch in sixth grade. The captured shadows branded onto walls, the charred bodies, and all those people in the hospitals. And they just filmed it like it didn't even mat-

ter that the people whose bombed bodies they were document-
ing were completely raw, almost jellied; they just let the cam-
eras roll. I always wondered what those cameramen had eaten
that day, pears or sweet rolls, rice cakes, carrots, whatever, and if
they had been able to keep it down. What did they do when they
were finished shooting that evening? Did they take a bath? Did
they touch themselves? Did they stare at their skin in the mirror,
waiting for it to move? Needless to say, this is not an association
you want to make just before your premier sexual experience.

"I think you're going to live through this, Duncan," I told him.
"In fact, I'm sure of it."

"Yeah, what makes you so sure?"

"Well, last night I had this dream that we were old, ninety-five
if we were a day, and we were sitting in a porch swing attached
to this tree that I'm sure didn't have nearly as many rings as we
had wrinkles, and 'Take the Skinheads Bowling' was playing in
the background. We were talking about the concert we went to
last week like it was the good old days. And then we started comparing scars. We both had scars all over our pruney bodies. I had
a cool fish-shaped one across my stomach. You were impressed."

Duncan laughed. "At night I see my scars in my mind, and I
watch them disappear as if someone had pulled up the plastic
sheet on a Magic Slate."

I noticed that Duncan was clad head-to-toe in blue. Usually he
wore ten or twelve competing bright colors, and you could only
look at him for so long before things started vibrating, visually
speaking. But today he had on a navy blue bowling shirt that said
"Earl" on the pocket, blue jeans, blue Converse high tops, and a
blue bandanna around his ankle; a small blue marble dangled
from his ear. "Say, what's with this color-me-blue look?" I asked.

"It's chromatherapy," he said. "I saw it on Oprah or Sally Jessy,
something. Different colors have certain effects on you emotion-
ally and physically. Red is a stimulant. If you surrounded yourself

with red, you'd constantly be doing chin-ups or something. Blue is supposed to be healing." He shrugged his shoulders.

That's one of my favorite-favorite things about Duncan, how he gives anything or anyone a chance. He accepts without complaint the absurdity that's as prevalent as ether and knows anything is possible, even good weird things.

I told him about the bats and about Mrs. McCorkle. Duncan loved Mrs. McCorkle because she always said outrageous things even when she *remembered* to take her medication. Once she told us if she were president, she'd impose capital punishment only for excessive chatter in movie theaters. "That would rid society of an insidious element," she said, "*and* help defray the population explosion." I think she meant it too. Duncan wanted to send her blueberries and morning glories.

I showed Duncan the bats. They were resting again, the withered foliage shtick.

"Are you sure they're bats?" Duncan asked. I pointed to the peaches near the top and showed him the ones clenched tight under leaves. "Wow," he said. "They're so beautiful. They look ancient and sacred. Like something in cave paintings." Duncan's voice began to crack. He gently placed both his hands on my breasts. "Do something for me," he whispered.

My breasts were tingling, hot-wired, bubbling with current. "All right," I said.

"What do these bats eat?"

"Insects mostly."

"What time do they start feeding?"

"I don't know. Around sundown." I began to wonder what it was I was going to end up agreeing to do. I had a feeling it wasn't what I had thought it was.

"Green and yellow are good colors, too," he said. "Restorative. I'll be back," he said, walking away. He turned around. "Tomorrow night."

When Duncan showed up, he was wearing only a busy madras pair of Bermuda shorts—no shirt, no shoes, nothing else. I hoped his scars wouldn't glow in the dark. He was carrying a jar full of blinking fireflies and a coffee can full of dead bugs. "Will you humor me, Ive?" he asked.

"This isn't going to involve like chicken blood, is it?"

Duncan smiled and shook his head. "What are your 'rents doing?" Duncan had this very serious look on his face; he looked sort of like Spencer Tracy in *Guess Who's Coming to Dinner*, like he was getting ready to make an eloquent speech on a touchy issue.

"I don't know. Watching a miniseries or something."

"Will they come outside for any reason?" Duncan grabbed my arm like he wanted me to think before I answered.

"Not likely. Unless the couch catches fire."

"Good. What about the Dorsetts?" He nodded his head toward their house.

"I haven't seen them. I think maybe they left town."

"Cool," he said. "Where are the bats?"

I pointed to the streetlight; a dark halo circled around it. "A couple stick around the tree and dive at the porch light occasionally."

Duncan took hold of my shoulders and led me under the canopy of the tree. He raised my arms and pulled my T-shirt over my head.

"Couldn't we at least use a tent or something?" I asked. For most things you can count me in; my name and the word *trooper* come up a lot in the same sentence, but an exhibitionist I'm not. I don't even like to undress in front of a mirror.

Duncan spread my shirt on the grass, pushed me down to my knees, then lowered me gently to the ground with my head in his hand, as if he were baptizing me. Out of the corner of my eye, I saw a bat dive into the light. Duncan took the dead insects out of the coffee can and arranged them on my stomach: a June bug, a cricket, some flies and moths.

"Duncan, you know, this is weird."

"I know," he said.

"I refuse to eat them, if that's what you had in mind." My stomach itched, but I was afraid to scratch, like any movement might activate the insects and make them bore into my navel or something, as if Duncan had preprogrammed them. Stepford bugs.

"You don't have to eat them," he said.

I was relieved. Around Duncan I do things that under any other circumstances would lead me to believe I'm certifiably off my noodle.

Duncan sat down next to me. He took some fireflies out of the jar, held them between his fingers, waited for the blink, and crossed himself, smearing the phosphorescent abdomens onto his chest. He lay back. Duncan scissored his arms and legs like he was making snow angels, only I guess they were actually earth angels, invisible. "Close your eyes," he said, "and do like I'm doing." I flapped and kicked, and it felt sort of nice, like I was a low-flying, upside down bird.

I felt something brush against my stomach. My skin was sparking, crackling with heat. I felt my stomach and my heart lift out of my body, finally striking out on their own. My legs shook. I let myself feel it.

Lifelines

RITA CIRESI

From *Mother Rocket* (1993)

The spring I worked in the Dairy Queen I hated everything: school and home and work, my teachers, my manager, my mother, myself. I was always walking toward something, always waiting for something wonderful to happen, waiting for a card or letter from my father, waiting for love to strike. But I bumped into more things than I consciously found, and I lost things habitually. Either I was shedding or I had bad luck. In any case, I lost two sets of house keys that spring, and every other day before I walked to work I lost a quarter in the school Coke machine. I lost so many quarters I went to our principal, Mother Superior, and complained.

"If you lose something, you ought to know what to do," she said, gazing down at me through her silver half-glasses.

"Go look for it?" I said.

"Wrong. Pray to Saint Anthony. He has divine intercession and can find you anything."

My mother snorted when I told her what Mother Superior had said. "Can the great saint find me my lost youth?" she said. "And can he find me a man? That's what I want to know. I'd believe in saints if I could see miracles like that."

My mother was old at thirty-five, and looked worn out. I was seventeen and I didn't believe in saints either. I didn't believe anything lost could ever be found, at least not in its original state. Still, I wanted to grab on to things, seize them, get whatever I could get, even if I couldn't hang on to them.

Wanting steady things to surround me came from moving place to place. My father worked construction, and we moved up and down the coast, following the jobs. For every place we lived I found a special shell on the beach. "Why do you want to carry those broken shells around with you?" my father asked.

"They wouldn't get broken if we didn't move so much," my mother commented before I could even answer.

"If we didn't move so much, she wouldn't have the chance to find them in the first place," my father said.

"If we didn't move so much and everything else wasn't so topsy-turvy, she wouldn't want to collect them," my mother said.

"You think everything's topsy-turvy?" my father shouted. "I'll show you topsy-turvy, my friend."

"Nothing's the way it used to be!" my mother said.

"It's always been the same, no matter where we moved: lousy, lousy, and lousy again."

"If it's so lousy," my mother said, "then get out."

My father got out. My mother chose Port Charlotte, sight unseen, for the name. "It's not a *beach*," she said scornfully. "It's not a *fort*, it's a port, and it's Port Charlotte. Charlotte, Charlotte— doesn't that name sound good and old-fashioned? Comforting?"

My manager at the Dairy Queen, Bob, said it sounded like the name of a Southern belle withering away on a sagging front porch. "Charlotte sounds like the name of some old maid saving herself up for some Prince Charming. Charlotte's wasting her whole life waiting for the prince to come along when there's somebody else just as good waiting on the front porch next door. She's a dying flower, that Charlotte girl." He winked at me.

I thought about my mother, shuffling around the house until noon on a Saturday in her slippers and thin, see-through nightie. When I told her to get dressed, she said, "I'm not going anywhere, so what's the point?"

Bob was as old as my mother, but he was more like my father. "I'm an enterprising fellow," he said one afternoon as he stood by the chocolate syrup machine. "I don't let anything stand in the way of what I want to get. You look like you're having a little trouble tying on that apron, Mary Ellen."

"I can get it myself," I said.

I didn't tell my mother that Bob and I worked the afternoon shift at the Dairy Queen alone. She would have disapproved. I was always careful to complain just the right amount about my job at home, but awful as it was, I sometimes looked forward to it. Bob and I usually worked without talking for the busy first hour. We bumped into each other sometimes as we backed away from the counters. The bit of Coke left in the can I finally had coaxed out of the fickle school vending machine tasted warm and flat, but familiar and good, and even though I watched it every day through the tall windows of the Dairy Queen front, there still was mystery in the way the Port Charlotte sky grew dark in the afternoon, and clouded over. Bob and I had made up a game called the Rain Game. Each person tried to predict the exact moment the storm clouds would break and pour down rain. The person who guessed closest to the minute won the right to sit down, while the other person had to serve the winner a miniature hot fudge sundae.

"Four-thirty," Bob predicted.

"Quarter to five, quarter to five," I sang. I felt smug when the hands of the clock edged past four-thirty and the sky turned pitch.

The first clap of thunder shook the building at 4:46, emptying the parking lot and reducing the music on the radio to static.

Bob switched it off. He grumbled as he held the plastic dish of ice cream under the chocolate syrup spigot. "You're a smart-ass," he said, "but you're my best girl. And you know why?" He winked at me. "'Cause you know who's boss around here."

"And who might that be?" I asked.

"Well, I've heard he's really smart and really good-looking," he said. "His name's B-O-B."

I shrugged. He laughed and handed me my miniature chocolate sundae.

Outside, the rain came sheeting down the tall windows. Bob pulled up a stool beside me. "Your skin's too pale," he said.

"So what."

"So nothing. It just means you probably don't get enough sun and fun. You like to have a little fun, I bet."

"I guess," I said. I kept on eating. The hot fudge was sickly sweet and I dug deep with my white plastic spoon to bring up the vanilla ice cream.

"Like right now," he said. "There aren't any customers, so we ought to have a little fun, Mary Ellen, just you and me."

"What's your idea of fun?"

"What's yours?"

"We could play a guessing game," I said.

"Go on, guessing games."

"They're fun if you try to guess the right things."

"Like what?"

"Like the kind of things you wouldn't find out about people in ordinary conversations. Things that tell you something about the other person, like what they wanted to be when they were little, and stuff like that," I said.

"Who cares about what people wanted to be when they were little?"

"It tells a lot about them as grown-ups."

"Yeah, well, I forgot what I wanted to be," Bob said. "Anyway,

I never turned into it." He sighed. He rubbed his hands back and forth over the stains on the thighs of his uniform pants. "Stop looking at me that way," he said.

"I'm not looking at you."

"It isn't the past that counts, anyway. It's the future."

"I guess."

"The Rain Game's enough of guessing games."

The chocolate syrup machine buzzed. The buzz died into a hum. Bob rubbed his hands together. "Time to get serious."

I thought he was going to suggest cleaning the counters. Instead, he examined his thumbnail, then suddenly looked up. "You like to read palms?" he asked.

"Psalms?"

"No, palms, p-a-l-m-s. Tell fortunes."

"I've never done it," I said.

"What do you mean, never? I thought that's what girls do at slumber parties. Sit around in their pajamas, talk about boys, curl their hair, read palms and jazz like that."

"If you're Catholic, telling the future is a sin."

"You gotta be kidding!" he said.

"I'm not."

"But don't they teach you that God's got it all figured out before it happens?"

"Sure."

"So don't you figure you got as much right as God to know what sort of things are going to happen to you?"

"I guess."

"It isn't God who's got to live your life."

"That's true," I said. "It's me."

"Isn't God who's got to get up and go to work every morning. Isn't God who's got to tell customers yessir and no ma'am. So why don't you put that sundae down," he said, taking it out of my hands. I watched him set it on the counter with regret. "Let's do a little palm-reading, a little fortune-telling, while there aren't any customers." He looked at me expectantly. I held out my left hand. He cleared his throat, moved his stool up closer, grinned, and took my hand. Chocolate syrup clogged his short fingernails; a smear of vanilla ice cream crossed the top of his hand. He turned my palm upwards and traced his finger across it. The skin on the tip of his finger was rough. Underneath my hand, on his hand, I could feel his calluses.

"This is the Lifeline," he said. "It tells you how long you're going to live."

"Don't tell me," I said. "I'm afraid to die."

He snapped his chewing gum and leaned closer. "Then I'm happy to report you're going to live a long and healthy life. But every break in the Lifeline—here, here, and here, man, you got a lot of them—means something traumatic is going to happen. Something B-I-G that's going to change your whole life. Now you're born here—" He jabbed his finger halfway between my thumb and index finger. "And then here's the first break less than a fourth of the way up your hand. So calculating you're about seventeen or so, I'll bet the first traumatic thing has already happened, might I be right?"

I nodded.

"And it seems to me the way this line moves—" Bob scratched his head. "I don't know, something about it—means it's got something to do with your parents."

I nodded.

"The line kind of splits and breaks off into two here. Your parents divorced?"

"So what?" I said. "Lots of people's parents are."

"Did I say anything moralistic?"

"That isn't a word," I said.

"You got a dictionary in your back pocket, Smartypants?"

"Nope."

He laughed. "You live with your mother?"

I nodded.

"Father left your mother, huh? For some other person, maybe, of the female sexaroo? Some lady friend?"

"What's it to you?" I said.

"It's all in the lines, you see. You see how this stronger line, this masculine line, breaks off? See how it intersections with this weaker line here, while the other, weaker line—meaning of the female sex—just wanders off on its lonesome without intersectioning with anything?"

"Inter*secti*ng."

"Intersecting, intersectioning, what's the difference? Either way your father gets the woman while your mother doesn't get anything."

I tried to pull my hand back, but Bob hung on to it. He looked me straight in the eye. Then he drew his stool closer with his left hand. The rain beat against the windows. Outside, in the parking lot, a palm frond ripped slowly off its trunk and fell like a feather onto the asphalt.

"So then your Lifeline continues," Bob said. "Because even though you thought maybe you would die when your father packed his bags and left you, you kept on living. And your mother, she kept on living too, right?" He cleared his throat, squinted his eyes, and concentrated on my palm. "But enough of that. Now you got yourself a Lifeline, and then, Mary Ellen, you got yourself a Loveline. You consult your Loveline to find out all about the loves of your life and whether or not you're going to win or lose at them. The Loveline, see, starts right up where the Lifeline begins. That means the closest love in your life is the love you got for your parents, and you can't get away from that, ever."

I nodded.

"Okay, so then after that comes the first crack in your Loveline. Quit turning all red there."

"I'm not turning red."

"You know what that means, I guess."

"It doesn't mean anything."

"It means enough to make your face turn red."

I pulled my hand away. One of his nails scraped the length of my pinkie finger. "It doesn't mean anything, because I don't believe in any of it."

"You think I was just making it up as I went along?"

"Yes."

He leaned closer to me and took my hand back. "So what's the matter, you don't admire a guy with a little imagination?"

I shook my head.

He let go of my hand. I turned my head so I didn't have to look at him. Outside, in the rain, a couple pulled up in a red Buick and ran up to the counter, holding hands and laughing. Bob jerked his head toward the counter and headed back to the coat room. "Looks like you have yourself a customer, Mary Ellen," he said.

I stood, and hesitated a little, the way I always hesitated when I stood up from the sand after lying too long in the sun on the beach. The couple knocked on the service window. They knocked again, and I went over and yanked open the glass. Hot, humid air hit my face. The rain splashed down on the asphalt.

They wanted banana splits. They wanted just a little syrup on the ice cream, the bananas cut up teeny-weeny, and heavy on the nuts on top. My hands felt funny. My fingers tingled and went numb. I clutched the dishes too hard and the wax coating flaked off underneath my nails. I was afraid I would drop the dishes.

"Not so much whipped cream," the man called out.

Bob came out of the coat room. "Give the customers what they want," he said.

The whipped cream piled up on the dish. I moved over to the chocolate syrup spigot. I put too much pressure on it, and syrup pooled up on top.

"Mary Ellen," Bob said. "Hey, Mary Ellen, what the hell are you doing? You heard the customer! Give the customer what he wants!"

He grabbed the dish away from me and threw it in the trash

can, where it hit the bottom with a thud. "You're good for nothing," Bob said, making up two more banana splits. "Just goes to show you if you want something done right, do it yourself."

The couple at the window snickered. I turned my face away from the glass so they wouldn't see me.

"And how many times do I have to tell you to close the service window?" Bob hollered, after the customers drove off. "You think we get our AC free?"

I untied my apron fifteen minutes early. Bob followed me into the coat room. "You taking off before the buzzer?" he asked, his voice apologetic. "Don't forget to punch out before you leave." As I pushed the back door to the parking lot, I heard him calling, "Hey, you're supposed to punch out, company regulation! And besides, your shift ends at six!"

I looked back and saw him standing in the doorway, hands on his hips, towel draped over his wrist. He waved. I walked away.

The rain had stopped as abruptly as it had started, but the air was still muggy. The traffic had cleared off Old Washington Road, but the sidewalks were cluttered with soggy pine cones, palm branches downed in the wind, and long, flesh-colored earthworms edging onto the cement off the grass. I gazed into the windows of the shops I passed: Quinlan's Grocery, where the drawers of the cash register were left open to prove to thieves they were empty, Miss Desiree's Salon of Beauty, where the chairs tilted at odd angles away from the mirrors, as if never expecting to be sat upon again.

No lights shone through the windows of the apartment, but because I was in the habit of lifting the top of the mailbox as quietly as if I were stealing something from it, I lifted it just as softly as I would have had my mother been waiting, and listening, on the other side of the door. Nothing inside. My mother was right; I looked in there too often. "So he sent you a birthday card," she told me last week. "You'd be a damn sight better off if he sent the alimony check."

I stood on the outside steps of the apartment, unlocked the door, and reached in to turn on the hall light. I closed my eyes and gave the cockroaches time to climb into the woodwork before I went in. I turned the box fan on high, lit the stove, and shoved some frozen fish fillets under the broiler. I changed into a T-shirt and shorts, and combed my long, scraggly hair. I was staring in the hall mirror, thinking *Someone just made a pass at me*, when my mother let the screen door slam.

I turned. But I couldn't look her flush in the face because I was afraid she might know what I had been thinking. She wore her white blouse and red skirt and the red criss-crossed sandals with the bright gold buckles. Her toenails were supposed to be painted to match the sandals, but the polish was too orangey to match the red. She carried a paper bag. "This is for you," she said. "And I'm sorry I couldn't give it to you on your birthday, but I didn't have enough cash to take it off layaway."

The paper bag fell to the linoleum as she pulled out and held up a white blouse which was a slight variation on the one she wore: sleeveless polyester, with a wide collar turned back into a V-neck, the breast pocket cut and stitched to resemble eyelet. I never had liked the blouse she wore, any more than I liked her red criss-crossed sandals, but once or twice I had told her she looked nice in it because I wanted to make her feel pretty. But she wasn't pretty. She wasn't vibrant, like my father's wife, Janine. Janine was my idol. "You're my candle on a dark night," my father once said to her, hugging her. Janine would never wear a sad-sack blouse like that.

"That's just like yours," I told my mother. The disappointment must have seeped into my voice; she dropped her arms and the blouse fell in her hands like a limp rag.

"I can't return it," she said. "I bought it on sale."

I reached out and touched the fabric. "It's really pretty," I forced myself to say. "And yours looks so nice on you."

"Try it on," she said. "See how it fits."

I turned my back to her and pulled my T-shirt over my head.

"Why don't you wear your bra?" she asked.

"It's too hot."

"You'll sag before you're twenty."

I turned around only enough to take the blouse from her. I slipped it over my head. She put her hands on my shoulders as if she were afraid I might bolt away before I looked in the hall mirror. Her hands were so much more gentle than Bob's; they used so much less force, but were still persuasive. But I didn't want to be persuaded. I didn't like Bob or my mother or the blouse, which hung down past my waist, covering my shorts. On the side of the blouse without the pocket, the dark outline of my nipple showed through the thin material. I looked naked.

"You look—very pretty," my mother said. I knew she meant it no more than I had meant it the one or two times I had told her the same thing. I shivered when I felt her warm breath tickling the hairs on my neck.

"Any boys yet?" she asked softly.

I thought of Bob. I thought of my father. "No," I said.

"People don't appreciate," she said. "Nobody appreciates what you have inside. It's all what you look like. It's all how well you can pass off being happy when really you're miserable inside." She sighed. "That Janine," she said. "Janine, Janine—doesn't that just sound like the name of some slut?"

"It does not."

"Whose side are you on?"

"Nobody's. I'm not on anybody's side."

"You could have fooled me," she said. Her fingers closed tighter around my arm. "Don't ever let me hear about you carrying on with any boys."

"I'm not."

"That's just the kind of thing your father would encourage."

"He would not!"

"They're all after one thing. And then they call you a tease, and worse, if you don't give them what they're after." She let go of my arm and inhaled deeply. "What's that smell?" she asked. She walked into the kitchen. I rubbed my arm. I heard her yank the stove open. I smelled the fish fillets crisping.

She came into the doorway. "I tell you time and time again, and still you don't listen. You don't listen—you don't listen! How many times do I have to tell you it's better to slow-cook something in the oven than burn it under the broiler?"

She was sleeping on the couch as I turned off the lights that night. The Lifeline couldn't register the small, horrible things that happened, like hearing your mother snore. It couldn't register the rustle of a cockroach exploring the inside of the paper bag my mother had left lying on the linoleum. Naked in front of the bathroom sink, I scraped my nails across a wet bar of soap, then took a metal nail file and pushed all the soap out. I couldn't get my hands clean enough.

The Ugliest Boy

DAVID CROUSE

From *Copy Cats* (2005)

Justin was in love with a girl whose brother had been disfigured by fire. The kids called him Barbecue, but only behind his back, because he stood over six feet tall, with thick biceps, a stomach hard from a regimen of sit-ups, and crossed daggers tattooed on his throat just below the scars. The face itself was a sort of tattoo as well—the smudged gray red of the skin around the cheeks, the even furrows across the forehead. The symmetry of the burns seemed artful, almost intentional. His sunken left eye was sealed closed, something white collected around the slit.

His real name was Steven Adams, and his sister's name was Gerri, and Justin didn't just love her, he ached for her. Her parents were away in Europe for the summer, and Justin had taken to staying with her often in her room. As they groped each other on her neatly made bed, he listened to the brother down deep in the house lifting weights—the clatter of the metal, the occasional grunting yell, and a faint rasping sound that may have been the air conditioner but Justin imagined as heavy breathing. It sounded a lot like their own breath—quick, desperate, and frustrated.

"Can you hear him?" Justin asked, throwing his legs over the side of the bed.

"Yeah," Gerri said. "He's angry."

"Yeah," he said, and he hunched there, his forearms across his knees, looking at her wall.

It was late June. Her parents would return in August, and Gerri's room would become as remote to him then as Europe was now. Listening to Barbecue and thinking about places he had never been, Justin became remote himself. "Nothing," he said when Gerri asked him what he was thinking. She put her hand on his bare back, and as she rubbed circles on his body, he felt something dark well up inside him—a self-disgust that made him want to slither out of his own skin. He tried to push it down by force of will.

"Are you sure?" she asked. This time he didn't bother answering. He turned to her, hand on her shoulder, lips against her neck.

"No," she said.

He had never given her an orgasm, never traveled anywhere distant with her, never revealed the worst parts of himself to her, never had his affection tested by crisis. He had never told her just how much he loved her, although he had said he loved her—but those two things seemed far apart at that moment in the dimness of her room. "I love you," he said forcefully but quietly, and he waited for the sadness that came into her eyes whenever he said these words.

Her hand was still on his back, but she was silent, and so he took hold of her arm and pushed her back on the bed. He didn't want tenderness from her—that was too close to pity. He could feel the blood pumping in her wrist. In his mind he was already looking past this to the time when she would be asleep while he was still awake, and then the next morning when he would run across town, first one mile, then three, then six and eight and nine. He was running ten miles a day lately.

"Stop," she said, so he stood without looking at her. It had been an empty gesture anyway. He wasn't even hard.

He left the room still not looking at her, sliding his fingers along the wall as he walked toward the lit room at the end of the upstairs corridor. In the bathroom he dropped his pants and listened to the water in the bowl. On the floor to one side of the toilet there were women's magazines and catalogs filled with oak furniture and cashmere sweaters. There were also a couple of recent postcards, one from Switzerland and one from Ireland.

Justin couldn't stop thinking about fire. It was what he thought about when he had twisted with Gerri on her bed, and it was what he thought about as the sound of water in the bowl quieted to a trickle and he held himself. He closed his eyes and wondered what it must have felt like for Barbecue—for Steve. If a person, an average person, were to tabulate his pain—all the cuts, scrapes, broken bones, and heartbreaks—would they add up to that one event?

Imagining that pain reminded him of his own—the sharp particulars of that one day in the woods. That memory was his. He possessed it the way Gerri's family possessed their house, and he entered into it with the same mix of trepidation and happiness: the walk by the hospital into the trees, emerging through the bushes and then kneeling by the shallow pond, the old shed across the water surrounded by rusted barbed wire and broken liquor bottles. And then they were coming out of the woods, and then his hand was slippery and he felt the shame, suddenly but with such familiarity that it was a seamless part of the pleasure. As he slid his thumb and finger down his cock he imagined Gerri opening the bathroom door, and that added to both the shame and the satisfaction—bound them together in a tight knot.

If she came in, he thought, then he would have to explain.

He found the washcloth he normally used on the bottom shelf of the cabinet, wet it, and rubbed it over his belly and privates. The cloth was cold—he hadn't let the water run long enough—but he didn't care. In the early stages of a jog, before he was in his rhythm, he often felt like his body was something separate from who he was—something that contained him but wasn't him. He felt that way as he pushed the cloth over his stomach, absorbed in the give of his muscles and skin. Semen had collected in his belly button. He cleaned it roughly with his finger, then wiped his hands and tugged up his jeans.

He didn't want to return to Gerri's bedroom, so he headed downstairs, where he killed time examining objects on the fireplace mantel—small oriental figurines with sly grins, intricately carved nonsense art, metal-framed photographs of Gerri's parents smiling in some desert climate. Bored, he crossed the room in the near dark and sat at the piano. He spun around one revolution on the oak stool, then raised his hands as if to bring them down with a clamor.

The first week Gerri's parents were away he slept in the guest room and upon waking in the morning he heard the piano and what he thought was the clatter of pots and pans from the kitchen. Sometimes in his drowsiness he assumed it was his mother, but then he remembered that he was in someone else's house and that the sound of the piano was Gerri practicing and the metallic clatter was Barbecue in the garage working on the Plymouth Road Runner—or maybe the Mercedes if he was feeling more generous. Justin felt a part of the rhythm of their house then, even if it was only till his feet hit the floor. He was always late for work and had to dress in a rush and push himself on the run there, up the long, slow hill that led to Main Street.

When he arrived at the service station and took a shower in the narrow stall out back, he would hold that memory of waking as the trickle of water came down into his cupped hands. He shook his hair dry, changed into his work clothes, and then he tried to hold onto it as he worked, in the way he held onto the melody Gerri had been practicing. He let it move through his head while he pumped gas and made change and stacked cases of oil, and it was enough to make him feel like an imposter in his day, because when customers glanced out their car windows and said, "Fill it up," they were speaking to someone in disguise. They didn't know where he had come from that morning, where he would return that night, didn't know his history. His face didn't even register to them, just his general shape—a dirty hand taking their credit cards.

You should just tell her, he sometimes thought in a moment of recklessness when they were speaking kindly to each other. But he couldn't. On her bureau Gerri had small ceramic statues of horses and rabbits and dragons that Justin had never touched. It hurt just to look at them. Her sweaters smelled of something sweet like baby powder, and they came in colors like *persimmon* and *peacock* and *charcoal heather*. "You look so collegiate to-day," he sneered at her when they weren't getting along, which seemed to be more and more as the summer inched forward.

Justin stood up from the piano stool, gave it another spin, and ran his fingers along the black keys lightly enough that they did not play. He tried to guess what it cost, and when he realized he had no idea, he stepped away from it into the next room.

The kitchen smelled of the strawberry candles Gerri was always lighting and placing precariously around the house. His own house smelled of his mother's cooking—pork chops, haddock, corned beef and cabbage—and her cigarettes, which she smoked standing in the doorway between the kitchen and living room so she could watch television while she cooked. Wicker baskets and strings of garlic hung from the beams above his head. The high ceilings in Gerri's house made Justin feel small—the way he also felt in relation to Gerri herself, he realized. She was lovely in a way that could make him feel diminished. Almost homely. "You're gorgeous," she told him once when kissing his chest, and it seemed like he had been chosen, the way he had been chosen at other times in his life—chosen to work for Sanborn's Automotive, a good, easy job he tried hard to dislike; chosen to be the son of a single parent; chosen that time in the woods near the hospital when he was ten.

The microwave clock showed it was past midnight. He felt like an intruder, and when he tried the fantasy on for size—when he imagined himself creeping through the house, rifling through drawers, stealing the mother's necklaces and rings—he was surprised to find that it fit relatively comfortably. Then he imagined Gerri catching him, and in the fantasy she knew him even though he was somebody else. She touched him and called him by name, and once again he was ashamed and pleased.

He switched on a light over the stove and grabbed himself a glass, feeling less like an intruder now and more like what he was—a visitor. As he poured himself some water he looked at his reflection in the window above the sink. He had never liked his nose. He didn't like his eyes either, he decided, although Gerri had said they were his best feature. He still didn't like his chest, almost hairless except for strands of blond and flecked with small red dots. He lifted the glass to his lips and drank it down, looking past his reflection at the yard.

That's when he noticed Barbecue standing on the porch smoking a cigarette and looking at the yard just as Justin had been doing. He was dressed in a white V-neck T-shirt and was smiling out one side of his mouth as he took a long drag. He held a Beck's bottle in his other hand, into which he tapped the end of the cigarette. Their eyes met. At first Justin didn't think Barbecue had noticed him, but then he made a short poking gesture with the bottle, calling him outside.

There were so many rumors about Barbecue that he seemed to be made of stories, like someone who has been dead for years existing only as photographs and words. There was the story about Providence, Rhode Island. Supposedly he drove down there every weekend and blew money on drugs and prostitutes. There was the story that his father—Gerri's father—hit him. Kids had seen bruises. But just one look at Barbecue—the knots of muscles in his arms and neck—and it was hard to believe that he wouldn't fight back. And if he fought back, wouldn't he win? His father was a thin man, short, with a hunched, nervous manner. A financial analyst in Boston.

Barbecue's face had been burned for as long as Justin could remember. Justin wasn't sure of the cause, although again there were rumors—a grease fire, an explosion in the garage, a lawn mower accident of all things. To Justin it simply seemed like Barbecue had come back damaged from a war nobody else had even known about. He set down the glass and headed out to the porch.

"Hey, hey," Barbecue said. "Welcome, fellow insomniac."

"Hello, Steve," Justin said without looking at him. He looked at the yard instead. They were both staring at the same dark spot as if something dangerous were prowling out there.

Barbecue snickered. "So," he said. "So, so, so." When he talked, his mouth moved from side to side as if he was gnawing something sinewy. "You like my sister," he said.

"Very much," Justin said.

"Very much," Barbecue repeated back to him as if it was something funny. He had Gerri's eyes, sort of. One of them anyway. The good right one looked like Gerri's, large and dark. "So," he pit-patted again. "So, so, so." Justin noticed then that Barbecue had rolled his cigarette himself. Barbecue inhaled deeply, blew sweet smelling smoke toward the yard, and said, "Are your intentions honorable? Isn't that what I'm supposed to ask? Are your intentions honorable?"

Justin didn't say anything.

"I'm just kidding you, man," Barbecue said.

"I know."

"But are they? Are they honorable?"

"I'm crazy about her, if that's what you mean," Justin said.

"Crazy for her, huh? Good for you. That's great. Star-crossed lovers. I can get behind that. I'll throw my support your way. My father, on the other hand, he's a different story." He took another long toke and continued. "She's going to Harvard or Yale or somewhere like that. Where are you going? That's the big ques-

tion, I guess. But I'm with you, man. I'm on your side. I sympa-
thize with the disenfranchised." He looked away from the yard
and at Justin now. "You try awful hard, don't you?"

Another silence. Then Justin said, "What do you mean?"

"I can hear you guys up there. I may look like Frankenstein,
but I'm not as dumb as him, you know. I can put two and two
together."

Justin wanted a drag on that cigarette. It would calm him
down, smooth him out. Maybe somehow it would bring them
closer together. He wanted to talk, but not like this.

"I'm just kidding again, relax," Barbecue said. "Just chalk it up
to bitterness. I'll give you three guesses why I'm bitter. You want
to guess?"

"No," Justin said. "That's okay."

"Okay, sure," Barbecue said and looked back at the yard.

Justin studied his face, and the more he looked at it, the more
he wanted to look. In the dark, the lines gouged in Barbecue's
cheeks seemed as much from age as violence. He decided he
could learn a lot from someone with a face like that. "How old
were you when it happened?" Justin asked.

"When what happened?" Eyes on the yard. Deadpan.

"You know."

"My virginity? Sixteen. A year younger than my sister." A small
pause. A bent smirk. A short drag. "But that's not what you mean.
You mean the face. That's what you mean. And the funny thing,
it's not even the worst part. The worst is down here where you
can't see it." He slid his open hand over his chest and belly. "Anyway, that happened when I was twelve. Gerri doesn't talk about
me, huh? I'm hurt." Another drag. Then he held out the shrunken
roach to Justin, who took it. "There you go," Barbecue said.

Justin blew smoke from his nose and mouth and passed back
the joint. He had never done this sort of thing with Gerri, and he
guessed she wouldn't approve of his doing it with someone else,
especially her brother, whom she spoke to only when asking for

something like phone messages. He had seen how they orbited around each other.

Justin tried not to stare. He stared anyway. A person with a face like that would understand.

Barbecue wet his fingers on his tongue, snuffed the joint, and said, "I think it's time for bed. Dream some nice dreams. Whisper sweet nothings in her ear or something."

Justin guessed that Barbecue hated and loved his sister fiercely in some gnarled combination of feeling. Justin could understand that. It was like he was seeing himself for the first time, he decided, as if Barbecue were a mirror. Some small part of himself—the worst part, he noted—hated her too, for being so pristine, so smart, for sleeping peacefully upstairs while he was awake, for the look in her eyes. He hated her for not giving him what he wanted, although he didn't know what that was exactly, and he hated himself for hating her, and what the hell was he doing out here anyway, smoking marijuana with her older brother? He took a deep breath and said, "Good night. Maybe I'll see you in the morning."

Justin waited until he heard Barbecue's feet on the stairs, then headed into the garage. The chrome on the Road Runner had been polished until it glistened. The hood was open, and when Justin bent down over the engine he saw that it was as clean as the outside. He reached in and touched the engine block and thought again of being caught, turning to see Barbecue in the doorway, but he heard no sound except his own footsteps on the cement as he walked around to the rear bumper.

Tools and spray cans littered the concrete floor. Barbecue had been grinding out a small rust spot on the fender. Justin knelt and rubbed the spot with sandpaper folded into a hard square. It wouldn't be that difficult, he decided, to get to know him.

The first time Justin had met Gerri she had surprised him. She had pointed at him and said, "You're that guy who runs around town. I've seen you in thunderstorms," and he had been startled to hear her voice addressing him. Then she had smiled and closed her hand into a fist and put it to her chin. He had come into the library to get a drink from the water fountain, and as he passed her she looked up from her books as if she had been waiting for him.

There had been stick drawings of animals in the margins of her notebook.

He had known her too, through the stories about her brother, and because her father was well known in town. He had even known her name and that she attended the private school in Exeter. He had known she played piano. When there was talk about Barbecue, it usually got around to her piano playing, which was supposed to be world class, according to one of Justin's coworkers at the station. There was even talk about her going to a conservatory, which he found out later was not true. She was not as good as people thought. "It's a way to keep me occupied," she said once with a laugh. "My parents are always trying to find ways to keep me *occupied*."

"He has an in-ground pool," Justin had told his mother the first time he mentioned that he was spending the night at his friend's house.

His mother was one of the few people in town who had avoided getting to know Barbecue by reputation, and she seemed happy to hear Justin had a close friend, maybe happy enough not to worry about not seeing him lately. "You spend too much time locked up by yourself in your room," she had told him more than once. "Or running. I read somewhere that it's not as healthy a sport as people might think. And there are the cars."

"Sure," he would answer as he headed to the bathroom. It was good to be away from there—he was especially sure of it whenever he got back. There was a sound she made when she sat down, a defeated sigh, and a strained groan when she stood up, and a small mirror in the bathroom with water stains across it that he had to look into whenever he brushed his teeth. There were old photos of himself in the living room, his hair wet from swimming. Looking at them, he wished they didn't exist.

"How is Steven?" she sometimes asked over dinner, and he wondered if she knew. If she did, he was sure she wouldn't say. That's how it worked between them. They had reached that agreement long ago.

"Pretty good," he said, and it wasn't really a lie, although it had started out as one, because as the summer progressed, as the postcards and packages arrived from different European cities, Justin and Barbecue talked more. The garage was cool and dark, and while Barbecue worked on his car late into the night, Justin sat against the brick wall, and Barbecue sometimes opened his hand and asked for a tool or the small rainbow-painted pipe with the blackened screen in its bowl. Eventually Justin began packing it himself and taking a toke when he first made an appearance, blowing the smoke out through his nose and closing his eyes.

"The Superbird. Now that was a car," Barbecue said once as he looked down into the engine skeptically. "Nineteen seventy was a great year for cars. It was all downhill after emissions testing."

"Sure," Justin replied.

"Not that I'm complaining. Nineteen seventy-four was a good year too. The last one. Pass me that rag."

The pool filter was humming out in the yard. Justin closed his eyes and listened to it, listened to Barbecue saying, "People think I am the way I am because of the accident. They think it's simple. But it's not. Ah, well. It gives me an excuse, I guess. It's worth something, or at least it was, once upon a time. When I was younger I was the little scarred angel. The accident was the reason for every bad thing I did. I'd steal a cookie. It was the accident. I'd shoot a pigeon with a BB gun. The accident. But there's only so much mileage you can get out of that. So what, though, right? I don't mind being the boogeyman. Take a look at this for me. It's all fucked up."

Gerri was upstairs during all of this, sleeping or mulling over one of their arguments. Justin and Barbecue never talked about her—they talked about the cracked carburetor in the Mercedes, the long stretch of hot weather, the ticking down of the summer days—but she was a presence nonetheless. One of the cars he was working on was for her, after all.

It had taken Justin a while to figure that out. There were two cars in the garage, two outside, one for each member of the family. Barbecue drove the Plymouth and the Explorer, which sometimes came home with long splatters of mud along the sides. Justin and Gerri did not drive often, but the first time they did—to a movie showing at the small one-screen theater in town—they took the Explorer. "She left the seat forward," Barbecue said the next night. "I hate when she does that."

"Yeah," Justin said, although it had been he who had driven.

"It'll be good when I get this done," he said, and he gave the Mercedes a tap on the fender, as if for luck. "That way she won't be messing with my shit anymore. She's going to love it too. She better love it anyway, right?"

"Right," Justin said. He pictured her stopped at a traffic light in Boston, two years older, head turned so she could look at the Charles River and the faces of the pedestrians coming toward her in the crosswalk—a collage of faces, some of them interesting. She would be thinking about her classes, the summer after this one, the rest of her life.

"I think the heat guard is loose," Justin told him.

"I know," Barbecue said. "Take a look at the manifold for me. Make yourself useful."

It was weeks later when Justin would finally tell him the story that balanced them—the story that explained. "I was ten years old," he would say, remembering that Barbecue had been twelve.

It was deep in the summer when Gerri said to him, "What's the matter? Don't you find me attractive?" She was straddling him, her hands on his chest, and her voice had the steady tone of someone who was more bored than annoyed. He gently pushed her off, stood up, and found his jeans on the floor. She watched from the bed as he slipped his foot into one pant leg, then the other, and pulled them on. When he made a move to leave, to walk down the hall to the bathroom and shut the door, she said, "Wait, Justin. Don't do that."

"Do what?" he said, as he tugged up his zipper.

"You *know* what," she said, and he heard anger in her voice, a coldness that reminded him of her brother.

"I don't know," he said, because that was all he could think to say. Although his fingers were working the buttons of his shirt, he still felt naked. She was staring him down from the bed as if the door was already open and he was huddled at the far end of the darkened hall. He imagined holding himself—eyes closed, wrist jerking—under that stare, and he grew flushed and hard, tight against his jeans. He wondered if she noticed.

"You know what," she said, "and so do I."

They were delivering the lines they had written in their heads all summer. He tried out another one just to see the expression on her face. "What do you know about anything?" he said. "Spoiled rich girl." He gave the knickknacks on her bureau as dark a look as he could and then opened the door.

He had taken a few steps down the hall when Gerri grabbed up one of her jewelry boxes and threw it after him. It struck the wall behind his head, not hard enough to break but hard enough that it popped open and sent earrings and necklaces to the carpet. He bent down to gather them up in both hands.

"Get away from that. Those are mine," she said. She stood over him, and he felt as small as he had ever felt in this house.

"Listen," he said. "I'm sorry."

She reached out to touch the top of his head. He thought of sliding up her body, kissing her mouth, pressing up against her and letting her discover how much he wanted her. Which is what he did. He wasn't quite aware that he was doing it. She put both hands against his chest and pushed him back. "Get out, Justin," she said. "Get out of my house." Those words, *my house*, were like another push, so he pushed her back. Her foot hit the jewelry box, and it made a small cracking sound. She glanced down at it and then at him—that same level stare—and he almost said he was sorry again. She stepped toward him, arms up, and then she was stepping backward again, her hand holding her cheek, and he was heading down the hall, saying, "I'm going now. I'm going."

Barbecue was in the garage polishing his car with Windex and a soft cloth. Justin walked in, rested his back against the cool wall, and watched him work. He would spray the hubcap, rub circles in it, stare at it, and then start over. After a while Justin slid down into a crouching position.

"I don't know what she sees in me," he said, surprised at his own words, and Barbecue's too when he replied, "That's easy. You're handsome." His face pulled into a gnarled smile, and Justin wondered if he had heard them upstairs a few minutes before. He had probably been sitting at the same wheel, shining the same hubcap, when Gerri had been throwing her jewelry box.

"It looks good," Justin told him, and they both scrutinized the hubcap.

"Thanks," he said. "I aim to please." He stood up and rubbed his hands on his thighs. "Do you want to go for a drive?" Justin said yes too quickly, and Barbecue's face ticked again. "Then you should probably buy a car one of these days, shouldn't you? Instead of running all around town, you could do what I do."

He thought of driving with his mother, the seat belts across their chests, the craning of her neck and the slow roll through the intersection—that feeling that something awful might happen any second.

"You're all fidgety tonight," Barbecue said. "More than usual."

"Yeah," Justin said, and at that moment he wanted an end to secrets. He wanted to see shock in Barbecue's face, buried in the gashes and bruised scars. He thought of the woods near the hospital, the pond and its fishy smell. Sometimes it was like it had never happened. Other times it was like yesterday—like it had been only hours since they told him that his skin was like cream.

"What time is it?" Barbecue asked him.

"I don't know."

"I guess you should probably head home, huh?"

"Yeah," Justin said, and he thought of Gerri reaching for her cheek as he turned and headed to the stairs. By the time he had reached the landing she would have been kneeling to pick up her jewelry. In his mind's eye he could see her still naked, three or four elegant necklaces looped around her palm. He wondered if the box had broken, if she had been crying, if she was crying now as he walked into the cool night air. Not knowing seemed a worse crime than the slap itself. The punch, he corrected, trying to find the right name for what had happened, the right place for it in his head. He couldn't remember if his fingers had been closed or open or the sound it made when he struck her.

The garage lights clicked off behind him, and he stepped down the walkway and around the side of the house in darkness.

"Ich wünschte du wärst hier," the postcard said. Three newspapers rolled into tight batons stuck up from the mailbox along with the postcard, junk mail, and a credit card bill for the meals Gerri's parents were eating in small Parisian cafes. Nobody had taken in the mail since Justin had been there two days before. During the past month, it had become his job. He slipped the postcard back into the mailbox, climbed the front stairs, and rang the bell.

When nobody came to the door, he took some of the small stones from around the shrubs, stones as white and smooth as teeth, and threw them at Gerri's window. The shades remained drawn. He thought about yelling up for her—or maybe stealing the mail and leaving. Anything seemed possible. It was raining lightly and his T-shirt was so wet that he could see through it. He had saved the largest rock for last. He threw it overhand, hard, and it hit the gutter with a bang. Nothing. He thought of Gerri sitting on the edge of her bed, a bruise on her cheek. He placed the bruise there carefully with his imagination as a way to punish himself. The slap had probably not been hard enough to cause it—his hand had been open, he was practically sure of it—but he wanted to make entirely sure. If he could see her, he could talk to her, and he could explain.

When he headed around the back of the house, Barbecue seemed to be waiting for him. "How are you doing?" he asked, and Justin thought that maybe this was the meeting he had actually come for.

"Fine," he said as he climbed the stairs to the patio. He looked up at the shaded windows.

"Why don't you give Gerri a little breather, okay?" Barbecue said. "You're upset and she's upset."

He wasn't upset, although being told he was upset made him upset. He said, "I just need to talk to her for a minute."

"Sorry," Barbecue said. He sounded like he meant it.

"A minute," Justin said.

"No," Barbecue said.

"No," Justin repeated, trying the word out.

"That's right."

He didn't really know what he wanted to do, except that he wanted to get into the house. He would figure everything else out after that. He ducked his head and stepped forward. Barbecue put his hand on his shoulder. It was the first time they had touched.

Justin turned and was going to say something when he realized that he was sitting on the grass. He opened his eyes and saw flecks of red on his T-shirt and expected a second punch, but nothing came. His hands were warm and wet and bloody, as if he had been the one hitting someone. Which he had been, he realized, just two days before. He felt some satisfaction from having the roles reversed. Maybe Barbecue did too.

Blood was running from his nose into his palms, but he didn't feel pain. He was more aware of the salty taste of the blood and the weakness in his legs, as if he had been running straight out. In a way Barbecue had saved him from embarrassment. If he had gone into the house, what would he have done, what would he have said?

He coughed and then vomited with a sharp hacking sound. A trail of spittle dangled from his mouth. He closed his eyes again and heard Barbecue say, "Oh, man."

They both looked down at what he had done. Then Justin heard himself say, "I'm sorry." He coughed again and wiped his face with the back of his hand.

A noise came from the house. Gerri was practicing. He could hear the piano faintly from the porch, and he understood better than ever why people might think she was going to Julliard or somewhere. Distance gave it false poignancy—delicate music almost not there at all. And there was the house—windows with fake black shutters that didn't really close, the door with its circular stained glass window, the piano hidden somewhere inside, and the player hidden too, her long blonde hair tied back, her body at attention. Of course she would have sounded beautiful, to the mailman, say, delivering a postcard from Portugal.

"Don't try to stand," Barbecue said. "Give yourself a minute."

"Okay," Justin said, but he struggled to get to his feet. He knew what he had to do.

This would be the way to tell Gerri. Give the story to her brother and let him pass it along to her. He staggered up and coughed again. "I have something to tell you," he said.

"What is it?" Barbecue asked.

"Well," Justin said, "it's complicated," and stepped back onto the patio.

Barbecue laughed. "It always is."

"That's true," Justin said. "That's true." And he took a step down, then another, until he was standing on the grass again. He started to talk. Then he told him. "I was ten years old," he said.

It had happened out behind the playground near dusk, when the pool was closed and most of the kids had already gone home in groups of two or three. The playground didn't exist anymore, or the woods behind it, but back then you could walk a rocky trail that led to a pond where kids sometimes caught frogs. That's what Justin was doing—looking for frogs. He must have figured it was a good time to look for them. The streetlights were on. It was quiet.

"There were two of them," he told Barbecue. He remembered this part vividly—kneeling down, the plastic toes of his high-top sneakers spattered with pond mud, then looking up and seeing the two men. He remembered two of them, although sometimes their faces were the same face, one face shared between the two. One of them made a guttural sound like *excuse me*, like *what are you doing here?* Or maybe it was one of the frogs.

They said something to him, something friendly, something coaxing. One was standing slightly in front of the other, and for a second Justin thought they were carrying something like a heavy log or stick, but they weren't. It was just the way the shadows were falling. Maybe they were and they dropped it as soon as they saw him. The grass was tall, up to his knees. "My feet were covered with mud," he said.

He remembered this much—one was fat, one was skinny, gawky almost. They both wore baseball caps. What did they say? It was hard to remember, hard to see them even, in that dusky light, like shining a flashlight down a well. They separated, one stepping clockwise around the pond, one counter-clockwise. Although they didn't separate so much as blur, like the lens of his memory was moving out of focus. It was confusing trying to remember exactly what had happened.

Sometimes they wore the same face.

"I didn't move an inch," Justin said. The nearest house was half a mile away. A family was eating dinner there, or watching television. He remembered walking past once and seeing the blue screen through the window.

Something was almost comforting about the way they held him, one around the shoulders, one around the waist, and pushed him down. The mud was warm and smelled of tadpoles, but cooler beneath the surface, like something half cooked. He made his hand into a fist and felt the coolness squeeze through his fingers. He bit down on something. His tongue. They were talking to him quietly, repeating each other's words. There was a weight, a pressure, on his shoulders and the small of his back. Was there pain? There must have been pain.

They were pulling down his jeans, tugging at his shirt. They hushed him the way the doctor hushed him, reassured him, told him it was okay, and he felt like he had to believe them.

Not less than a hundred yards away kids were playing on swing sets, tossing basketballs, seeing how much time they could squeeze out of the day before heading home to supper. Which wasn't right. There was no one else around. But still he swore he heard something. "I thought I heard kids laughing," he told him, "and then I remember worrying about dinner."

He was going to be late. But maybe not. They were quick about it. They were efficient. They told him not to worry and not to tell anyone. He remembered them telling him please. Please don't tell anyone. There was shame in their voices, although maybe not, because that seemed unlikely, and maybe it was just one voice. The voice told him that he was pretty and talked about his body parts. Broke him down, subdivided him. Nice lips. Nice legs. Nice ass. He didn't know how he'd ever put himself back together again. He clenched at the mud and hoped they wouldn't take his money, because he had five dollars in his wallet.

Justin didn't tell Barbecue everything, of course. He didn't talk about how strong he felt afterward, walking home, because that seemed absurd. Why would he feel strong? But he did. He did tell him, though, how he threw away his shirt, his underwear, his jeans, his socks even. He put it all in one of the trash bags of leaves he had raked that weekend to earn the five dollars they hadn't taken. He put the bag out behind the shed on the outskirts of the property. A neighborhood dog was with him when he did it, circling around his feet.

"Two of them?" Barbecue asked. Something about that did seem insane, impossible. Justin could see Barbecue's confusion somewhere in the gnarled expression as he tried to grasp it, measure it against his own pain.

Justin shrugged and moved to go. His nose was still bleeding, and now it was starting to hurt. He said, "I just wanted to talk to her."

"She doesn't want to see you anymore, you know," Barbecue said. "She's been thinking about it for a long time, but she hasn't had the heart. She waited too long. That's what I told her. Way too long. But she felt sorry for you. And she was hoping."

"She was hoping," Justin said.

"That's right," he said. "She was hoping."

Justin turned and looked back at the yard, then up at the windows on the second floor of the house.

"She has a lot of hope," Barbecue said, and after thinking for a second, "She's full of hope." The way he said it sounded almost paternal but also bitter, as if he had said, she's full of it, full of shit. Despite himself Justin felt almost insulted on Gerri's behalf. It was Barbecue's smile that did it. Justin didn't like it when he smiled like that.

"Well, tell her," Justin said. He felt a lump in his throat. He put a foot on the first step again, his hand on the railing. "You know, tell her."

"I'm not going to do that."

"Why?"

"You know why."

Justin stood there looking up into Barbecue's face. He felt like he could stand there forever and that Barbecue could stand there forever too, looking deeply into each other. The piano was playing from inside the house.

On the way home he crossed through downtown, past the library with its rickety clock tower, past the bank signs blinking the time and temperature, walking on the side of the road against a steady flow of headlights. Sometimes he noticed the face of a driver watching him as the car slipped past. They must have wondered where he was going and what had happened to him. He had not bothered to clean his face or his shirt. He could feel the blood around his nostrils. The rain was warm and he was strangely happy.

He crossed against the light, past a middle-aged woman looking at him from inside her Civic. He was a mystery to her, he decided, and the thought made him feel tougher in his isolation. He was a story they were going to tell over her dinner table that night, but not the *right* story. He jumped to the curb and jogged down the sidewalk into an alley.

When he arrived home he went inside and thought briefly about heading to the bathroom so that his mother would not see his face, but instead he stood there on her braided throw rug and waited for her to come in. She was probably upstairs in bed, awake, listening to talk radio. Then he could hear her moving around—her steps soft as if she did not want to be heard.

She did not gasp or even look very shocked when she saw him. Her hands didn't rise to her mouth in surprise. She didn't yell. She said, "What did he do to you?" and anger was in her voice. She knew who had done it. That much was easy to figure out.

"It was just a little fight," he said. She was rubbing a warm cloth down his face. He hadn't even realized she had gone to get it until he felt it against his skin. "Don't," he said. "That hurts."

When he ran through the city that September, nose swollen, both eyes black and yellow like a mask, people waved and yelled out to him. They wanted to talk to him, because the break had been so bad, because the family had been rich and they had given Justin's family—Justin's mother—more than a little money, and because the punch had been thrown by one of the toughest kids in town. The daughter, the one who played the piano, she was at Princeton now, wasn't she?

Justin stopped and as he stretched his calves, they asked how he was doing, and if he could breathe okay, running the way he was with his nose busted up like that. He straightened up and motioned north and talked about the house where he had spent his summer. It was like he had just returned from a faraway country and he was talking about his trip. The story he told them grew shorter as he learned how to tell it, one variation for the concerned mothers, a different one for the girls his age, another for the joking middle-aged men. "But you should see the other guy, right?" one of them said, and then he slapped his shoulder and smiled as if they were friends.

Sometimes Justin saw the Road Runner parked around town, straddling two spaces at the edge of a parking lot, and he thought about lingering there—leaning on the warm hood—but he never did, and he didn't see it often, and then not at all.

Two Piano Players

CAROL LEE LORENZO

From *Nervous Dancer* (1995)

The old blue afternoon air sticks to the roof of my mouth. My cousin, Jewel, dogs me all the way through the Florida heat to the back of the church. Our feet stir a breeze, but it stings. I've been pointing out new sights to Jewel all day. My hands feel too tired for a piano lesson.

"I don't want to go in the back door of any church," she tells me. Jewel is on her vacation from up in Georgia. She pulls her skirt so tight I can see the split between her legs. She does not trust me as a long-term friend. Only two days here and she feels that I am already wearing thin. But she will sit through my church piano lessons with me because she doesn't want to get lost in Florida. So she stays close, walking in rhythm with the jingle of my bracelet collection on my arm.

Jewel complains, "You can't play piano good at all."

I tell her, "It's my mother that wants to learn to play piano. But she won't take lessons. I have to take and then teach her."

"You are going to bore me," Jewel confides.

At the church door, slick dark birds come from nowhere, settle and argue in a tree. Jewel is fighting to get in the church first. "Gia! Gia! I'm afraid of birds."

"Birds?"

"Wild birds!"

I don't like to touch my cousin. Jewel's thin hair has gone sticky with Florida humidity, and her hands feel as hard as weapons. To make her calm down, I pull at her blue clothes; she's wearing something old of mine. She wears it but says it's not too pretty. She tells me I'm not too pretty either because I have too much dark hair and my mouth is mean. I tell her my mouth only looks mean because I'm shy. She tells me I look like the foreigners that work on the Boardwalk. I tell her it's just that I tan too easily, that I'm not a foreigner because I'm her real cousin. She makes a face.

I get her into the back hall where it's as cool and dark as the inside of the minister's nose. I have seen up the minister's nose. I dare to take communion, but I watch out for the minister. He looks down at me kneeling with my friends. All my friends are baptized. I go with them to the rail. I'm the only one who takes the Body and the Blood and then can't swallow. And cries because I'm not supposed to have it. And the minister knows.

When I'm in the living room begging to be baptized, my mother and father turn their smooth faces together, then look at me and say, "Gia cannot be baptized because she doesn't yet know what she's doing." So I punish us all by playing my piano sideways, pecking into its face until it slips and scratches the white off the living room wall.

With a clatter like rings dropped to the bottom of a bottle, here come the minister's sons. Sometimes I think the two of them came out of his nose. In this cool, cool corridor, the minister's twins are coming toward us with sweat under their arms.

Immediately Jewel sits on her legs on a yellowed corridor bench. She looks awed, but she isn't. She has tea-colored hair, but it's her albino eyelashes that give her that peculiar stare. She sits on her legs because they are her best feature.

Jewel says, "What are they carrying? Teeth?" Long, whitish things are in their hands. Of course, they live for tricks.

Really, it's the ivory tops of piano keys. Miraculously, they have pulled them off in whole pieces. Who knows what rooms they have been in.

Close, the boys smell as strong as onions. One shows us that he's all muscle, but all his muscle is in his stomach. He shoves his stomach out and it makes his pants snap open.

"You're in for trouble with those piano keys," I say.

"Oh no we're not," one says. "It's as good as never doing it, cause we never get caught."

The minister's sons get bad grades, but they are very bright. "We are looking for your legs. Do you have any?" they ask Jewel.

I tell them to stop. "Jewel doesn't take jokes."

The only sound comes from Jewel, her teeth tapping together like tiny feet running away. Her legs are good from playing hardball with boys in her backyard dust. I love boys in secret. She does things with them, she says, and then she cusses them out loud to their faces. But now she won't talk to boys, not in hot Florida. She opens her mouth and breathes humidity.

I try to stay still, but I only get a cramp in my leg.

When nothing is said, one swells his lip and says, "You better leave us alone or our father will damn you to hell."

"He can't hurt me," I say quite certain. "I've not been baptized, so he can't do anything to me yet."

The doors in the church won't stay closed. The piano teacher opens the door to the practice room and creates a suction. So another door down the hall gasps open, and another slams shut.

We go in watching out for our fingers. Jewel is introduced while she's heading for a chair against the far wall. She sits and presses her skirt into her lap. It's hard for her to be still if she's not asleep. Jewel has lots of energy. She eats too much sugar. She's allowed because her mother has no patience to teach her differently. She puts her head back, trying to fall asleep. She will not listen to me play because she has perfect pitch.

The blue cotton top that yesterday was mine overpowers the

thin blue in her eyes till they look as empty as her drained glass at lunch. She never leaves anything of hers behind. In fact, though she's here for a stay, she won't unpack and merely nods her head into the old hard suitcase each morning, chooses for one day only, and slams it shut. That's why a mistake was made—I have on short shorts and she has on a skirt; once done, Jewel does not reverse.

The piano teacher says, "Pleased to meet you," but warns her, "Learn something by staying awake right in this room. Have you ever been taught piano?"

"I won't play anything," Jewel says, "except by ear."

She and I have tried: "Blue Moon," "Chopsticks," and "Detour, There's a Muddy Road Ahead," which I told Jewel was a Methodist hymn and she slapped me.

My teacher has on her perfume today. It gives her a deep smell and makes me feel tipsy.

At first I sit at a paper keyboard laid out on a table. Using my ears as my barrettes, I hook my long hair back to rest my neck. My mother wants to cut it. My father won't let her. "Whores have long hair." My mother's words, hardly heard, have played across the cords in her neck. "His whores." She capitalized *His* and let the words drain back down her throat so my father couldn't be sure he'd heard. I love the word *whore* and wrote it down immediately; it will be my favorite word one day.

As of late, my mother has let her short hair grow. She has tried to stretch it with her fingers.

The piano teacher asks me to remove my bracelet collection for the lesson. I push them high up my arm till they stick. I hear my teacher suck her tongue, so I let them off my arm and they ring down beside me on the table. I play finger exercises on the tabletop to no music at all.

The real piano is under a Jesus-on-the-Cross. The practice rooms electric light runs down his wooden legs. Whether truth or a trick, it makes his legs look broken. Teacher sits in a chair beside me. She strokes the backs of her hands, loving to be the example. She doesn't look down. By habit, she watches Jesus on his cross and plays by feel.

One chord; unexpectedly she sings. "AAAAAh," the world's longest vowel, pitches out of her throat. "I've touched Jesus's wounds!" She sticks her fingers in the air. So the ivory keys were lifted from here, too. "The minister's twins," I tell immediately and taste my lips. But no one likes tattletales.

"You play, Gia." Her hands dangle in her way and she paws her own breasts with embarrassment.

The sounds of my playing on old glue and spoiled wood seem to stain the room brown. My tune is too simple and plodding. Plus I'm playing it wrong. I will have to hide this from my mother. I'm supposed to be teaching her, but she couldn't resist showing me how to do it wrong.

My teacher is confused by my inabilities. Her breasts point at me sharply through her full dress. I hate breasts. I'm afraid my mother won't ever let me have any. She tells me I don't need them now. But I think, secretly, that boys like them very much. She tells me out loud she will be happy if I never let anyone love me like "this and that."

The piano squeaks and I'm tired of my lazy little talent. I catch my teacher pushing the bar up higher on the metronome, making me faster. She watches her watch and cleans her shoulders. The teacher's nervousness must be what keeps Cousin Jewel awake.

"Over," says the teacher, and she pulls her pocketbook out of hiding. I count my bracelet collection on the table and string them back up my arm. Jewel and I can't stand to walk out beside a teacher. We hurry, but the teacher succeeds in leaving with us.

Outside is too green and blue after the pale church and its bottled-up air. My eyelashes try to sweep the sun away.

The piano teacher hurries for her bike, she has laid it against the shade on the church wall.

Jewel calls, "Why is she running beside that bike?"

"Because," I say, "she has to jump over the boy's bar."

"She shouldn't do that. She could hurt herself." Jewel is a tomboy, my mother says. Then why does she get so sick at accidents?

My piano teacher grips the handlebars and her old pocketbook, which is so flat as to be uninteresting.

"That's a man's bike," calls Jewel again.

"Well, I'm off to see a man," the teacher announces and mounts her bike on a fast trot.

A boy comes out of nowhere, covered by the blast of sunlight. The piano teacher's bike wobbles and hits him. It's a lone twin. For a moment he dances on air, screaming, "Okay, okay, okay!" before he lands catching his balance on two feet. The piano teacher is down, gear grit on her dress. She pushes herself up, saying, "I'm sorry. I apologize." The twin seals his lips, but the spit in his smile crests at the corners. She kneels to the twin's bare summer skin and checks it over. "Thank God I didn't leave any marks on you," she says.

The teacher knocks the sand off her bike. She loves to talk so much to me, I've noticed, so she even talks to the silent twin. "Today I have many things to do. First I'm going to visit my old father, but he's disoriented. If I'm not on time I'll disorient him more. He thinks things happen that don't. We often spend our time together talking about things that don't really happen."

"Boy, is she rattled," says Jewel.

The piano teacher coughs and runs and jumps the man's bar again. I gasp but she makes it. Her pocketbook caught underarm, she sets off determinedly on her bike. She bumps up off the seat to pull at her skirt and make sure it has not been eaten.

Jewel says, "Jesus, she's sure got looks from behind."

"I hate behinds," I say. "Let's go. I want to go home and play with my wild birds."

"I'm sure you do." She wags her head.

Passing through downtown, Jewel struts among strangers,

wearing my clothes. Rows of dull heat waves stretch down the street. We pass stubs of stores and go into a short street where my father's business is. It's really where my father works for someone else, but my mother calls it his business anyway.

The back door to the offices opens. "Let's go look," says Jewel. She pulls up her underpants through her skirt. But Myrna, the woman who works with my father, steps into the flickering blue shadow of the doorway and gets in our way. In the heat, her hair has run into one long, thin tail which she lifts, then lays against her shoulder.

She has two cigarettes with her, she feeds one from the other. The short one falls at her shoe. She looks skinny and childlike. She pulls at the cigarette twice, and twice again.

When we get too close, Myrna laughs. "Don't you come in here, cause he's already gone," she says.

"She means he left for home," I say. We retreat to the sharp edge of the building. "She doesn't talk to me this way when my father's around."

Jewel stares at her over the albino rims of her eyes and says loudly, "I'll just bet she doesn't."

The air wrinkles Myrna's dress. But it's not air, it's heat waves because Myrna's body ripples, too. "Hey, you with no hair on your head—aw, forget it." She doesn't finish, but slings her cigarette onto the street with a hard crack of her thumbnail.

Jewel grunts. Myrna's gone. I go put out both of her cigarettes with my hot sandal.

Now the heat waves are as fine as the mesh on my bedroom window screen. Heat splashes over my open shoes onto my feet. Jewel won't walk. But I won't wait. So Jewel says, "Oh," and adds a funny, starchy twist to her walk. The white sidewalk looks closer than it is; it looks like it's jumping.

The thin wall of Jewel's face draws tight. "Oh, I don't feel too good," she says. "I have to go." She laughs with a tiny terror, and speaks to me in thumps like her heart has popped into her cheeks.

"I have to go to the bathroom. If only your father had been where he was supposed to be. Because I have to go right now!"

"*I* don't," I say cruelly.

"It burns," she says, agitated. "It burns."

"I'm not sure what you mean."

"Don't say 'lemonade' to me." She is desperate now. She twists like a mad dog with fleas everywhere.

"Lemonade, lemonade, lemonade," I sing into the glare that ricochets off the storefronts. The glare is running all over everything, the color of lemonade; it runs down me, both my legs. I giggle from shock. It is I who have peed. I pee right down into my footprints.

"I told you not to say it," says Jewel, so relieved that my clothes on her quiver.

"I don't feel like I have to go anymore," says Jewel minutes later and flatly.

Lucky for me, my footprints steam quickly and dry up behind me. Not so lucky with my outfit—the center of my cool summer shorts feels like wool.

"Don't look up," cautions Jewel. "Some things you do are just too disgusting."

She pulls out an albino eyelash to measure it against the color all around us. The eyelash is a used-looking white. Trying to throw it away is hard. Her eyelash sticks to any finger that touches it. Finally she leaves it on the side of the bank.

There is only one bridge in town, a steel spiderweb. Crossing it makes Jewel uneasy. The creosote and fish smell of the river's edge rises under us and Jewel holds the sides of the bridge like she's on a melting ice staircase.

On level road again, she zigzags, feels her face, and says she's overheated. She wants to hurry to my house and sit down. "Then let's go have a Brown Cow. You ask for it," she says.

The sprinkler is out on our lawn, throwing stitches of water. We stay out of the water, afraid the colors of our clothes will run.

But the white car has broken the stitches of spray, and my father has left his fresh, wet tracks through the shade to the front door.

The porch of our house is made of glass slats. They are called jalousies. We can see out through them, but the neighbors can't see us inside. I really call them jealousies because when my mother is jealous my father he walks and talks her out to the porch. Then she has to stop accusing him, otherwise the neighbors will hear what she thinks my father has done. He keeps her from taking their arguments too far.

Jewel likes the yellow chaise behind the jalousies. She wants an ice cube for her temperature. She would like for me to get it for her. At the same time, she doesn't want me to touch it. She gets it herself, sits in the chaise, and holds it to her face.

My father's smooth voice glides through the house, calling to my mother. I hear the bedroom door close and I go to it. Lightly, I knock. He opens the door just enough to not let me fit through. He smiles my name, "Gia, you're home." He's the one who named me. He says teasingly but meaning it, "No, Gia, don't disturb your mother, she's going to rest." In the dark hall, where I feel I am turning into a shadow, his eyes stay a pale blue. He closes the door easily so as not to let the sound hurt my feelings.

Now I can't get the pee-pee off because their door is next to the bathroom and I'm not supposed to stay that near. I do wait to hear what they're doing—and it turns out they are making little sounds of surprise to each other.

After a while my mother comes out, wearing her hair up.

"May we have a Brown Cow?" I say. Then I hurry to get fresh, while my mother shouts, "Gia, don't you dare take another bath. Too many baths make you skinny." She doesn't stop talking, but dry sniffs in the middle. "I thought I smelled cat pee."

She is digging at the hard vanilla ice cream with a big spoon when I come out with my skin and clothes freshened. My mother pours the Coke over the vanilla ice cream for a Brown Cow. She looks pretty. "That's Daddy's shirt," I say sarcastically. No one answers me. "Why are you wearing it?" I persist. Why must she wear my father's clothes with nothing under it?

Jewel and I sit across from each other at the dinette. Jewel eats the foam off her Brown Cow with her front teeth. I hold the foam with my top lip and swallow the strong Coke quickly.

My father roams in and out of the kitchen. Though this is the end of the day, he's put on another clean shirt. How broad his arms are. He tells me he only *thinks* at work. So why does he have those long, smooth muscles?

He wanders when he's home early—dropping sounds through the house, clinking keys, tapping his teeth, ruffling for things in a drawer. He doesn't seem to know where things are at home.

The birds in the outside cage are talking nonsense; I listen to them mixing up all the words we've taught them. Jewel watches me. "When I'm here you're not supposed to bother with pets," she says. She scratches her face hard. She may be getting ready to tell on me. My peeing is a joke she can make to get my mother's attention. A swallow of Coke backs up my throat.

It's then that I remember the dirty words list I've been working on. "I can tell you the meaning of things now. They're in my room," I whisper when my mother turns on the water to rinse. I lead Jewel back to where we both sleep on matching cherry-wood beds. Because Jewel is here, my parents have taken down my sleeping rope and hidden it. It's used to rope up the sides of my bed so I won't go to sleep and fall right out of bed. I've always done that. My cousin knows it, but we don't want to remind her. I'm trying to sleep without it, but my mother is nervous.

I open my dresser drawer. "These are all the words you said last time you were here. Now I have the meanings for you." I take out my chocolate box. On the first layer are unwanted candies with fallen fillings.

Jewel looks at them. "Let's eat some," she says.

"Don't touch them. I bit all the bottoms off and put them back. I only taste each one once, I don't eat candy."

"But your mother says you can have all the candy you want."

"She gives me candy cause she never has to worry about me eating it. She says it proves how nice I am," I say.

Under the false floor of the chocolate box are the pieces of paper with dirty words on them. I begin to read what all these dirty words mean. I'm the one who wants to know exactly.

Jewel paces and then shouts at me, "Where did you get those answers? They are not definitions. Those are daffynitions. Did you get them out of a dictionary?"

I say, "I tried to." Air stops in my throat; a bubble lodges. I speak through a tiny pinprick hole. "I had to make them up. They weren't in the dictionary."

"You mean you're reading me what *you* think those filthy words mean?"

"Then what do they mean?" I ask.

"You will never mature if you make up definitions." She strains her patience with me till I think her eyelids will tear in two. "Now listen and remember. I'm not telling you again," she says.

"I thought you didn't know the definitions," I wail.

"What I know is not to say everything I know out loud."

She slaps my wall and leaves my room. I bend over my dirty words.

Night comes with a slow moon. Because Florida is flat, sunset takes forever. On the jalousied porch, I try to play gently with my cockatoo. Jewel braces her hands to screen the bird off if it flies at her face. She says, "Birds in the house mean bad luck. Something dies."

"They're pets," I say.

"Nobody's tamed them." She scuffs her voice at me.

With his hooked beak, the cockatoo bites me in the quick of my cuticle. I return him to the outside cage. I put my fresh water offering on the cage bottom. The birds perch near the roof.

Their mouths are closed, no song or imitation human words come out.

With the birds falling asleep, the air seems so still. I play "March Militaire" for Jewel. My fingers touch the keys but seem to clang at the roof of my mouth.

The phone rings and rings. Someone is not giving up. My parents don't want to talk to anyone on the phone tonight. My father kisses my mother's neck because she has left her hair up. "Ouch," she says about his kiss, "that's hot."

The phone rests. Then it starts ringing again.

The moon looks breakable. I ask Jewel not to point her finger at it.

My father joins us and sits on the small of his back. His legs are getting longer; he is stretching out. We have him on the porch with us. He doesn't read; he holds the paper on top of him.

Caught at the phone, my mother looks at the wall and listens.

A mosquito sings. Jewel kills it. For this summer, she's calling my father Uncle Daddy. We giggle. Mother's voice on the phone has gone tart. We press our fingernails to our mouths and our knuckles stop-up our noses. My hands smell very good. Jewel says she's making fun of me, the way I sound when I call him Daddy. "You get too sweet when you try to talk to your daa-dee. It's enough to make me heave hot vomit." We talk about my father as if he were deaf, but he's only bored. We are hysterical with this exchange.

"Shut up," calls my mother. The phone has made her irritable. And my father has to go inside; my mother tells him to.

In the kitchen, my mother and father mumble to each other and make coffee. "It will keep them awake and nervous all night," promises Jewel.

They bring their cups to the porch. "Have some coffee, darling," my father says to me. I love him so much but I won't drink after him. I'm afraid I'd be able to taste my father.

He tells my mother to sit with him on the rattan settee and

make him comfortable. She puts her leg over his. My cousin sees this and quickly she cleans out the corners of both of her eyes.

"Something has happened," says my mother. "The phone. Your piano teacher has had a terrible accident."

"Did she hit a car or a truck?" asks Jewel.

"No. Not a wreck. Someone."

I remember the twin frantically running in the air. "Did she hurt someone?"

Jewel has reached for one of her eyelashes. She may pull it any minute.

My mother says, "You must practice very hard and make her feel better. She's been raped."

My father slides his leg from under Mother's and now he rests his right ankle on his left knee.

"It's already happened to her. Don't cry."

I laugh. Ha, ha, ha, chopping it into three bites. *Rape* was one of the words on my list.

"They haven't caught him yet. We don't know who he is."

"Then how do they know it was a man?" I say. My stomach laughs now, in and out like it is riding a horse.

My father pets the leather of his new shoes.

"For some reason," she says to my father, "she's just not getting it. Growing up. She'll never know how to take care of herself."

My father says, "You don't have to worry about her. She's so young that she's a little knock-kneed and still swaybacked. Men won't be after her yet." They laugh with their joke and they seem so happy that I make the mistake of laughing with them.

My laugh cools my mother off. She pulls out the pins in her hair and watches me, but I don't jump.

Jewel and I go to bed, because we feel like it. She is wearing see-through pajamas and I can see the lamp through the side of her pajamas. My mother has set my rubber baby doll at the extreme foot of the bed, hoping I will wake when I roll onto it instead of fall. "You still like to sleep with dolls?" asks Jewel.

"No." I force my toe into the doll's mouth. It is not quite a lie, but I have told my doll she will be mine forever.

Instead of prayers, Jewel croons, "So-o-o, your teacher was raped, w-e-l-l, we don't really care." She flips off my light. I find my rubber doll by feel and stroke her stiff, hard-rubber face.

It has been raining. The ground takes it and then gives it back up, standing water. Our shoes have been wet for two days and have sand specks dried into the white polish. We are all over inside into everything. What we do not know is that on this day my mother is hiding her birthday. Then at dinner she tells us she's had her 35th birthday. "I didn't want it anyway," she says to my father, "but you did forget it."

"*When* did I forget it?" my father asks.

"Today," my mother says. She needs to blow her nose. But no one has a Kleenex. Except Jewel, who uses them to fill her first training bra. Jewel stretches the neck of her T-shirt and pulls out a Kleenex from what she calls her right cup. My mother laughs and tells Jewel, "You look like you've collapsed a lung." She doesn't want to use Jewel's Kleenex. Jewel refuses to wear it again. No one wants it on the table. My mother looks angrily and then sickly at it. She has no choice but to blow. Her nose now sounds empty. Then she stretches the napkin longways and wrings its little neck. Jewel has to be the one to get up and carry it out of the dinette.

We decide to finish fast and go play in the black grass of the backyard where the moon isn't. My father follows us. "Tomorrow early, get flowers for your mother," he says. He gives me the exact name of the arrangement. In the moist backyard, he makes me turn my chin up at him to read his lips. He's not sure of my memory. He gives me money between a paper clip. I promise not to forget.

When he steps out of our dark, Jewel asks me, "Don't you get it yet? He still doesn't want to give your mother flowers, he's making you give them to her." When she slits her eyes to laugh, I slip away.

The next day Jewel and I take the hot spidery bridge to downtown and I hand the florist my father's words and money. I remember my mother's nose when she doesn't want to blow it. When we get home, my mother takes the flowers in their paper lace collar. She doesn't inhale the flowers, but she blows on our bridge windburns to cool us. Then my father comes home and says, "A nosegay for you," to my mother. "No," she says, "Gia called it a nose gauge." They laugh together, but when it dies my father tiptoes out of the room. He smiles around the house but he is staying too careful.

In a few days we are up in the tiny raw wood attic investigating for something forbidden. The wood we are on is a rough fur of splinters. Jewel and I are too excited to be careful because we have to sneak fast. I breathe hot air out of my mouth and the same air back into my nose. We want to find the box of dresses my mother wore when they danced together before I was born. She won't even let me touch those dresses. We want to put them on and play house in rhinestone straps and black eyelet and black sheers.

The dresses are gone. The box is gone. Jewel doesn't care because she's hurt her fingers. I've hurt my fingers, too.

Mother finds us on our beds with needles trying to work out our fine splinters. "What are you two sewing? Your own skin?" I blurt out, "Where are the dresses I'm not supposed to play in?" She tells. She has given them to that skinny Myrna who works with my father.

After dark, when the breeze reverses and Florida cools off, she surprises my father with what she's done. "You made me eat and get fat." I can see that my mother is not fat—merely grown-up.

One-sided conversations excite Jewel, who has been painting her toenails in the living room; some of her toes are stuck together. She whispers to me, her voice thin as a stem, harsh as a broom, "Don't you know that Myrna is your father's girl-friend?"

Dark drops in front of my eye. I brush at my hair, thinking it has fallen in my face. "How could you know that?" I ask as I bend over her toes. "You only saw her one day last week."

"You shut your eyes and sleep at night. I stay awake and listen. You ought to be more nervous."

My father's breath saws across me to Jewel. "What did you say, Jewel?" She grunts. But I think my father has heard because he leaves the room in his beautifully clean and pressed clothes, his pants flicking at his legs.

We pull Jewel's polished toes apart. Jewel crosses her legs and counts her naked toes. I don't hear how many. A funny soft cloth seems to be wiping my eardrums clean.

Our house can't get to sleep tonight. Jewel and I are in bed in the dark. The attic fan kicks on. The refrigerator makes ice, pushes it, drops it. The tap drips hot water, I know. A night bird, not a singer, shrieks.

Then sound is in our house that gets behind my eyes and claws. It sits Jewel up in bed. "My God! Who screamed?"

My mother has screamed, "Let Myrna wear them."

"She and I work together." My fathers voice. "You be careful!"

Don't they know where I am? That I'm here, listening. Jewel's shadow lies against the wall, a dry paper doll.

Now the house doesn't make a sound. "Why—why don't you leave me?" he asks.

"Because you love me," she answers.

My heart runs on high, thin toes. The dark has another sound now. It's a pair of bird wings folding, stretching, and being preened. I say to Jewel, "Sometimes I'm afraid my father will get hurt."

"Don't you know," she says, "it's your mother that you should worry about?"

All day, something hurts my stomach like I have taken in what my body cannot handle. My mother and father won't look at each other, and when he nears her she jumps a little, and for his part, he will not eat her special banana pudding. A pain climbs and scratches and swings inside me all day. I practice piano standing up because it feels awful to sit. I am getting ready for my first lesson with my teacher since her rape.

Late afternoon, I am wet between my legs. Cousin Jewel is busy stretched out on a chaise wearing my jewelry. In the bathroom I pick up my summer skirt and look. I don't have to turn on a light; I am bright red. I rush to tell Jewel. I need to give her this news. "Look, I'm wet as paint." I lift my skirt.

She springs up, the chaise webbing snaps its fingers under her.

Then I say, "Have I lost my virginity?"

"Who told you that one?" says Jewel, and then she runs from me.

I give chase. "I got it first. I can explain it to you."

She tells me abruptly to shut up.

"It feels like a baby already inside," I shout to her, but I can't catch her. I chase her into the backyard. I run her into the flowers. Though the yard isn't fenced, Jewel runs only so far and then back, never leaving the privacy of our yard.

My mother stops me because she says you shouldn't chase a guest. "What could make you two not get along?" she asks. There is wet laundry on the line and I stand near it. My mother likes for the breeze to whip it dry.

"Look." I lift my skirt.

"That's ugly, put down your skirt." My mother speaks softly. Still her voice makes the backyard air ring. "Damn Jesus. Goddamn Jesus to hell," my mother says. "The damn piano teacher gets raped on a bicycle and scares the period out of you." She leaves on the heels of her thought with me. She half turns, remembering, and says into her shoulder, "Jewel, stop whirling like a dervish. What an idiot my sister's child is. Always thought so; never could take her for long or short."

Inside the house she gives me the white thing. "Do you know about this?"

I try to rhyme "administration, ministration, minister, menustration."

"My God, Gia." She tells me, to make herself feel better, "I would be so happy if you never get married."

Outside, when I'm together again, I can see Jewel has put on socks to protect her legs. I call to her because she won't get near, and I tell her I'm wearing a sanitary pad like the one I tried to look up in the dictionary. "Now I'm not making up the answers. It fits and feels like I'm wearing my bicycle seat." I laugh, but it's hard to do.

Jewel says, "You're terrible. But I don't want to go back home and leave you. I'm sorry you were snooping in dirty words and got your period. I don't want to go, but they'll make me go now." She adjusts her socks.

My mother and father say, "We must make her feel welcome and then get rid of her." They hurry into the backyard to play with her. She plays ball with them in her dress and socks. She holds out the lap of her skirt and they throw the ball into it. That night, after I get used to my period being with me, I feel better; I put my hands against my face and my heart pounds only in the heels of my hands.

The inevitable phone call is made. My mother makes herself do it and holds onto me for support, she says, and rubs the hair on my arm the wrong way. She says, "We think Jewel should be out of this. Gia's piano teacher has been raped and what with Gia starting her period, there's been so much." I take my arm away and excuse myself to go ease up the extension in the next room.

My mother's sister is saying, "Well, that's why I sent her. You know how much Jewel's been through. And me, too, so much,

what with my foul divorce and my foul life with him and him being her lousy father. Me, too. I was just, well, beating her every
day. You know? Put her back on the bus. I don't want the poor
thing in it. She's practically pulled out her eyelashes over my divorce; she sheds them in the ashtray and you know I smoke. And
did she do this there, did you hear her grunt—little grunts? She
grunts because she says she can't think of what to say anymore."

The house feels busy now. We go for a ride when we are supposed to be asleep in bed. My father, my mother in front with
him, takes us to a place where I don't think he can get us and
our big white car through. The sides of the road are high with
hard, full mounds of saw palmettos. Sand blows like clean smoke
along the road. Jewel asks to stop ahead at the Silver Palomino
Motel. In the roadside sand and ragged grass is a concrete horse
outlined in neon. Jewel is very attracted. Since she is strong-
willed, my father lets her have her way. The car gives sideways
into the soft side of the road, and I hope my father can get us out.
He lights his cigarette on the orange ring of the car lighter and
laughs, "Careful, that's a big horse."

Jewel and I go alone to approach the palomino. We check back
toward the car. My mother and father have their hair together
under the white cap of the top.

"Well yes," says Jewel, at the big concrete hindquarters. "Its
a male, a stallion." There's a reflecting pool, too, and water lilies and the reflections of our faces float on it. I put my hand deep
down into the water and through my face.

I've left a puddle of lily water on the concrete and Jewel stands
in it to reach as high as she can for the staff of neon over the
horse's huge haunches. She gets it and moans, a quiet sound only
I can hear. Then she does a funny thing with her pelvis. Kick,
kick, kick, Jewel punches her pelvis forward. My high-pitched
laughter does not break her concentration. Her body turns into a
tongue that shouts without sound. I am jealous of her doing this.
My mother is rushing toward us, each step sounding like she is

stripping grass. Then Jewel breaks her hands up into the air; I clap wildly to celebrate.

My mother rushes at Jewel. "What do you think you're doing?"

"Being electrocuted—don't you know?" says Jewel.

"Don't give me that. Bump, bump, bump," says my mother. "You were making fun of what we do."

"What do you do?" asks Jewel politely.

My mother rattles breath around in her mouth.

"It hurt me," Jewel says. "I stuck to electricity and it ran all through my private places." Her face has clear sweat on it like spit. "Let's not ever tell how I looked being electrocuted," says Jewel.

My mother's eyelid ticks like a pulse, and she agrees.

When we get back in the car, we sit still. Small bugs fly in the car dome light. My father spins and rocks the car onto the weathered road. The bugs fly out with the breeze. My mother sits sideways, maybe so Jewel can't stare at the back of her head.

"Thank you for tonight," Jewel says to herself. Her words fall down the front of her dress. Her teeth smile at me; they are moist.

It is the morning that I'm losing my cousin and I'm in the dressing room with its perfume stains on the carpet. "Hurry," my mother says. "Brush your teeth and blow your nose." I find I can't do both at the same time. She combs my hair. Jewel darts behind us and her smirk leaves a streak across the mirror. She says, "She cuts your meat at the table; you can't tell time or comb your hair. And there are things you don't know!" My mother catches her, waters down her head, and takes a spare to scrape at Jewel's tea-colored hair. When she finishes, Jewel's hair looks like it has been sewn on. "You made my hairdo hurt," complains Jewel, and my mother sticks the teeth of the comb into the back of Jewel's hair and lets her walk away with it riding on her.

Finally Jewel shakes it off and my mother flings one hip out in an ugly way she has and leaves us. Jewel says, "I pretend that your mother is pretend."

On the way to the bus, Jewel insists on hanging her elbow out her window. My father puts on the air-conditioning anyway, so it is noisy in the car, a loud baffle under which I can talk. I'm in a hurry. I need to tell Jewel all the ugly things about me that I hide because I'm afraid to be so ugly alone. I try to tell her so she can take it away in her head. But my cousin won't listen. "I can't," she says. "Listening is a waste of time." She lets the wind blow in her ear.

At the bus station, both of us grab at her old hard suitcase. Neither of us will let go, so we run raggedly, bumping it between us, to the waiting spot where the bus will come in, drip oil, and leave.

When we settle, she thumps me on my head to make me think hard. "I don't remember what my father looks like," she says.

"I do. I remember."

"Do I look like him?" she asks.

"No," I lie. Because I know her mother hates her father and so Jewel doesn't want to be his image, she *has* to look like her mother.

The bus comes, blowing its warning horn. Jewel is stuck on calling it a trumpet. She is the only one leaving town today.

Without me, she is climbing up the steep bus steps. It sounds like she is walking in rubber shoes, but it's the steps that are padded. I don't take my eyes off of her; she stands sideways to me and I can see through the clear cornea of my cousin's eyes. I never could hold her attention.

Jewel is busy choosing a seat. The bus backfires a vivid metal blue cloud. My mother says, "Close your mouth, Gia, you'll get cancer." I keep waving good-bye, I can't find Jewel. Finally, the bus driver waves good-bye to me.

At night, my father and I take two fat parakeets from their outside cage and bring them in. We put them in my dollhouse and they go upstairs and downstairs and room to room for us. "Are you two playing house, dears?" my mother laughs at us. My father goes to the bathroom to get ready for bed, and I've got a rough sore throat from trying not to cry for somebody I see every half a year. I start to the kitchen for milk and meet my father again in the hall. He is in his stiff undershorts. "Night," he says, oblivious that his fly is gaping open. I am as transfixed as if I'd sniffed pepper. I have something new to tell my cousin already. What I saw has shocked me more than what I had imagined. I saw hair.

Next day, I stop talking so much and start thinking.

The weather is dry; the grass sounds like a rug to walk on, the sky and the clouds are almost no color, and the air smells like Clorox. The dry heat gives my mother a temper. She listens to weather reports and taps the barometer till it breaks; she has lost her willpower to be nice.

Alone I hunt the breeze, standing on the bridge and sitting on shaded benches. When I go home, my mother is ironing my father's khaki pants. I begin to talk about the boys playing in the park. My mother says I'm boy crazy. She punishes me for looking at boys. She tells me to take off my top because it's too hot. I tell her I'm too big now and she says I'm flat as an iron. She makes me take off my pretty top. I won't walk around now, so I sit and my flat boy's chest tingles with all that attention. Because she's mad at me, my mother works the steam iron over the legs of my father's pants and nails them so tight with the iron I doubt that he'll ever get back in them.

Next, she has an argument with my father. I mean he stands and takes it, looking out the same direction she is, on the porch. I knew it was about him and his sorry ways.

She corners her eyes at me when I take up for him. "Your father is unmanageable." She gets mad and wears her wedding ring on the wrong finger. She calls my father's boss and gets my father fired. Myrna, the woman she'd given her clothes to, is accused of adultery with my father, but her husband stands by her anyway. Only my father lost.

"I've broken your wings," she tells my father. "Now you won't fly." My father receives his punishment and it's true he doesn't seem so good-looking. She has brought down my father. The problem is that we are a family, so we are all attached.

Today, the air conditioner shivers like the nervous system of the church, cooling with used air. I am in the practice room. My piano teacher comes to me. I hand her what my mother has made me bring—cut flowers and a Hallmark occasion card, for her rape. She rubs the flowers against her face and twirls them into what had been her drinking water for when she went dry listening to me play. "I want to hear your fingers," she says. I play on the table for control, then the piano. She holds the card while I play with muscles that hurt inside my hands. "You try too hard," she says. I want to wring my hands, but I wring my dress instead.

The church's air-conditioning shuts down. "Let's just stop the lesson," says my teacher.

"We're moving away," I say, making sure I don't tell her where.

She reads the card. I see now that she needs glasses because she has to move her lips to read silently. She polishes the slick surface of the card along her dress. "Tell your mother they never caught him. Tell her your piano teacher's father *thinks* your piano teacher got raped. But he tells your piano teacher that he *knows* he's so old he makes up things."

The air conditioner does not come back on. She takes up my sheet music, and this time she keeps it. She slides her pocketbook out of hiding. "No!" I say. "My mother said he took *all* you had, every old thing, and you've still got your pocketbook." Her hand hangs onto her neck. Under it is a blush spot, I think. Then I see it might be a gouge mark.

"This time I won't leave with you," she says, and puts her pocketbook back in hiding. She helps me from the bench for good-bye. Where she's touched my dress, it stays stuck to my skin. I try to smile ahead of myself.

The halls are humid. The minister's twins are exploring the church with a screwdriver that has a long yellow handle. They snicker air up through the hairs in their noses.

"The church stinks," they tell me.

"Well, what do you expect? The air conditioner is on the blink."

The skin around their eyes stretches with laughter, and I know what they're up to—they have shut the air-conditioning off. They love to break things.

So we throw away, give away what can't come with us, and sell, and move to Jax. My father sets out like it's a Sunday drive for the town he only calls by its nickname. In Jax, we start over.

My mother chooses the new empty house; it's on the ocean-side. In its rooms you can hear the waves rolling toward us. Even when she tells me that the tide is going out, it is rolling toward us. My mother gets too close to my father. Her eyelashes brush into his; I don't know if she tickles. They are both really very beautiful, I realize.

I sit with a whole box of stationery. I will send letters to Jewel. This is my first one. "We are in Jax now with the birds, but my mother won't let them live outside. She's put them in little cages inside with us. The piano came, too, so I *will* have to take lessons. But I *don't* have to teach my mother. She found out she can't learn."

Next thing I say is "Uncle Daddy," to make Jewel laugh. (She has smiled at me, but laughing, of course, is something very different.)

I underline and try. "*Uncle Daddy* has a night job loading trucks, so he's tired all the time. I don't like the looks of my father asleep in daylight. My mother says the words that scare me: his wings are broken. I will also tell you that my father has hair—only I bet you can't guess *where*. We don't go to church anymore. Instead, I go to the library. I don't have to *wonder* about being baptized. Remember my rubber baby doll? She's gone. Do you know where she might be? I told my father that in my prayers I wanted to ask God where she was. You know what? He said why don't I shortcut it and just ask you. You may not even smile at my letter. But I always knew, Jewel, that you don't take jokes. I don't take jokes either."

What I can't say yet—maybe next letter—is I'm afraid now. Under my blouse are "you know whats," soft little marshmallows that will worry my mother if she finds out about them. I can't say the word for it from my dirty list because now I know the meaning.

Idling

TONY ARDIZZONE

From *The Evening News* (1986)

Sometimes when I'm hauling I drive right past her house. The Central Avenue exit from the Kennedy Expressway, and then north maybe two, three miles. The front is red brick and the awnings are striped, like most of the other houses on Central Avenue. Her name was Suzy and she was the kind of girl who liked cheese and sauerkraut on her hot dogs. She was regular. She went in for plain skirts, browns and navy blues, wraparounds, and those button-down blouses with the tiny pinstripes all the girls wore back then. She must be as old as I am now, and the only girl ever to wear my ring. She was special. Suzy was my only girl.

I met her at a party at a friend's house. A Saturday night, and I was on the team, only I had pulled my back a couple of days before—too serious to risk playing, they said, sorry, we think you're out for the season. I'd been doing isometrics. And though they gave me the chance to dress and sit with the team, I said the hell with it, this season's finished, get somebody else to bench warm with the sophomores.

Which was okay, because the night I met Suzy the team was playing out in Oak Park, and had I gone I'd have met my father afterwards for some pizza, like we usually did after a game, but instead I went over to Ronny's. The two of us hung around the back of his garage, talking, splitting a couple of six-packs, with him soaking out a carburetor and me trying to figure if what I had done with the team was right. Ronny told me stuff it, you can't play you can't play. There are things nobody can control, he said. You just got to learn to roll with the punches. He was maybe my best friend back then and I was feeling lousy, here it was not even October and only the second game. Let's get drunk, Ronny said, laughing, so I said stuff it too, there's a party out in Des Plaines tonight. So we got in his car and drove there. Then some of the game crowd got there, all noisy and excited, and I met Suzy.

It went real smooth and I should have known then, like when you're beating your man easy on the first couple of plays you should know if you've got any sense that he's gonna try something on you on the third. I started talking to her, thinking that since I was a little drunk I had an excuse if she shut me down—maybe I even wanted to be shut down, I don't know, I was still feeling lousy—but she talked back and we danced some. Slow dances, on account of my back. And when I told her my name she said you're on the team, I saw you play last week. I said yeah, I was. She seemed impressed by that. But she didn't remember that it was me who intercepted that screen pass in the third quarter, and damn I nearly scored. She smiled, and I held her.

Things went real fine then. We danced a lot, and later Ronny flipped me his keys, and me and Suzy went out for a ride. Mostly we talked, her about that night's game, and me about why I'd decided not to suit up, which, I told her, was really the best thing for me. There's something stupid about dressing and not playing. If they win, sure it's your victory too, but what did you do to deserve it? And if they lose, you feel just as miserable.

I took her home then and told her I wanted to see her again, and all the talking made me sober up, and that started it.

I don't know if you've ever had duck's blood soup. It's a Polish dish, and honest to God it's made with real duck's blood, sweet and thick, and raisins and currants and noodles. Her father, the father of three beautiful little girls, with Suzy the oldest, took all of us out to this restaurant on North McCormick Street and he ordered it for me. He said the name in Polish to the waiter, then looked at me and winked. He even bought me a beer, and I was only seventeen. The girls watched me as I salted it and kept asking me how it tasted. I didn't understand. I said it tasted sweet. Then Suzy's mother laughed out loud at me and told me what was in it. I think she wanted me to be surprised.

Suzy went out with me for her image. There was no other reason, it was as simple as that. Now there's no glory in dating a former defensive end. Suzy went out with me because the year before I had dated Laurie Foster, and Laurie Foster had a reputation at Saint Scholastica, where Suzy went to school. This is where everything gets crazy. Laurie somehow had a reputation, which I don't think she deserved, at least not when I was taking her out. We never did much really of anything, but because I had dated her I got a reputation too, and I never even knew about it. I guess there was some crazy kind of glory in dating and going steady with a guy who had a rep.

She said let me wear your ring, hey, just for tonight, and I said sure, Suzy. And she asked me if I liked her and I said of course, don't you like me? She laughed and said no, I'm just dating you for your looks. I was a little drunk that night and she said do you ever think about it, Mike, do you ever just sit down and think about it, and I said what, and she said going steady. I told her no. Then she asked me if I wanted to date other girls, and when I said no I didn't she said well, I think we should then, and finally I said it's all right with me, Suzy, if you think it's that important, and she said it is, Mike, it really is. She wore my ring on a chain around her neck until she got a size adjuster, then she wore my ring on her hand.

Pretty much of everything we did then was her idea, not that

I didn't have some ideas of my own. But Suzy initiated pretty much of everything for a while back then. Ronny was dating a girl who lived near Suzy out on Touhy Avenue, and I remember once when we were double-dating Suzy and I were in the back seat of the car fooling around and she said can't you unclasp it, and I said oh, sure. And that time we were studying at the table in her kitchen—her mother was down in the basement ironing and her father was still at work—and she says not here, Mike, but hey maybe in the front room.

She said hold me honey, hey, and she touched me and I touched her and she was wet and smelled like strawberries and her mouth nipped my neck as I held her. She said Mike, do you like me I mean really do you like me, and I said yes, Suzy, that's a crazy question I really like you, and she held me and made me stop and we sat up when we heard her mother coming up from the basement.

The next weekend I bought some Trojans, and Ronny lent me his car for the night. But before I went to pick her up the two of us got a little drunk in his garage. Ronny said I'd better try one first to make sure they weren't defective. He said people in those places prick them with pins all the time just for laughs, and I said yeah, I sure hope this thing'll hold, and Ronny said there's seventeen years of it built up inside of you, remember, and I said damn, maybe she'll explode, and he said she'd better not on my upholstery, and we laughed and he threw a punch at me and we drank another beer and then blew one up and it held good and we let it fly outside in the alley.

The back seat was cold and cramped, and Suzy cried when it was over, and we wiped up the blood with a rag. It meant something, I thought, and I started taking going steady a little more serious after that.

It must have been the next month that her mother started in on me. She was young then and still very pretty for a woman who'd had three kids, and she began out of nowhere saying little things like here, Mike, take a chair, and did you really hurt your back or is there some other reason why you quit the team? I had always tried to be polite to her. Then Suzy started to get on me, asking me sometimes exactly what was I doing when I pulled my back, how was I standing, and couldn't I maybe try out for track or baseball or something in the spring? I couldn't figure where they were coming from, and I tried to explain that even before I got hurt I hadn't been that good a football player, that I'd been on the team simply because I'd liked to run and play catch with my father on fall afternoons. Suzy's father seemed to understand, and he'd tell me stories about his old high school team, funny stories about crazy plays and the stuff the players wore that was supposed to be their equipment, and then sometimes he'd get serious and say it wasn't a sport anymore at all now, that it was a real butcher shop, a game for the biggest sides of beef, and if he had a son he'd let the boy play if he wanted to but he'd hope his kid would have the good sense to know when to quit. Because all athletes have to quit sooner or later, he said. Everyone quits everything sooner or later. The trick is knowing how and when. Toward the end I got to know him a little. I'd go over there sometimes even when I didn't feel like seeing Suzy but when I knew there was a game or something else good on TV, and once the three of them came over to my house in the city and the three of us, me and my father and Suzy's father, sat around and shot the breeze and had ourselves a good time, and we must have drunk a whole case of beer, and Suzy and her mother ended up out by themselves talking in the kitchen.

Suzy's father asked me how I quit the team, and told me once he had worked for a guy and after a while he realized he was getting nowhere. He said even though they already had Suzy and needed every penny they could get, one day he sat down with his boss and told him that he simply couldn't work there any longer. He said Mike, there are things sometimes that you just have to do, but you need to learn that it's almost as important to go about doing them in a decent way. I told him that maybe I had been a little hotheaded with the coaches.

He said he respected me for what I did, on account of it showed that things mattered to me, but maybe staying on the team and picking up a few splinters on the sidelines might have been a better way to go about doing it.

I knew even back then that me and Suzy weren't going to last long, and then I started realizing that what we were doing was serious business, especially if Suzy got pregnant. I was cool toward her then. It was around this time that I found out from the guys at school that she had gone out on the sly with another guy. This guy, she told me when I asked her about it, was her second cousin who was having some temporary trouble finding himself a date. I laughed good at that and said damn it, at least if you would've told me I wouldn't have had to hear it from the guys, and we both found out then that I really didn't much care. We had a long talk then, and then for a while things went okay.

For a while. Until May, until I was walking down the second-floor corridor at school and I got wind from Larry Souza, a guy who was dating one of Suzy's friends, about a surprise six months' happy-going-steady party Suzy was going to throw for me, with all the girls from Scholastica and the guys from Saint George invited too and even some kind of a cake, with MIKE & SUZY in bright red icing written on the top, and me and Ronny were sitting in his garage late one night drinking some beer and talking, and then we were thinking wouldn't it be something if I didn't show, wouldn't that be a real kicker, and then the night of the big party comes along, with me expected to drop by at around nine, just another date, Mike, maybe we'll stay home, sit around and watch a movie on TV or maybe if the folks aren't home we can sneak downstairs after the little ones go to bed and you know what, and at eight me and Ronny are in his garage scraping spark plugs and still talking about it and laughing, and at eight-thirty we need just a drop more of beer so we drive out, and by nine we're stopping by the lake because Ronny thinks he sees an old girlfriend racing down Pratt Street on her bicycle and I'm saying damn, Ronny, that girl must be thirty-five years old but we drive there anyway and end up sitting on the trunk of his old Chevy sharing another six-pack, still laughing, and then we meet some kids who've got a football and Jesus it's a beautiful night, a gorgeous night in May, and we pick sides and then some girls come along and we ask if they want to play, it's only touch, and below the waist and not in the front, honest, and we've got some beer left in the car if you're thirsty first hey come on, and I'm guarding this goon who couldn't even tie his own shoes by himself let alone run in a straight line and on the very first play Ronny is throwing to him high and hard and the clown falls down and I move up and over him and make the interception, easy, and I'm laughing so hard I stop right where I catch it and let the boob tag me, here, tag me, I'm going nowhere, I'll tag myself, hey everybody, please tag me, laughing so hard and we play until past eleven when a police Park Control car comes crunching up the cinder track and this big cop gets out and says all right kids, the park is closed, and one of the girls says please officer please, have a heart, why don't you take off your gun and stick around and play, and the big cop says sorry, wish to Christ I could, and we all laugh at that, and then Ronny and I say hey who wants to go for a ride and two of the girls say sure, where, and Ronny looks at me and shrugs and I say damn, anywhere is okay by me, so we all get in and we drive and drive and drive, nearly all the way up to Wisconsin, the four of us drinking what beer is left and stopping here and there along the road to see if we can buy some more, I'm sorry, come back in three years, they say, and I'm telling this girl who looks like the Statue of Liberty holding up her cigarette the way girls do in the dark car with the tip of it all glowing all about what I did that night, and she says can you picture them all waiting and then you don't show, surprise, and then we have ourselves a contest to see who can guess what kind of cake it was and Ronny says chocolate and his girl guesses pineapple but my girl comes up with angel food and we laugh and say she wins, I give her her prize, a kiss, and damn she kisses back, hard, and then Ronny stops on this quiet road in the middle of the blackness and says hey, where do you want to go now, and I say Canada, and my girl says take a left, and Ronny turns and says what's left, and his girl says we're left and I want to stay right here, and damn that is funny and we drive and drive and drive, and it's long past three and silent like a church when I finally get to my house.

My dad is awake and angry, worried that I'd been in an accident. They called here four times, Mike, he says, and what can I tell them I don't even know where my own son is. When I tell him what happened he says that was a downright shitty thing to do, then he shakes his head and says what would your mother have thought? I think of Suzy's father, how I never thought that he might have been worried, and my father says you should call them right now and apologize. I say it's late, too late to bother them, and he says you're old enough now to think for yourself, do what you do, I'm going to bed.

I didn't call there for a couple of days and by then Suzy had found out what happened. The first thing she said was when can you pick up your ring? I said hey Suzy, I don't want you to give me my ring back, and she said that ring must've cost you forty dollars, and we start to argue.

Her youngest sister answered the door, looking like Suzy must have when she was that young, and you know I bet like her mother too, clean-faced, eyes all shining, with freckles across the bridge of her nose. She tells me to come in. I try to smile to make her smile, but then her father comes down the stairs coughing into a handkerchief and holding my ring in an envelope. I tried to talk to him, to explain, but I didn't know what to say.

Now I drive for Cook County. A GMC truck and mostly light construction materials for building projects. It's not a bad job. A year or so after I finished high school Suzy's mother died, some kind of crazy disease that I guess she knew all about before but didn't tell anyone about, and when I heard I drove out to the house. Her father came to the door and told me Suzy was out. I said I came to see you. He nodded then, looking at me. Then instead of inviting me in he told me that he was busy packing to move to his sister's out East, and then he said he'd tell Suzy I stopped by and that I should be sure to thank my father for the sympathy card he'd sent.

When we'd kiss she'd close her eyes and keep them closed, tight, and I'd look at her sometimes in the back seat of Ronny's old Chevy going up the street with the bands of light moving across her face. And once when we were at the lake she took my hand and said Mike, do you ever just think about it? I asked what, and she said oh nothing, Mike, I guess I just mean about things.

The coaches hollered at me after that interception, like I was a damn rookie sophomore. They said I caught the ball and stood still. But they were wrong—as sure as I know my own name I know I ran. My body moved up and toward the ball, it struck my hands and then my numbers, I squeezed it and went for the goal line. I think about that sometimes when I'm hauling, and sometimes I pull over on Central Avenue and look at the red bricks and striped awnings. I think of Suzy and her father. I grip the truck's wheel, my engine idling.

No Lie Like Love

PAUL RAWLINS

From *No Lie Like Love* (1996)

Down Theil Road outside of Washtucna, Washington, the cobalt blue of the south horizon at sunset marks the far-off line the sailing men of Christopher Columbus feared. A mile off West 26, first to the north, then to the south, you'll see white houses, and they'll each have a barn and a couple of silos, a windmill, and a pine windbreak. And around it all, in front to the highway and behind back to the edge of the world, is grain and grain and grain.

It's two hundred plus miles to Seattle, and that sunset takes up a curved third of the sky in oranges at the middle, through dirty roses, and into gray violets and blue. The whole outdoors curves with the line of the sky like an amphitheater, and you'll see a tractor and harrow in silhouette on a hill for contour to add to the ramshackle lonely off West 26.

Mauren Cowley, the girl I was seeing last summer, wondered who put up phone lines along every mile of highway and down every crossroad. It breaks my heart to think about it. And I will not, not for anything in this world right up to the very edge, stay here and be a farmer.

Dad thinks I'll come around and study agricultural science here at WSU.

"A college degree is worth something these days," he says. "Everything is agri-business now. College will gear you up for the market end of things."

He sees a future in organic farming.

"The people want it," he says. They want food that's clean and safe, environmentally responsible, au naturel. If they want it cut with a sickle and bound in shocks stacked like little sheds, he'll oblige if it adds up to a nickel more a bushel net. My dad is a farmer who works the land. He loves it like a tool, not for how it smells after rain or how it feels to crumble a clod of it between his fingers—not if that clod has too much clay or sand; not if there are too many stones or there is too much alkali. No one abuses the land like farmers, who pour their crankcase oil down a ditch bank or use old tin rubbish for landfill and leave rusting machinery to rot. It's the farmers who erect and string and repair endless lines of fence, chopping up the countryside in what amounts to a bigger task than the telephone lines all down Highway 26.

"What do you know about it?" my dad said to me once.

"As much as I ever will," I told him straight.

Last summer, on Tuesday nights and Friday nights, I drove West 26 to see Mauren Cowley, the short-order girl at Mackenzie's Drive-in. I'd take her home so she could shower off the grease smell and change. Sometimes I'd hang out with her little brother while I waited and shoot frogs with his .22. He didn't care whether I or anybody else took Mauren out or not. He bummed rides in my convertible, swearing that he could drive while Mauren dried her hair.

Then Mauren and I would drive the forty-five miles down 26 into Othello to be someplace different. We'd drive past wheat and into hay and the sprinkling pipes along Irby Road, stretched out like high kickers arm in arm, swirling water out in feathers and crawling on their wheels. By the time we were over the tracks and past the old elevators by Lucy Road, the water in the fields was flashing like high beams out of the end of the rows, and I'd play the stereo so loud Mauren and I couldn't talk, while we blasted down the highway till the flashing yellow STOP HERE at the weigh station and then the flashing red at the crossroad for Othello and Yakima or Moses Lake. Then I would turn the music down and ask Mauren what she wanted to do.

Mauren Cowley would shrug; then we would go eat and then most times see a movie.

I liked Mauren Cowley without ever meaning to and without ever loving her. Mauren Cowley was dumb and she had a horsy face. She looked walleyed when she had her hair pulled back, the way she wore it when she was slopping together shakes and dagwood sandwiches at Mackenzie's. Which is where I met her because you wouldn't meet her anyplace else. She looked good from a distance, through the glass of the kitchen window from the gas pumps. She looked like some mousey-haired girl in a pink T-shirt and rolled-up jeans who you didn't know.

Inside, I was disappointed by her horsy face, but by the time I got home I wasn't remembering her as being so bad. When I went back the next week, she looked more tan, which seemed to help, and so did some of the hair that had slipped out of the ponytail.

I said hello when I paid for the gas, and I looked at the name on her blue badge. I asked her could I get a cheeseburger.

"Uh-huh," Mauren said.

While Mauren got started on my quarter-pound double cheese at the grill, a short woman in cat-eye glasses and an apron came out of the Ladies. She asked had I been helped.

"Mauren's fixing me up," I said. Mauren stopped, and if you can know someone's smiling while their back's still turned, I'll say she did.

Cat-eyes rang me up after Mauren finished, and I asked what time they closed.

Cat-eyes squinted and checked my receipt in her head.

"Eleven o'clock," she said. "Twelve on Fridays."

Mauren Cowley came out about 11:20. Cat-eyes came out behind her and locked the door. A fat man in a pickup was waiting for one of them.

Cat-eyes looked straight at me and she said, "You need a ride home, Mauren?"

"No," Mauren said.

"I'm her cousin," I said from across the parking lot.

"Like hell," Cat-eyes said. She got in the truck with the fat man, and they sat with the motor running and the headlights off.

I walked over and asked Mauren if she needed a ride, and she told me no.

"Do you work every night?" I said.

"No."

"What nights don't you work?"

"It changes."

"What nights usually? What nights next week?"

"Tuesday," she said. "And Friday or Saturday."

"Do you want to go somewhere Tuesday?" I said. Mauren shrugged, and I edged up beside her.

"Who's that?" I said. Cat-eyes was watching, so I pointed at her.

"Clara," Mauren said.

"She looks like the wrath of God."

"I work with Becca sometimes," Mauren said. The fat man switched on his headlights and pinned us to the wall like escaping prisoners. I turned my back to them and stood in front of Mauren.

"What time are you off Tuesday?" I said.

"Five o'clock," she told me. "In the afternoon."

All summer long we blasted down 26 with the music loud enough to make our ears bleed and the wind blowing out whatever Mauren had done with her hair, until she stopped doing anything at all more than washing out the smell of the grill and tying it back into its ponytail.

We ate at drive-ins. Mauren liked it when we went to an old-type A&W where you ordered over a speaker in the lighted menu and the girls brought your food out on a tray they hung from the window of your car. She liked to make the orders difficult. She'd order without pickles and want root beer and ice in separate cups.

"What do you do that for?" I said. "You like pickles."

Mauren shrugged. "Sometimes," she said. She'd watch the girls in their short, candy-striped skirts and chew at the corner of her mouth.

Then mostly we'd see a movie, where Mauren would do everything she was supposed to do. She would laugh when things were funny, and when things got close she would squeeze my arm or my hand, and if the movie got scary she would scream and sometimes pick her feet up off the floor, as if under her chair was a space like under her bed, with hands waiting to reach out and grab her and pull her down to someplace dark. We would kiss a little in the movie, and then more somewhere along the way home. Sometimes back behind the old elevators by Lucy Road, or down some other crossroad and out in a field, with the top always down and the stars always up. And once on the train tracks, waiting to feel the tremors and the rumble.

The rain was the most lonely thing out on our place. I would lie on my stomach and watch out the front door. The house was dark as twilight inside, and the rain outside was cold and fell in big drops and straight lines. It fell on the fields all the way to the edge of the world.

I would call Mauren at work. I would try to make my voice sound like I thought her father's would, and I would ask to speak with her please.

Becca would call for her, or Cat-eyes would bark, "Mauren."

"What are you doing?" Mauren would say after she said hello.

"Nothing," I would tell her.

"Why aren't you working?" she would say.

"It's raining. Why aren't you?"

"Troy," she'd say quiet into the phone, "I'm going to get in trouble."

"So?" I'd say.

"Troy, I gotta go."

"Go," I'd say. "Good-bye."

I'd call her back all afternoon, and Mauren would be scrambling to answer the phone. She would make up things to say out loud for Becca or Cat-eyes to hear. She would say, "No, she isn't working this shift. I don't know, but I can check the schedule." And I would tell her, yes, check the schedule. I would tell her sometimes, "Check and see when Mauren Cowley is working," and she'd read back to me her own days on for the next week: "Monday, Tuesday, Friday days; Wednesday, Thursday, Saturday close."

She would quote prices to me.

"That would be $2.99. Plus tax. It's on a special." Always plus tax. Or it would be the gas price.

"A dollar twenty-three. But there's three cents a gallon discount for cash, and that would be a dollar twenty."

And a hundred times she only said, "I'm sorry, you must have the wrong number. This is 7879."

Becca would beat Mauren to the phone sometimes and tell me that Mauren had run off with a trucker or something. Cat-eyes would gripe at Mauren about how she wasn't getting paid to talk on the phone and this was a business number, hand her the phone every time, then scream at her when she hung up, Mauren told me.

If I picked up Mauren after I had called her all afternoon, Becca would tell me I was silly.

Mauren always said, "I'm going to lose my job."

"You don't like your job," I'd say.

"It's the only job there is."

We had rain almost two straight weeks in June. And I lay in the dark, calling Mauren at work to get her to the edge of trouble. Mackenzie's was the only job there was.

Mauren asked questions like a baby doll, like nobody had told her anything, not ever in her life. She asked me once, "What's special about unleaded gasoline?"

"It's lighter," I told her.

She asked me where I was going to college in the fall.

"Let's go see," I said.

Mauren put on my sunglasses, and we drove a hundred miles an hour to just outside of Pullman. We crept once around campus for a look and then turned around and rocketed back to Washtucna.

"What are you going to take at college?" Mauren asked me.

"Women," I said. It's what I always said.

"What else?" Mauren said.

"I don't know. Maybe business, maybe science, some sort of engineering."

"I'd like to go to travel school," Mauren said. "My dad says go learn to cut hair, but I'd like to go to travel school and learn all about traveling." Her dad did say that; he said he wished he knew how to cut hair. He would set up a shop in his spare room and barber for three dollars a head on weekends and make a mint.

"On who?" I'd ask Mauren.

"Have you been in an airplane?" Mauren said.

I said, "Yes." I lied.

"Where did you go?"

"Texas," I said. "To see my uncle."

And once, while we were parked out in a field, with the sky down low being a tease about rain, my lips were bruised from kissing and cut one place from a jagged crown Mauren had on one front tooth. Mauren had her legs stretched out over my lap and was trying to roll the window up and down with her foot.

She said, "Sometimes can you wish for things and then still get them?"

"Not that I've ever seen," I said. She reached her hand over the car door without thinking about it and tugged up a stalk of grain.

"No," she said. "It doesn't ever seem like it." She was weaving the stalk into her hair, winding it around the ponytail till the head of grain stood up like a single feather in an Indian bonnet.

"Pocahontas," I said, "white squaw."

"Didn't you wish for this car?" she said, looking around the field. "Isn't this the kind of car you wish for?"

"No," I said. "I bought it."

I taught Mauren how to downshift and power into a turn, showed her peeling out and burning rubber, made her pump gas and check the oil.

When we caught air coming off bumps down the dirt roads, she said, "Isn't it bad for the car?"

"When it's gone, it's gone," I told her.

I taught Mauren how to swear, something she could use.

I worked all day that summer for wages from my dad. I rode in a high-cabbed tractor with my shirt off and the radio turned up and chopped grain for miles. I could drive half an hour in one direction and cut a twenty-foot swath that added up to nothing. If I stared at the horizon, the edge, I'd be standing still, like I was on a giant paddle wheel, and the grain moved past in a river along my side and underneath me.

I used to climb up on the cab and yell. I bounced up and down in the seat till I broke the springs, and I jerked the steering wheel at the same time, trying to yank it free. I spit out the window at the grain and took leaks on it and practiced all the words I'd teach Mauren and make her yell out the car into the wind on Highway 26.

Mauren and I went to Othello to see fireworks on the Fourth of July. She was late getting off work. I waited for her outside of Mackenzie's, lighting off firecrackers in a ditch down the road with a bunch of little kids.

"We've been swamped," Mauren said. Her hair stuck to her face and she flapped her T-shirt because it was sticking, too. "Clara wasn't going to let me go."

Clara was watching us through the glass, and I held up a dud firecracker like I was going to flip it at the gas pumps for her to see, until she started around the counter.

"Let's go," I said.

Mauren's family was loading into a pickup when I pulled onto the lawn.

"I'll hurry," Mauren said. "What time do they start?"

"When it gets dark," I told her.

After her family left, I walked into Mauren's house. I heard the shower going, and a radio. The radio was in Mauren's room, the one she shared with two little sisters. There were bunks, and under an open window with yellow curtains a twin bed that would be Mauren's. The bed was white with a metal-gate headboard like in old hospitals. The room was picked up neat except for Mauren's jeans and T-shirt on the floor.

When the shower stopped behind me, I waited for her, standing in the doorway. I had never seen Mauren even in shorts yet. She took her time, and she came out in jeans and a sleeveless sweater, toweling her hair. She stopped when she saw me. "Did everybody leave?" she said.

"Yes," I said. She waited for me to move before she walked into the bedroom. I stood back in the doorway, and Mauren put on her canvas deck shoes.

"Do you like fireworks?" she said.

I shrugged.

Mauren pulled her hair back into the ponytail and daubed on lip gloss. "Do you want to eat here? There's salads and things. My mom left a note," she said.

"You don't want to," I said.

"We could," Mauren said. Then she shrugged away the offer and dropped the lip gloss and some gum into her purse.

We watched fireworks from the car, picking through cartons of Chinese food she had wanted to try, but she didn't like it, only the little strips of meat and the pea pods. The fireworks, the gold ones that hung and dripped, made me think of willow trees, I told Mauren. She was leaning on my shoulder, sucking on snow peas and pointing.

"What makes the colors?" she said.

"It's minerals. Sulphur is the blue; phosphorus is white; cadmium makes red." I made it up. "I don't know what makes the green."

"Sugar," she said. "Sugar burns green."

I didn't know if it did or not.

"My mom's going to Seattle," Mauren said after another burst, the ones that pop into screaming tadpoles in the sky.

"What for?"

"Dancing," Mauren said. "She goes every year. She meets her old girlfriends and they go out dancing and see movies and flirt with men." We watched a huge blast, a ball of red, white, and blue that exploded out and down and down so that we ducked.

"What does your old man think of it?" I said.

"He sends her," Mauren said. "He doesn't like to dance." I figured then Mauren's father was about as dumb as his daughter.

"Do you ever go?" I said.

"No," she said.

I told Mauren my dad didn't even take the holiday off. Her father was a mailman of some sort, but not the kind that delivered house to house.

"He picks it up in Pullman," Mauren said. "He takes mail to all the little towns."

She said did I know their cat had died of old age.

She said she liked Washtucna.

A white comet went straight up from the ground and didn't explode—it just tipped over and went out.

We sat till midnight listening to the radio play in the dark, watching the cars pass. We drove home at the speed limit, with our eyes open for cops.

Mauren started wearing rings on her thumbs, then two or three on a finger, stacked above and below the knuckle. She kept them in her purse and strung them on or swapped them around, and that would keep her attention for ten or twenty minutes while we drove.

"They look like pull tops" I said. They looked like silver, but they stuck to magnets. They would suck up in the car vac like loose change. I'd find them down my shirt when I undressed at nights. When I gave them back to Mauren, she'd dump them in her purse.

Sometime she switched her gum to sugarless and bought sunglasses of her own.

Mauren is the first girl I slept with, which is a funny way to say it, since there wasn't any sleeping. It was down by the grain elevators, just off the tracks, waiting for the train again. I thought it would be like the music, when it's so good you want to take it inside of you and the only thing you can do is turn it louder and then louder, until your stomach starts to shake and you're waiting to come apart. I thought it would be like that.

She's the only girl I've ever slept with; then she cried on the way home.

Sometimes, after I'd drop Mauren in Washtucna, or on nights when I couldn't see her, Sunday nights, I drove the road myself. I would putter down to Washtucna like taking a lap up to the starting line, and then I would drive the distance back to Othello as fast as I could, and sometimes without lights, which was like holding my breath, waiting for something to happen. And I wanted to be standing alongside the road to hear myself tear by, like a rush, a bullet. And to hear the screaming fade, and to reach out and touch the red flash without breaking my hand, only burning the tips of my fingers.

Sometimes I imagined dying in a crash. Mauren would come to my funeral and those little silver rings would drop off her fingers into my casket.

Mauren told me in August, "I don't want you to come see me anymore."

"Why, do I scare the customers?" I said.

Mauren only looked at me funny.

"What's the matter?" I said.

She looked down at her shoes that were fuzzy from the soap she used to mop the drive-in floor. "I've got a boyfriend," she said.

"What boyfriend?" I said. "Who?" She wouldn't tell me anything about it.

Her dad came in the pickup and waved to me. Then he looked at Mauren, looked puzzled, and she climbed in. I shrugged, and he waved again and drove Mauren Cowley home.

On Sunday at home I washed the car and listened to Dad yammer off the front steps. The same old thing.

"Pull up the Lincoln and do that, too." After the soap and wax, halfway into the buffing, he'd say, "Do it right."

In the afternoon I drove out to the motocross at Washtucna. Mauren's brother was there, like she said he always was on a Sunday, nosing around and trying to score rides. He was sitting on a Kawasaki decked out in muddy chrome and lime-green plastic.

"How old is your sister, really?" I said.

"Fifteen," he said. "Hey, what happened, man? I seen her new boy."

"Nothing," I said.

"Hey, check this," he said. He laid out on the bike with his face stuck over the handlebars, gritting his teeth in the imaginary wind while he twisted the throttle and squeezed the clutch.

There is no lie in this world like the lie about love. The lies of science explain it best. Valence shell electron pair repulsion theory and gravity and the polar ends of magnetic fields. The logics of repulsion and attraction and the fascination between two bodies—that I underlined in a notebook because I thought I knew what it meant. I'm learning all the things I didn't know about the world now, taking physics and chemistry. I'm pulling mediocre grades, having a hard time with the math. Dad says no more meal ticket next year. He pats the hood of my car and says there's tuition and books, right there.

There are two things you do here in college, and they are the same everywhere, I guess, and they are to drink and to get laid. I can't drink. I get sick. My body has no tolerance, not even for beer. I've known this since I was fifteen, and at first I tried to get around it. I drank and I got sick, but I told myself it was like lifting weights and building up your wind with distance running, but I still got sick every time, so I quit.

And I've cut out the other for a while, too. Not that it isn't easy to come by, not that it isn't dropping down from the trees and crawling in through the window. Not that I don't know my roommate's lacrosse stick outside the curtains means I'm on my own to find anywhere to go but home for the next hour. But I've figured something out, something about the lie of it all.

Sometimes when I think of Washtucna, and the fields, and the roads with the telephone lines swinging down them off West 26, I swear I'll just keep going east. Down to Cheyenne and Chicago, Cleveland, all the "C" towns, not for "Cowley," but just because one comes after the other in a line.

And I think that someday maybe I'll be in love, and that could make the difference.

CONTRIBUTORS

TONY ARDIZZONE is the author of *The Evening News*, which won the 1985 Flannery O'Connor Award for Short Fiction. He is the author of seven books of fiction, most recently *The Arab's Ox: Stories of Morocco*. His novels include *The Whale Chaser, In the Garden of Papa Santuzzu, Heart of the Order*, and *In the Name of the Father*. His work has received the Milkweed Editions National Fiction Prize, the Chicago Foundation for Literature Award for Fiction, the Virginia Prize for Fiction, the Pushcart Prize, and two National Endowment for the Arts fellowships, among other honors. Born and raised in Chicago, he currently lives in Portland, Oregon.

RITA CIRESI won the 1992 Flannery O'Connor Award for Short Fiction with her short-story collection *Mother Rocket*. She is author of the novels *Bring Back My Body to Me, Blue Italian, Pink Slip*, and *Remind Me Again Why I Married You*, and the story collections *Sometimes I Dream in Italian* and *Second Wife*. She is a professor of English at the University of South Florida in Tampa, a faculty member for the Bay Path University online MFA program in nonfiction, and fiction editor of *2 Bridges Review*.

MARY CLYDE is the author of *Survival Rates*, a Flannery O'Connor Award winner in 1999. Her short fiction has appeared in journals and anthologies, including the *Georgia Review, Quarterly West, Boulevard*, and *New Stories from the South*. She earned an MA from the University of Utah and an MFA from Vermont College. She has taught undergraduate writing and literature and graduate creative writing. She lives in Phoenix.

DAVID CROUSE is the author of *Copy Cats*, which received the 2004 Flannery O'Connor Award for Short Fiction, and *The Man Back There*, which received the Mary McCarthy Fiction Prize in 2008. He is full professor of English at the University of Washington and also serves as the director of the MFA Program. His stories have appeared in such publications as the *Massachusetts Review*, *Beloit Fiction Journal*, *Chelsea*, and *Quarterly West*.

CAROL LEE LORENZO is the author of *Nervous Dancer*, winner of the 1994 Flannery O'Connor Award for Short Fiction. She currently leads the fiction workshops at the Callanwolde Fine Arts Center in Atlanta. She has taught creative writing at Emory University, Oglethorpe University, and Georgia State University. Her short stories have appeared in *Five Points*, *Epoch*, *Pennsylvania Review*, *Painted Bride*, *Chelsea*, and *Sou'easter*, among other literary journals. Lorenzo is also the author of three novels for young adults.

ALYCE MILLER is the author of *The Nature of Longing*, which won the 1993 Flannery O'Connor Award for Short Fiction, and four other books, *Sweet Love*, *Skunk*, *Water*, and *Stopping for Green Lights*. She has also published 250 poems, essays, short stories, and articles. Her work has appeared in more than one hundred and fifty journals, including *Ploughshares*, *Iowa Review*, *New England Review*, *Southern Review*, *L.A. Times Summer Fiction Issue*, *Kenyon Review*, *Michigan Quarterly Review*, *Story Quarterly*, *Story Magazine*, and *American Fiction*, among others.

DEBRA MONROE is the author of *The Source of Trouble*, which won the 1989 Flannery O'Connor Award for Short Fiction. She is also the author of the story collection *A Wild, Cold State*; two novels, *Newfangled* and *Shambles*; and two memoirs, *On the Outskirts of Normal* and *My Unsentimental Education*. She lives in Austin, Texas, and teaches in the MFA program at Texas State University.

RANDY F. NELSON is the author of *The Imaginary Lives of Mechanical Men*, winner of the 2005 Flannery O'Connor Award for Short Fiction, *A Duplicate Daughter*, *The Overlook Martial Arts Reader*, and *The Almanac of American Letters*. His stories have appeared in such publications as the *Gettysburg Review*, the *North American Review*, and the *Kenyon Review*.

224

ANDREW PORTER is the author of *The Theory of Light and Matter*, which won the 2007 Flannery O'Connor Award for Short Fiction. He is also author of the novel *In Between Days*. His award-winning fiction has appeared in *One Story*, *Ploughshares*, and the *Pushcart Prize Anthology* and on NPR's Selected Shorts. A graduate of the Iowa Writers' Workshop, he has received a variety of fellowships, including the 2004 W. K. Rose Fellowship in the Creative Arts, a Helene Wurlitzer Fellowship, and a James Michener-Paul Engle Fellowship from the James Michener/ Copernicus Society of America. Porter is a professor of English and director of the Creative Writing Program at Trinity University in San Antonio, Texas.

PAUL RAWLINS's short-story collection *No Lie Like Love* won the 1995 Flannery O'Connor Award for Short Fiction. His fiction has appeared in *Glimmer Train*, *Southeast Review*, *Sycamore Review*, and *Tampa Review*. He has received awards from the Utah Arts Council, the Association for Mormon Letters, and PRISM International. He lives in Salt Lake City.

BARBARA SUTTON won the 2003 Flannery O'Connor Award for Short Fiction for her short-story collection *The Send-Away Girl*. Her stories have appeared in *Agni*, the *Missouri Review*, the *Antioch Review*, the *Chicago Quarterly Review*, the *Harvard Review*, *Image*, and other publications. She works as a government speechwriter in New York City and blogs at *Sketches by Baz*.

KELLIE WELLS was awarded the Flannery O'Connor Award and the Great Lakes Colleges Association New Writers Award for her 2002 short-story collection *Compression Scars*. She is also author of the novels *Fat Girl*, *Terrestrial*, and *Skin*, and the short-story collection *God, the Moon, and Other Megafauna*. Her work has appeared in the *Kenyon Review*, *Ninth Letter*, and *Fairy Tale Review* and was selected for inclusion in the 2010 anthology *Best American Fantasy*. Wells is a graduate of the writing programs at the University of Montana, the University of Pittsburgh, and Western Michigan University.

NANCY ZAFRIS is the author of *The People I Know*, recipient of the 1989 Flannery O'Connor Award for Short Fiction. She is also the author of two novels, *Lucky Strike* and *The Metal Shredders*. Her second collection of short stories, *The Home Jar*, was named one of the top ten books of 2013 by the *Minneapolis Star Tribune*. After serving as the fiction editor of the *Kenyon Review* for nine years, she became the editor of the Flannery O'Connor award series for several years. She has recently finished a new novel.

HESTER KAPLAN, *The Edge of Marriage*

DARRELL SPENCER, *CAUTION Men in Trees*

ROBERT ANDERSON, *Ice Age*

BILL ROORBACH, *Big Bend*

DANA JOHNSON, *Break Any Woman Down*

GINA OCHSNER, *The Necessary Grace to Fall*

KELLIE WELLS, *Compression Scars*

ERIC SHADE, *Eyesores*

CATHERINE BRADY, *Curled in the Bed of Love*

ED ALLEN, *Ate It Anyway*

GARY FINCKE, *Sorry I Worried You*

BARBARA SUTTON, *The Send-Away Girl*

DAVID CROUSE, *Copy Cats*

RANDY F. NELSON, *The Imaginary Lives of Mechanical Men*

GREG DOWNS, *Spit Baths*

PETER LASALLE, *Tell Borges If You See Him: Tales of Contemporary Somnambulism*

ANNE PANNING, *Super America*

MARGOT SINGER, *The Pale of Settlement*

ANDREW PORTER, *The Theory of Light and Matter*

PETER SELGIN, *Drowning Lessons*

GEOFFREY BECKER, *Black Elvis*

LORI OSTLUND, *The Bigness of the World*

LINDA LEGARDE GROVER, *The Dance Boots*

JESSICA TREADWAY, *Please Come Back To Me*

AMINA GAUTIER, *At-Risk*

MELINDA MOUSTAKIS, *Bear Down, Bear North*

E. J. LEVY, *Love, in Theory*

HUGH SHEEHY, *The Invisibles*

JACQUELIN GORMAN, *The Viewing Room*

TOM KEALEY, *Thieves I've Known*

KARIN LIN-GREENBERG, *Faulty Predictions*

MONICA MCFAWN, *Bright Shards of Someplace Else*

TONI GRAHAM, *The Suicide Club*

SIAMAK VOSSOUGHI, *Better Than War*

LISA GRALEY, *The Current That Carries*

ANNE RAEFF, *The Jungle around Us*

BECKY MANDELBAUM, *Bad Kansas*

KIRSTEN SUNDBERG LUNSTRUM, *What We Do with the Wreckage*

COLETTE SARTOR, *Once Removed*

PATRICK EARL RYAN, *If We Were Electric*

ANNIVERSARY ANTHOLOGIES

TENTH ANNIVERSARY

The Flannery O'Connor Award: Selected Stories,
EDITED BY CHARLES EAST

FIFTEENTH ANNIVERSARY

Listening to the Voices:
Stories from the Flannery O'Connor Award,
EDITED BY CHARLES EAST

THIRTIETH ANNIVERSARY

Stories from the Flannery O'Connor Award:
A 30th Anniversary Anthology: The Early Years,
EDITED BY CHARLES EAST

Stories from the Flannery O'Connor Award:
A 30th Anniversary Anthology: The Recent Years,
EDITED BY NANCY ZAFRIS

THEMATIC ANTHOLOGIES

Hold That Knowledge: Stories about Love
from the Flannery O'Connor Award for Short Fiction,
EDITED BY ETHAN LAUGHMAN

The Slow Release: Stories about Death
from the Flannery O'Connor Award for Short Fiction,
EDITED BY ETHAN LAUGHMAN

Rituals to Observe: Stories about Holidays
from the Flannery O'Connor Award for Short Fiction,
EDITED BY ETHAN LAUGHMAN

Spinning Away from the Center: Stories about
Homesickness and Homecoming
from the Flannery O'Connor Award for Short Fiction,

EDITED BY ETHAN LAUGHMAN

Good and Balanced: Stories about Sports
from the Flannery O'Connor Award for Short Fiction,
EDITED BY ETHAN LAUGHMAN

CPSIA information can be obtained
at www.ICGtesting.com
Printed in the USA
LVHW030028110221
678953LV00002B/124